"Lord knows how I didn't visit you last night. I came close."

"What stopped you, Drake?" Nicole picked up a pebble and sent it skimming across the water. The movement startled a flock of white corellas that exploded into the air in protest.

"I have to let you decide what you want." He glanced down at her. She wasn't wearing makeup—she didn't need any with her skin—not even lipstick, which he found strangely erotic. "Which isn't to say I'm going to wait a long time."

"For me to decide to sleep with you?" Her head tilted, her eyes more green than blue in the shade of the wide-brimmed Akubra.

"You will, whenever, wherever. We both know it."

She looked back at the peaceful, unspoiled scene. "It could be a mistake. Neither of us is exactly reconciled to the past."

"I'm trying, Nic. You find it very hard to trust."

"I'm concentrating on getting my life right."

"You think increasing intimacy with me will interfere with that?" His tone was deeply serious.

She nodded. "I can't deal with you like I've dealt with other men in my life."

Dear Reader,

Home to Eden is the final book in the KOOMERA CROSSING series. I hope both my loyal, much-valued readership and welcome newcomers will have enjoyed the previous four in the series. I burned the midnight oil on one of them. I'll leave you to guess which!

Throughout the series, indeed my long career, you will have noticed I enjoy writing about families—in particular, dysfunctional families. These problematic families crisscross society, from the most privileged to the severely disadvantaged.

Small wonder I'm drawn to exploring family life. There are so many mysteries connected to families: past secrets, double lives, things that are never spoken about but forever hover in the consciousness. Most bondings bring comfort, friendship and support. Some emotional attachments, however, can go beyond the norm. I've drawn on this for *Home to Eden*, coming at it from the angle of obsessive attachments. One can readily see such attachments could be a by-product of certain conditions such as loneliness and isolation. Families who live in remote areas are more dependent on each other for survival and emotional support. Outback stations certainly qualify as remote. The wonderfully inspiring, frightening and funny, tragic and violent stories of Outback life are legion. There are heroes and heroines and, inevitably, as anywhere else, villains.

The heart is a very strong yet very vulnerable organ. Love and hate coexist there. Human beings can love fiercely, yet still be capable of hurting the object of that love. Jealousy has to be regarded as a great catalyst for disaster. Some jealousies pave the way to tragedy and death. *Home to Eden* is such a story. My aim, as always, is to give my readership good stories they can enjoy. I hope I've succeeded with KOOMERA CROSSING.

Best wishes,

Margaret Way

Margaret Way
Home to Eden

HARLEQUIN®

TORONTO • NEW YORK • LONDON
AMSTERDAM • PARIS • SYDNEY • HAMBURG
STOCKHOLM • ATHENS • TOKYO • MILAN • MADRID
PRAGUE • WARSAW • BUDAPEST • AUCKLAND

ISBN 0-373-71183-2

HOME TO EDEN

This edition published by arrangement with Harlequin Books S.A.

® and TM are trademarks of the publisher. Trademarks indicated with
® are registered in the United States Patent and Trademark Office, the
Canadian Trade Marks Office and in other countries.

Visit us at www.eHarlequin.com

Printed in U.S.A.

PROLOGUE

TWELVE-YEAR-OLD Nicole Cavanagh in her lacy white nightdress stands at the first landing of Eden's grand divided staircase nursing a terrible apprehension. Her small fists are clenched tight. She can't seem to get enough air. She is trying to guess the reason for all the commotion downstairs, even as the thought keeps rising that it is all about her mother, Corrine. The thought is terrifying.

It is barely dawn, the light seeping in through the great stained-glass window directly behind her in waves of jeweled splendor: ruby, emerald, sapphire, topaz, amethyst. Nicole pays no attention even though the effect is entrancing.

Something is wrong. Something is terribly wrong. There is always turbulence when her father, Heath, is at Eden. Suddenly overcome by a gnawing premonition, she starts to tremble, reaches out to grasp the smooth mahogany banister as though she's gone blind and is petrified of falling. Her ears strain to pick up exactly what the voices are saying. Her father's voice blustery like wind and thunder overrides all others. He is such a violent man. She can easily pick out Aunt Sigrid's tones, clipped but slightly hoarse; Aunt Sigrid once had a tracheotomy. Her aunt is a severe woman, her manner imperious, a consequence perhaps of being born a Miss Cavanagh of Eden Station. She is quite without her younger sister's beauty and charm— "Left you in the dust, didn't she, Siggy," was her father's cruel comment. But her aunt has always been good to Nicole in her fashion. As had Louise, her lovely grandmother, a kind and devoted woman who now sounds shaky and deeply worried. Grandfather Giles's cultured tones reassure her, calm and reasonable as ever.

Nevertheless, Nicole can measure what it all means. Child of a highly dysfunctional family, she has inbuilt antennae that track trouble. A frantic family row is in progress—she picked up on that almost from the moment she swung her legs out of bed. Aunt Sigrid always says she is way too knowing. From the sound of his voice, her father has worked himself into a frenzied rage. She has learned over the years from her practice of eavesdropping—the only way she can ever find out anything—that her often absent father is, as Aunt Sigrid said, "a disgrace to our proud name, an adventurer, a compulsive gambler, money spills through his fingers like water, he brought nothing to the marriage. Even the big diamond engagement ring he presented to Corrinne is a fake."

Yet he is very handsome in a dissolute kind of way. Nicole has looked that word up in the dictionary. Dissolute. It meant all those things. Perhaps that was what brought her mother to the marriage, his sheer animal sex appeal. Aunt Sigrid never failed to point that out. Aunt Sigrid's own husband, Alan, "largely maintained by Father," is nearly devoid of that quality and has no hope of ever gaining it.

She can't hear her cousin Joel's voice. Almost four

years her senior, already six feet tall, Joel is probably fast asleep. Joel's ability to tune out family arguments is impressive. He professes to despise his father for being such a wimp, hates his mother's constant nagging—who doesn't?—calling his grandfather a "throwback to the feudal age" with his insistence on the importance of family, the proper respect, good manners, the sense of responsibility that should go hand in hand with privilege. Joel is something of a misfit.

"I love only you, Nikki. You're beautiful and good. You're the closest person in the world to me."

She isn't good at all. Even at twelve she is, as her aunt puts it, "hell-bent on establishing her place in the world." That means eventually inheriting Eden. Her grandfather has promised it to her. She loves her historic home with a passion. She has that in common with her grandfather and her aunt Sigrid, but Aunt Sigrid will never inherit. Nor will Joel. That, too, her grandfather has confided. Eden is hers. She is the chosen one with special qualities which her grandfather claims he sees in her. Her grandfather's love and faith sustains her. He plays the dominant male role in her life. He is Sir Giles Cavanagh of Eden Station.

Her father starts to roar again, a sound that reverberates through the house. She steps back instinctively, overcoming the sensation he has actually struck her. Which he has on occasion and she never did tell Grandpa.

"I'll tell you who she's with. Bloody McClelland, that's who. The arrogant bastard. Always thinking herself a cut above me. But she chose *me,* not him. Now she's picked up with him right under your noses, the arctic bitch.''

''And where have you been all this time, Heath?'' Her aunt's voice cracks with contempt. ''What do you get up to in Sydney apart from gambling? You're never far from the racetrack or the casino. Do you think we don't know that? You're an addict. Gambling is a drug.''

''There's more attraction in gambling than living here,'' her father answers furiously. ''The lot of you looking down on me. The Cavanagh black sheep. Always so chillingly polite, but you bloody hate me. You just don't have the guts to say so. What is a man to do when his wife doesn't return home? To be humiliated like this! I tell you she's finally gone off with that bastard. He never stopped loving her.''

''What you're saying is crazy!'' Now her grandmother speaks with intensity. ''Corrinne would never leave her child. She adores Nicole.''

''But she's done it this time, hasn't she, dear Louise?''

Nicole's grandfather cuts in as though he's reached breaking point. ''Instead of your usual ranting, Heath, I'd be obliged if you'd focus on what might have happened to your wife. I very much fear an accident. Instead of wasting time, we should be organizing a search party. Corrinne has the Land Cruiser. It could have broken down somewhere.''

''In which case she'll soon be home.'' Her grandmother sounds to anyone who knows her achingly unsure. ''Corrine is a loving mother. She would never abandon Nicole. Never.'' She repeats it like a mantra.

A low growl issues from her father as if he'd momentarily turned feral. "Who are you trying to convince, Louise? Your beloved Corrinne is no more than a common whore. You realize you're admitting she's taken up with McClelland. She'd leave me, but never Nicole."

"I have no idea," her grandmother, so proud, lies. "You were the one who snatched her away from *him,* Heath. Almost on the eve of their wedding. To think I was the one who invited you here for Corrinne's engagement party. You were kin, after all. A Cavanagh. I felt sorry for you. I felt the family was too hard on you. How you repaid us." A wealth of misery and regret in her voice, she went on, "You broke up two families who'd been the best of friends. The Cavanaghs and the McClellands. We've been here since the earliest days of settlement. The Cavanaghs even before the McQueens. We all stood together in this vast wilderness in order to survive. Our families would have been united but for you. Do you think I'd be speaking like this if you were a good husband and father? But you're not, are you. I know you're still obsessed with Corrinne. I know the black jealousy that prowls around your brain and your heart. Your mad suspicions. You never let her alone. But you scarcely have time for your own daughter, Nicole."

No hesitation. A thud like a hand slamming down on a table. "If she *is* my daughter," her father snarls.

Chaos is easy to create. It takes so few words. Glued to the banister, Nicole has trouble breathing.

"She's yours, all right." Aunt Sigrid is all contempt—and something more. What?

Grandma's quavery voice gives the impression she

is on the verge of tears. "How can you say that, Heath?"

"Sorry. I need proof." Her father laughs. Not a nice laugh. A laugh utterly devoid of humor.

Her grandfather intervenes, speaking with grave authority. "My daughter would never have married you knowing she was carrying David's child."

"Perhaps she didn't know at the time." Her father produces another sneering laugh followed by the sound of boots scraping on the parquet floor. "To hell with the lot of you! You all idolize Corrinne, but she's a cruel bitch. God knows why she married me. It had little to do with love."

"Lust more like it!" The words seemed ripped from Aunt Sigrid's throat.

Another mirthless laugh. "I bet you've spent a lot of time weeping over what you've never had, Siggy." Her father speaks as though his sister-in-law is trash, not one of the Cavanaghs of Eden. "I'll get this search party started. I can do that much. My bet is we won't find her. She's gone off with McClelland at long last. And none of you could stop her."

At that, twelve-year-old Nicole collapses on a step, starting to succumb to a great sickness inside her. "Please, God," she begins to pray, "don't let anything bad have happened to Mummy."

"For God's sake, Nicole, what are you doing there?" Her father unleashes another roar, striding out into the hallway only to see her hunched up on the stairs. "Answer me, girl."

No answer. No point. Not anymore. He isn't her father.

"Leave the child alone, Heath." The iron command

in her grandfather's voice then changes to tender, protective. "Nicole, darling, go back to bed. There's nothing for you to worry about. Go, sweetheart."

Go? When her mother is out there somewhere in the desert? "I'd rather go look for Mummy." Nicole finds the strength to pull herself up, though her legs are wobbly with shock. "Please, Granddad, may I go with you?" She cannot bring herself to address the man, Heath, standing tall, staring up at her with his black eyes. Probably seeing her mother. Doesn't everyone say she's her mother's mirror image?

Grandma rushes into the entrance hall, crushing one of her beautiful lace handkerchiefs to her mouth. "No, Giles!"

"There may be comfort in it for the child." Sir Giles draws his wife tenderly into his arms.

"I wouldn't be in the least surprised if the secretive little bitch knows where her mother is." Heath Cavanagh spits anger and venom. Definitely not Daddy anymore. "Corrinne takes her everywhere. Tells her everything. Where's your mother, girl?" he thunders.

In a flash, the secret forces within Nicole gather. It's as though she can see through her mother's sightless eyes. Searing whiteness. Nothing.

"Gone forever," she says.

CHAPTER ONE

NICOLE WAS NEARLY twenty minutes late arriving at the Bradshaws' splendid East Side apartment, although, Carol had confided earlier, she was the guest of honor. Today was her twenty-sixth birthday and Carol had arranged one of her "little dinner parties," which usually turned out to be sumptuous affairs with glamorous and often famous people in attendance and "someone special" for her to meet. Carol, who had all but adopted her as the granddaughter she'd never had, was determined to find her the right husband and thus keep her in New York, or at the very least within easy traveling distance. That didn't include far-off Australia, the home of her birth. The Outback was worlds away from New York, the fabulous hub of the New World.

The Bradshaws had taken her under their wing almost from the time she'd arrived in New York two years before, fresh from a three-year stint in Paris where she'd been living and studying painting. As fate would have it, the Bradshaws were visiting a SoHo art gallery the same afternoon Nicole took shelter there. The rain was coming down in buckets with intermittent booms of thunder. As she'd removed her head scarf, Carol Bradshaw, standing nearby, had burst out with, "What lovely hair! Like a glass of fine wine held up to the light."

From that chance meeting a genuine, mutually rewarding friendship had evolved. The Bradshaws had lost their only child, a brilliant young man with the expectation of a full life ahead of him, to a freak skiing accident when he was about Nicole's age; now stepping in to fill that gap was Nicole, a young woman reared in the isolated Australian Outback but severed from her country by a family trauma about which she hardly spoke.

Just once in the early days did Nicole confide in Carol about her mother's tragic death, saying only that she was killed in a car accident when Nicole was twelve. She never divulged that the accident was on her family's huge historic cattle station. She never said it was she who had led her poor grandfather, now dead from shock and grief, to the four-wheel drive at the bottom of Shadow Valley; she who first sighted the bodies in the sizzling heat. Her beautiful mother thrown clear of the wreckage, body splayed over an enormous boulder, sightless eyes turned up to the scorching sun; the man's body still behind the wheel of the vehicle, windshield smashed, blood all over his face, just as dead. The man was David McClelland, whom her mother had jilted, on the eve of their wedding to marry Heath Cavanagh, a distant cousin and the black sheep of the family.

So many lives ruined all in the name of love!

The coronial inquest had brought in an open finding, leaving both families to endure years and years of cruel speculation, not the least of it the tricky question: who was Nicole Cavanagh's real father? Everyone

knew about the old love triangle, comprising Corrinne
Cavanagh and the two young men who'd loved and
fought over her. Inevitably doubts about Nicole's paternity were sown. Rumor had it the victims of the
accident may have been arguing—which was likely,
given the highly explosive situation that promised to
get worse. Corrinne may have made a grab for the
wheel, causing McClelland to lose control of the vehicle. The vehicle went over the escarpment plunging
to the floor of Shadow Valley. Heath Cavanagh's ac-
count of his movements was accepted—one of Eden's
stockmen vouched for him in any case—but the enmity between Heath and David was legendary. Two
neighboring pioneer families, once the greatest friends,
had been estranged for several years after Corrinne
had jilted her fiancé, David McClelland. Somehow the
families had patched it up in a fashion to accommodate Nicole, who was the innocent victim of all this
unhappiness. This allowed her to form a deep attachment to the young scion of the McClelland family,
Drake. But the early estrangement was nothing compared to the bitter war that broke out after the tragedy.

Without the evidence to prove it, everyone in
Koomera Crossing and the outlying cattle stations held
Heath Cavanagh responsible, as though he were a demon capable of being in two places at one time. Either
that, or it had been a murder-suicide, which no one
wanted to believe. Nevertheless no one was really sat-
isfied with the theory of death by misadventure. As a
result the speculation continued to run wild.

Nicole told her American friends none of this. Like
her, they'd known family tragedy, but not so much as
a whiff of scandal had touched their respected name.

In the Bradshaws, Nicole saw two handsome, aristocratic people in their mid-sixties who were friends when she truly needed them, alone as she was in another country. They became like family to her.

It was the Bradshaws who had found her her light-filled SoHo loft with its vast industrial windows. The Bradshaws who had introduced her to their wide circle of friends, a good many with sons and daughters her own age. When the Bradshaws saw her paintings, they'd insisted on helping her to get them shown. Through his contacts, Howard Bradshaw had even engineered her TV appearance that afternoon. Brief but important. She'd been introduced as a "sunny, up-and-coming young Aussie artist." As near-perfect a misnomer as Nicole could think of, for her background was too full of black trauma. One day she reasoned she would confide in Carol fully, but not yet. The past was too close. Too filled with grief. Grief was the worst illness of all.

Carol came to the door to greet her, her face warm and welcoming, shining with pleasure.

"Nikki, dear!" They kissed. Not air kisses, but real displays of affection.

"So sorry I'm late. Traffic, forgive me."

"Of course. You're here. We watched your guest spot. You came over wonderfully well. So beautiful and articulate. Howard and I are proud of you."

"It would never have happened without you and Howard," Nicole said, smiling, then arm in arm with Carol accompanying her across the spacious and sumptuous entrance hall. A magnificent neoclassical parcel gilt console stood along one wall, overhung by an equally magnificent black lacquer and gilt mirror with two antique English gilt figurine lamps to either side of an exquisite flower arrangement. The Bradshaws were wealthy on a scale that made her own family's fortune modest by comparison. She could see the elegantly dressed people gathered in the living room, which Carol had recently had made over—God knows why, for it had been beautiful before. Several heads were already turned in their direction. A little knot of people broke up, parting to either side.

Shock sucked the breath from her lungs as she felt the color drain from her cheeks. She put out one hand, then the other. Her mother was staring at her intently from across the Bradshaws' opulent living room. The most marvelous apparition, astonishingly young and beautiful, a half smile caught on her mouth, her whirling auburn hair floating around her bare white shoulders.

The long years were as nothing. Yesterday. Whoever said time heals all wounds? Someone incapable of great depths of emotion. True love is eternal. Unchanging. It endures beyond death.

The apparition was very slender and delicate, like a fine piece of porcelain. She was wearing Nicole's favorite color—violet-blue—with an all-over glitter of silver. A beautiful, feminine gown. Shimmering, light as air. Romantic.

Just like hers.

Rapture drained away as pain and despair flooded in. The long wall facing her, she saw now, was set with tall mirrored panels to reflect the chandeliers, the museum-quality antiques and the paintings. There was no apparition. She'd had no miraculous acquisition of psychic powers. How ridiculous to think so.

What she'd seen was her own reflection. An out-wardly composed, inwardly disturbed young woman. One who had suffered a shocking childhood trauma and had never broken free of its horror. All those years of therapy, futile. There was no hiding place from grief. The memory of her beautiful mother still held her in its spell. She wanted her back so badly she was capable of unconsciously conjuring her up.

"Nikki, darling, whatever is the matter?" Carol held her arm, gazing at her in dismay. "You're not ill, are you?"

Howard, tall and distinguished, a worried frown on his face, hastened to their side. "Nikki, dear?" He bent his silver head solicitously to hers.

"I'm so sorry." From long practice Nicole held herself together. Tried to smile. "I'll be fine in a minute. I felt a little faint, that's all. Too much rushing about and the excitement of appearing on the show." How could she possibly say she thought she'd seen some-one long dead?

"I imagine you haven't taken time off to eat," Carol scolded gently. "Never mind. I've got all your favorite things. There now, your color is back," she exclaimed in relief. "Howard, be a darling and fetch us both a glass of champagne."

"Of course." He hurried off.

Steady, Nicole thought. Steady. She took a calming breath, aware that a silence had fallen over the huge living room. She ran the point of her tongue over her lips. Her mouth was bone dry. A reaction to what she thought she'd seen, no doubt. But Carol and Howard were so very kind, she knew she'd be able to get through the evening.

IN THE EARLY HOURS of the morning the phone woke her, shrilling her out of the tormented dreams that had ceased to plague her for many long months but had returned suddenly in full force. The brain had an extraordinary power to relive the past just as it chose to throw up impenetrable walls. Though she returned to Eden only twice a year—for a short visit at Christmas and for her grandmother's birthday in June—she couldn't drive out its demons. They walked with her, talked with her, slept with her, appeared in her paintings, but never, ever would they reveal their secrets.

Moaning softly, her head muzzy, mouth parched, she rolled to the right-hand side of the bed, picking up the receiver without bothering to turn on the bed-side lamp. All these years she'd been unable to sleep in complete darkness, so it was her practice to leave a light on somewhere in the loft. The digital readout on the clock radio said 3:24 a.m. She could think of nothing but trouble.

She spoke into the mouthpiece, straining ineffectually at the top sheet that wrapped her like a mummy. "Hello?"

"Nicole?"

Her heart spasmed. She tried to focus on one of her paintings that hung on the opposite wall. A painting of the ruined tower on Eden. It was where her mother and her lover used to go. Hadn't she followed them as a child, already tuned in to tragedy?

"Nicole, are you there?" Aunt Sigrid spoke across thousands of miles of underwater cable as though she were no more than a block away.

"Siggy, I was asleep. Do you know what time it is

here?'' She glanced again at the luminous dial of the clock.

"To hell with that!'' Siggy, being Siggy, replied. "It's the early hours, but I had no option.''

Knowing her aunt so well, Nicole snapped together, throwing off the nightmare that clung to her like a shroud. "Bad news?'' Why ask when cold certainty assailed her?

"It's not your grandmother,'' Sigrid said, obviously following her niece's line of thinking. "She's fine. But you have to come home. Your father has found his way back to Eden.''

"Father? What father?'' She felt it like an electrical jolt, kicking out wildly to free herself from the clinging sheet. That wicked man she'd once called Daddy? Never!

"Your father, Heath,'' Sigrid reminded her curtly.

"I don't know him as my father.'' Nicole could hear the coldness in her voice.

"He's your father, Nicole, much as you've disowned him.''

"Oh, that's good!'' Finally she was able to sit up, absolutely astounded by the way her aunt kept pulling the rug out from beneath her feet, championing Heath Cavanagh at the most inappropriate times. "I was raised to believe he was my father. That all changed the day they found my mother.'' She lost control, finding herself shouting into the phone. "Your sister, Siggy.''

"Don't try to rattle my cage, girl,'' Siggy warned. "You'd feel sorry for this creature if you saw him. He's come to Eden to die, Nicole. He's got nowhere else to go. His whole life has been one terrible failure.''

Nicole rolled her eyes. ''And you're asking me to feel sorry for him? That's one heck of a request. Correct me if I'm wrong, but doesn't the whole Outback believe he killed my mother and David McClelland? The McClellands sure did.''

Sigrid protested strongly. ''There was absolutely no proof. It was a terrible accident. Your mother was known to have a hot temper just like you.''

''Don't talk like that, Siggy!'' Nicole cried. ''My mother was a victim. Dead and not even yet thirty-five. A victim of either David McClelland or Heath Cavanagh. She was not suicidal. She would never have left me, I know it. But we'll go to our graves with all the doubts they left behind. How dare that wicked man come back to Eden when Eden belongs to me.''

''You'd think you deserved it!'' Her aunt's voice rose as though she, too, had been dealt a rotten hand. ''What right did *I* have to inherit, after all? I was only the other daughter, the plain one with the sharp tongue. What right Joel, my son? It had to be you, Corrinne's daughter. And Heath Cavanagh's. She was madly in love with him once, I can tell you that.''

''You could tell me lots, but you never have,'' Nicole retaliated sharply. ''I'm not coming, Siggy. He can stay if there's nowhere else for him to go, but I never want to lay eyes on him again.''

Sigrid's anger vibrated over the line. ''What makes you think you can treat him like a leper?''

''Sure you weren't in love with him yourself?'' Nicole challenged, her mind in a chaotic whirl. ''He's not my father. And he's the one who said that, not me."

"He only said it because he was in a terrible state. He thought Corrinne had left him. He was obsessed with her from the moment he laid eyes on her."

"So she betrayed her fiancé." Her throat constricted. *Don't cry. Don't cry.* She swallowed and the awful feeling passed.

"Precisely! She couldn't help herself. Heath was a magnificent lover."

"And how would *you* know?"

"My sister told me," Sigrid said, seemingly untouched by her niece's implication.

For an instant Nicole hated her aunt utterly and completely. "No more than that?"

"No more. For God's sake, Nikki, what are you on about?" Sigrid demanded furiously. "We're talking about your poor father. He's in dreadful shape, cirrhosis of the liver. He hasn't got long. Your grandmother wants you to come home. It's unforgivable the way you flit in and out, can't wait to get back first to Paris, now New York. Anywhere else but Eden, where you belong. God knows we've all given you time. You should be here. That's why my father left Eden to you."

"But surely you enjoy playing boss, Siggy," Nicole retorted, stripping away all pretense. "We're made of the same stuff, aren't we? We're not crazy about men. We're crazy about a grand historical station called Eden. When it suits you, you forget Dr. Rosendahl thought it crucial I get away. I was only twelve when I found my mother dead, not a great age to be crushed by horror, so hold on to your compassion."

Sigrid's harsh, impatient tone softened. "Do you think I don't feel for you, girl? You've got plenty of guts. You were always strong, even as a child. More guts than my boy. Listen to me now. This is very, very important. I swear on your mother's grave, David McClelland wasn't your father. I beg you to believe me. Even the McClellands never entertained the idea you're one of them, even if you liked to rouse the devil in Drake by suggesting you might be cousins."

Nicole gave a brittle laugh. "Is he married yet?" She'd never be sufficiently free of her memories of Drake, so glamorous and charismatic in manhood; the boy she'd looked up to in childhood, though she'd had the companionship of her cousin, Joel, Siggy's son, who'd harbored a nasty jealousy of Drake.

"Why would you be interested?" Sigrid asked dryly. "Hostility between the two of you is the norm whenever you chance to meet. But no, he's not. Too busy buying up properties. You might consider this. He wants Eden."

"Be serious, Siggy!" She spoke through clenched teeth. "He'll never get it." Yet wasn't she plagued by that very fear? Siggy was right. Her real place was at Eden, guarding her inheritance.

"I wouldn't be too sure about that," Sigrid snapped. "You're no match for Drake McClelland, I can guarantee that. He's as tough as they come and a brilliant businessman. He's taken off like a rocket since he inherited Kooltar. It's no secret, either, he has no love for us Cavanaghs. He could destroy us all."

Nicole's answer was unimpressed. "Let him try. I'm not in awe of Drake. We grew up together, remember? I mean, come on, once we were pals."

"That's quite a while ago, Nikki. The tragedy changed everything, even if his family couldn't block him from seeing you. I know some sort of bond still exists, but Drake is the one person who can bring us down. You must know that in your heart."

Nicole felt cornered by her aunt's charges. She had seen Drake during her adolescence—they were both invited to every social function that came along as a matter of course—but past events had destroyed any chances of their sunny childhood relationship blossoming into something else. She was hated if only for her looks, which had once belonged to her mother. Still, like Siggy, she had the unshakable conviction Drake McClelland would play a major role in her life.

As the McClelland heir, he'd possessed a juggernaut drive toward achievement. It wasn't just fame and fortune, and the power that went along with them; Drake wanted a real stake in the country's future. He wanted to make a contribution, building on everything his forebears had achieved. Eden in anyone's language was a rich prize.

"Are you there, Nicole, or have you gone into a trance?" her aunt asked testily.

"I'm here," she answered. "Sorry, I did drift off."

"And I'm almost out of strength." Suddenly Sigrid's voice had a weak flicker. "Are you coming home?"

"I don't think I could with that man there."

Sigrid didn't pause. "Your father. He's in a sorry plight even if he did bring it all on himself. But I'm sorrier for you, Nicole. You haven't got a heart."

Nicole was so shocked tears sprang into her eyes. "Thanks a lot, Siggy. If I don't have a heart, how

come I didn't toss you and your dear husband out?''
Now she didn't fight the urge. She slammed down the
phone, feeling intense pressure build up in her chest.

If only she could be perfectly happy with the life
she'd made for herself here. Why she couldn't was a
great puzzle. She had the Bradshaws with their endless
kindness. Through them she'd made her own circle of
friends. Attractive, accomplished young people, full of
hope and ambition. She'd even met someone tonight
she felt it might be possible to fall in love with. But
the passionate love her mother had inspired in two
very different men had destroyed her. And them.
Small wonder Nicole had a profound distrust of strong
emotions.

She did have her painting, though. That was her
release. And she'd been assured by people whose
opinion she valued that she had a genuine gift. It was
Dr. Rosendahl, healer and mentor, who'd first suggested she use her gift as therapy to exorcise her demons. Rosendahl who had actively encouraged her to
continue further study in Paris. Her cup should be
overflowing.

Except it wasn't. Despite everything going so well
for her, she was haunted by a strong sense of loss. She
had frequent mental images of her desert home. The
Timeless Land, where the ancient earth was a rich
fiery red, where the sun looked down in unwinking
splendor from a cloudless opal-blue sky. Birds were
the phenomena of the Outback, and here great colonies
of birds screeched their lives away: brilliant parrots,
white cockatoos, the gray and rose-pink galahs, the
myriad small birds of the vast plains, orange and red,
the great flights of budgerigar wheeling and flashing

green and gold fire. Endless varieties of waterbirds lived in the maze of waterways, lakes, swamps and billabongs that crisscrossed the vast inland delta that was the Channel Country, a region of immense fascination, rich in legend.

A desert yet not a desert. She knew all it needed was the miracle of rain to turn into the greatest garden on earth.

The station had been named Eden for the impossible, wondrous blossoming in that vast arid wilderness. To be there was an experience forever retained. In her SoHo loft she could almost smell the perfume of the trillions of wildflowers. She could see herself as a child swimming through infinite waves of paper daisies, pure white and sunshine yellow, rushing back to her beautiful mother, standing a little way off, with a chain of them she had fashioned to adorn her mother's glorious hair.

She knew she wasn't as beautiful as her mother. She couldn't be. No one could be. Yet they had had to bury all that beauty on Lethe Hill. Had to leave it to the silence of the desert in plain sight of the eternal red sand dunes that ran to the horizon in great parallel waves.

Nicole settled back on the bed, running her hand through her auburn hair that fell in long loose locks over her shoulders and down her back. What was she to do? Siggy had confirmed her niggling fears. Drake wanted Eden. Why wouldn't he? It was a strategic, important station with permanent deep water. Maybe he even wanted to raze the historic homestead to the ground and rebuild. Drake had worshiped his only uncle just as she had worshiped her mother. The friendship they'd once shared had proved impossible to sustain; it was as though each was constrained to blame the other for the sin that had been committed. Each had armed themselves with a long sword, letting fly whenever chance brought them together. Their relationship had been damaged beyond repair. These days she seldom surrendered to the luxury of giving her mind over to memories of Drake.

But he was there all the same.

CHAPTER TWO

THINGS DIDN'T RETURN to normal after Siggy's phone call. Or what passed for normal for her, though recently she had begun to feel her life was starting to come right. Only there was no escaping the past. The more one tried to push it away the more it fought back like some noxious weed that festered and spread.

The truth was, Siggy's news had upset her badly, bringing back a sharper agony than she'd known in a long time. It stirred up all her old memories of the tragedy that had alienated two families and sent her fleeing halfway around the world in an effort to rebuild her life.

So Heath Cavanagh had landed on Eden's doorstep to die? He had no right whatever to be there.

Unless he's your father?

She could never escape that voice in her head. If only she knew without resorting to DNA testing. That would be too humiliating, except it could uncover a huge truth. Or a lie. Though she'd searched for evidence of him in her face and in her behavior, she couldn't or wouldn't recognize any Heath Cavanagh in her. No characteristic, no expression. Neither could she mark any resemblance to David McClelland. So who would know? She'd had to totally reappraise her mother's life. Her adored mother had not been Miss

Goody Two-shoes; most certainly David McClelland had been her lover. Before and after her marriage. Well, they'd certainly paid an appalling price for their infidelity.

Her grandparents had refused to talk about it. Siggy was adamant Heath was her father. While she was vocal in condemning him, Siggy could, on occasion, defend him with vigor. One had to wonder why. From all accounts Siggy had been jealous of her beautiful sister. Was it crazy to think at some stage Siggy might have indulged in some petty revenge by stealing Corrinne's husband, if only one single time? Either that or she'd fallen under Heath Cavanagh's spell and couldn't help it. So much that couldn't be spoken of. No wonder she'd been desperate to get away.

Her grandmother always understanding, never demanding, would love to have her home, though her grandmother had been the first to say the family should listen to Dr. Rosendahl's advice and send her away from Eden. At least until such time as she felt she could cope.

Who said she could cope now, even after five years of living abroad? Was she strong enough to confront the lingering ghosts? To visit the escarpment, Shadow Valley? Basically she was scarred, and those scars weren't going to go away. Sometimes she thought she would never be free to get on with her life until she had the answers to all the questions that plagued her.

Perhaps she could find them if she returned home. She was older, a survivor, albeit with unresolved grievances. In some ways it seemed the decision had been made for her. If she found Heath Cavanagh wasn't in the terrible condition Siggy would have her

believe, she'd send him packing. Then there was the
threat of Drake and his ambitions. She needed to be
home to keep an eye on him. She could see the big
advantages that would open up for him and the
McClelland cattle chain if Eden fell into his hands, but
Eden was her ancestral home. He would never take it
from her.

Nicole checked out Qantas flight schedules on the
Internet. By the time she disconnected, her plans were
already made. It may not have been exactly the thing
to do, but she had no intention of notifying the family
until the last moment. She'd arrive quietly, before
Siggy could cover all bases.

A WEEK LATER she arrived in Sydney thoroughly jet-
lagged but thrilled to be back in Australia. She'd left
a subzero winter in New York and arrived to brilliant
blue skies and dazzling sunshine of summer in the
Southern Hemisphere. She always found it impossible
to sleep on planes, so she was groggy with exhaustion,
her body clock out of whack. She was in no condition
to take a connecting flight to Brisbane, so she booked
into a hotel and slept. The next day she awoke re-
freshed, ready for the hour's flight to Brisbane midafternoon. That meant another night in a hotel and more
phone calls before she could arrange a flight out west
to the Outback that lay beyond the Great Dividing
Range, and from there a charter flight to Eden.

Flying was a way of life in the Outback, with a land
mass that covered most of the state of Queensland.
The Channel Country where she was heading was
home to the nation's cattle kings. Her people. A riverine desert, it provided a vast flat bed for a three-river

system that in the rainy season flooded the distinctive maze of channels that watered the massive stretch of plains. The Channel Country covered a vast area, one-fifth of the state, with the nearest neighbor—in Eden's case the McClellands—one hundred and fifty miles away. Chances were she'd be completely played out by the time she got home.

AT EAGLE FARM AIRPORT in Brisbane, the same old routine, minus the intensive obligatory checks that had taken place when she'd arrived from overseas. A lengthy process she accepted without complaint in this new dangerous age. Passengers resembling a benign flock of sheep headed off to Baggage Claim, where they milled around waiting for the luggage to come through. When it did, within moments a crush of bodies appeared at the conveyor belt, all eyes glued compulsively on the flap. As the luggage made its way around, it was seized triumphantly and hauled away.

She couldn't sight her matching Louis Vuitton bags, a going-away present from her grandmother years before. A young woman behind her suddenly rushed forward, nearly knocking her over, and heaved off a great canvas bag covered in travel stickers.

''Sorry!'' A rueful grin.

''No problem.''

After a while she began to get worried. Everyone else was picking up their stuff, so where was hers? Maybe someone had taken a liking to her expensive luggage. Absurd to spend so much money on luggage when it got treated so roughly, she thought wearily. Just as she was starting to feel this was no joke and her luggage had been left in Sydney, the first of her cases tumbled out onto the conveyor belt.

Thank God! Still she'd have a battle to get two of the heavy suitcases onto the trolley. She moved forward, prepared to marshal her fading strength.

HIS DRIVER was a short round balding man who stepped forward to identify himself.

"Mr. McClelland?"

"Yes."

"Jim Dawkins," the man said cheerfully. "I'm here to drive you on to Archerfield. Mr. Drummond sent me."

"Yes, I know. I spoke to Harry last night."

"Just the one case, sir?"

Drake nodded briefly. "It was only an overnight trip."

"I'm parked out front and down a bit."

"We might as well get under way."

"Right, sir." Dawkins took charge of the overnight bag.

God knows what made Drake turn back to look around the airport terminal. And at that precise moment. But if he hadn't, he'd have missed her. For a moment he stood immobilized by shock, feeling as if a hand had reached in and twisted his heart.

Nicole Cavanagh. He could count the days since he'd last seen her. June, when she'd returned briefly as she always did for her grandmother Louise's birthday. June and Christmas, like clockwork before she flew away again.

She had her back to him, standing at the conveyor belt waiting for her luggage. He'd recognize her anywhere by that glorious mane. It was difficult to describe the color, but it always made him think of rubies. Today the familiar cascade of long curling hair was pulled into a loose knot. As she turned—a young woman keen on collecting her luggage surged forward and nearly knocked her down—he saw that flawless skin, milk-white with fatigue, large, blue-green eyes set at a faint slant. Even at that distance, he could see they were shadowed with exhaustion.

Not that anything could dim her beauty and the aura she gave off, a mixture of cool refinement and an innate sexiness he knew she was almost totally unaware of. Every woman he met fell short of Nicole. She was wearing a sleeveless, high-neck top in a shimmery golden-beige, narrow black slacks, high heeled sandals, a tan leather belt with an ornate gold buckle resting on her hips. She looked what she was. A thoroughbred. High-stepping, high-strung and classy. No matter their dark history, he found it impossible to quietly disappear, to simply go on his way and ignore her. He'd heard Heath Cavanagh was back on Eden. Obviously Nicole was returning home to assess the situation.

"Wait for me, could you?" he asked Dawkins who, as an employee of an employee was obliged to do whatever he wanted, anyway. "I've just spotted a friend."

"Right, sir."

A friend? he asked himself, feeling his nerves tighten. These days they were more like veiled enemies. Too much history between them, old conflicts aired whenever they came face-to-face, but the magnetic attraction that had grown out of their childhood bond somehow survived tragedy and loss. Probably the tensions between them would never go away. But Nicole, like her tragic mother, took hold of the imagination and never let go.

He moved toward her, glad for the little while she couldn't see him but he could see her. Words would only tear them apart.

NICOLE HAD READIED herself to grab the first case, when a man's arm shot past her and a familiar male voice said near her ear, "Won't you let me? The Vuitton, is it? What else?"

She was paralyzed by shock, and her heart leaped to her throat. She spun around, feeling desperately in need of several deep breaths. "Drake?"

For a mere instant there was that unspoken recognition of their physical attraction. "Nicole," he answered suavely.

"You of all people!" She experienced a strong sense of dislocation, staring up at the commandingly tall young man in front of her. Two years her senior, Drake McClelland emanated strength and confidence, an air of authority he wore like a second skin. He had a darkly tanned face from his life in the sun, singularly striking hawkish features, thick, jet-black hair and dark eyes that were impossibly deep. "How absolutely extraordinary. I've hardly been back in the country twenty-four hours, yet you're one of the first people I meet. What are you doing here?"

He didn't answer for a few moments, apparently preferring to concentrate on collecting her heavy suitcases and depositing them on the trolley, a task he made look effortless. "Like you I'm a traveler returning home. You are returning home, Nicole?"

She ran her tongue over her dry lips. "Yes. Were you on the flight from Sydney? I didn't see you."

"Maybe I didn't want you to," he found himself saying unkindly, for he hadn't sighted her, either.

She winced slightly in response to his tone. "So things haven't changed, it seems." The last time she'd seen him, in June, it was at a picnic race meeting when inevitably their conversation, civil to begin with, had degenerated into passionate confrontation. Grievances were ageless.

"No." His features hardened, but there was also a kind of sadness there.

"Have you picked up your luggage yet?" she asked, simply for something to say. She was unnerved, amazed it was so, when for some years now they had lived in different worlds, coming into contact only when she was home. The place of her birth, though vast in size, was populated by a relative handful of people. Station people all knew one another. They were invited to the same functions and gatherings as a matter of course. She rarely refused an invitation when she was home, even if she knew perfectly well Drake would be there.

"I didn't have luggage, only an overnight bag," Drake replied over his shoulder. "It's with my driver. I'm flying out of Archerfield. The plane's there. How are you getting home?"

No smile. Curt tone. Always the overtones of authority.

"I'm not ready to go home yet, Drake." She studied his compelling face for a few seconds, then looked away. It made no sense to ache for what you weren't allowed. "I'm too tired. Too much traveling. I can't sleep on planes."

"Neither can I." He gazed down at her moodily. "So what's the plan? Stay overnight at a hotel and fly on tomorrow?"

"Something like that." She flipped back a stray tendril, conscious she was swaying slightly on her feet and unable to do much about it.

His hand shot out to steady her. "You look utterly played out."

"Thank you, Drake," she responded wryly, immediately aware of skin on skin, the crackling tension between them.

He dropped his hand abruptly. "Where are you staying?"

"The Sheraton."

"Then I'll give you a lift into the city."

She shook her head, feeling extraordinarily close to tears. Exhaustion, of course. "You don't have to do that, Drake."

"I know," he said, "but since I've known you all your life, I don't feel right leaving you when you're so obviously jet-lagged. My driver is waiting outside."

She hesitated, hoping against hope the usual antagonism wouldn't flare up. "If that's what you want."

"It is."

"Right, well…I have to say yes and thank you. But I'm taking you out of your way, aren't I?"

"It would hardly be the first time," he said tersely. "I suppose I could change my plans to accommodate yours. It won't matter much. We could fly back tomorrow. The alternative for you would be many more hours spent arranging connecting flights.''

"I can't ask you to do that." She spoke quietly, feeling all the distrust and conflicts just below the surface.

"Why not? It's not as though you don't have enough on your plate. I heard your father is back on Eden.''

She shrugged. "Heath Cavanagh?"

"There's no remote possibility your father is anyone else." The last time they'd met, they'd managed to fight bitterly about her paternity. Accusations full of impotence, despair and fury. The acridity still hung in the air between them.

"Don't let's go over that again." Her breathing was ragged.

"It'd please me greatly never to hear you insinuate it again.''

"What do you know, anyway, Drake?" She stared directly into his dark eyes.

"I know you're your own worst enemy." As had happened so many times in the past, their conversation jumped to the deeply personal. No in-betweens. "You're incredibly bitter about your father."

"And you aren't?" Her eyes blazed.

Briefly he touched her arm, a calming gesture that nevertheless had steel in it.

"No one could call us friends anymore, could they, Drake." She made an effort to pull herself together, conscious that people were looking their way.

Drake moved to the relative privacy of a broad column. "Fate took care of that," he said dryly, "but we're still neighbors.''

"So we are. We get invited to the same places."

"How else would I have seen you in the last five years?" he went on, looking into her face. "Christmas parties, a wedding or two, polo matches…the last time, a picnic race meeting. One has to be grateful for small mercies. Things could change if you really wanted them to, Nicole. You have one solution at hand for this ongoing cause of conflict."

Hope spurted, died. "You're talking my father, DNA?" She tipped her head. Tall herself, she still had to look up at him.

"It would settle the paternity issue once and for all." There was challenge in his voice.

"I couldn't bring myself to ask him."

"You don't have to ask him."

"I need permission. That's how it works."

He kept his eyes on her. "You have a question. I have the answer. The decision is up to you. So far you've just made things hard for yourself. And me, too."

She shrugged, conscious of the truth of his claim. "Have you seen him?"

"I don't normally pop over to Eden to say hello."

"Once you did."

"Yes." Images of her as a bright and beautiful young girl flashed into his mind. She'd been quite the tomboy, determined, adventurous, brave in her way. Never the sort of kid that tagged along like her cousin, Joel. She had a wonderful natural way with horses, too, which had created an additional bond between them, plus a great love of their awe-inspiring desert homeland.

"Heath is supposed to be dying," she found herself confiding. "At least that's what Siggy said."

"Why does it sound like you doubt her?" He couldn't help frowning.

"I don't want to talk about that," she said, stalling. "In fact, I don't want to talk about Heath Cavanagh at all. He's not a very nice man. He could have blood on his hands. You McClellands long believed it." She drew a breath, and her next words held a conciliatory note. "I'm afraid of going home, Drake. That's why I don't go home."

"Do you think you have to tell me that?" he responded, his voice rough with emotion. He wanted to reach out for her. Comfort her. Once he would have. "We'd better cut short this conversation," he suggested. "You're sagging on your feet. I can't leave you here while I fly back home alone. I just can't. I'd be abandoning you to a series of very tiring flights."

"Indeed you would, but I've survived so far." She straightened her shoulders.

"At this point I doubt much further." He put a supportive hand under her elbow. "Let's call a truce. We can go back to being sparring partners after I land you on Eden."

CHAPTER THREE

NOTHING HAD CHANGED.

From the air Eden looked timeless. Primordial. Majestic. The homestead and its satellite buildings nestled in the shadow of the ragged escarpment that commanded the empty landscape. The colors were incredible. They reminded her of the ancient pottery she'd seen in museums. Orange and yellow, fiery red, molten cinnabar, indigo, the silvery blue of the mirage that danced over the spinifex plains. Vast areas that in the Dry resembled great fields of golden wheat. In the shimmering heat of the afternoon, the lawns and gardens that surrounded the homestead, fed by bores, were an oasis in the desert terrain.

"Eden!" All her love for it was revealed in the one word.

"Home of the Cavanaghs for one hundred and fifty years," Drake said with a glance at her proud yet poignant expression. "No time at all compared to the Old World."

"But plenty of time to put down roots." She stared down at her desert home, knowing it might be already under siege from the very man who sat beside her at the Beech Baron's controls. "Eden is our castle and we guard it from all comers." Her voice was charged with emotion and more than a hint of warning. "The ruined tower…'' Her voice faltered. That was a slip. She never mentioned the tower.

"Is a relic from the bad old days when it was used as a lookout and fortress against the marauding tribes.'' He wouldn't force her to bring up the personal significance of the tower. "That's the story, anyway. Personally I think the Aborigines were only trying to defend themselves or cut out a beast for food.''

"We don't really know. There were mistakes on both sides. Eden and Kooltar suffered several incidents in the same years, the mid 1860s. So did the McQueens farther to our north. A member of my own family and two of the station hands were speared to death barely a hundred yards from the tower door.''

"With the expected reprisals afterward.'' His tone suggested the reprisals had been too severe. "Didn't a tribal sorcerer put a curse on the Cavanaghs?''

A faint shudder passed through her body. "Thanks for reminding me. No one took it lightly. We still don't.'' After the tragedy, hadn't her grandfather said repeatedly the family was cursed?

He glanced at her sharply. God she was beautiful, and in the way that most moved him. Yet everything about her was dangerous to him. Danger to his self-assurance, his assumption he was in control of his own life.

"It all happened, Drake.'' She paused a moment, twisting her fingers. "They went to the ruined tower to make love. My mother and your uncle.''

"There, you've said it.'' His eyes flashed triumph. "Uncle. That's it. My uncle. My blood relation. Not yours.''

"Whether I believe it or not is another thing,'' she

answered, knowing the subject always led to a fierce row.

Just to prove it, he snapped back, "I'm not your cousin, Nicole." His voice that could sound so attractive suddenly grated. "I have no cousinly feelings whatsoever toward you."

"Maybe not, but where did the affection we had for each other go? Remember how we used to roam? We'd ride miles into the desert. Come back overheated by the sun to dive into a cool lagoon. You used to let me ride your palomino, Solera, now and again. Even Granddad liked to see you, despite the troubles. He always said you had a great future."

"Not everything disappeared in a puff of smoke," Drake mused. "I'm building very successfully on the inheritance Dad left me. The McClelland Pastoral Company is doing well. Making money isn't hard. Sustaining relationships is a lot harder."

"So how do you regard me now?" It wasn't said provocatively, but very quietly.

"The truth?"

"I don't want you to lie."

"As your mother's daughter." The words came out in an involuntary rush.

She gave him a sad look. "In your eyes, then, a huge flaw. I am my mother's daughter, Drake, but I'm proud of it. She wasn't the only one who committed the unforgivable. Your uncle was her lover."

His remarkable eyes flared. "A very dangerous thing to be. Fiancée, then mistress. It brought their lives to an untimely end."

"All because they wanted each other. No one really believes it was an accident."

"Well, if someone else's responsible, they're still out there."

"Supposedly dying." Her tone was flat.

"I don't think your father had anything to do with it," he confounded her by saying. "For all his faults he was far too much in love with your mother to kill her. My uncle maybe. Not her."

The great shift in his thinking confused her. "What are you trying to do? Rewrite history? Why are you saying this, and why now?"

He shrugged, but kept his eyes on the landscape below. "When were we ever able to discuss the subject without anger? You've had five years away to think. So have I."

"But you believed Heath was responsible somehow?" she protested. "Your whole family did. No one more than your aunt Callista. She was the loudest in her condemnation."

"That isn't surprising. She adored her younger brother."

"So did your father, but he was never cruel. He and your mother simply withdrew into a shell. I heard your mother remarried?"

"Hardy Ingram, the M.P. We've known him for years and years. He's a good man. He'll look after my mother well, but he's no substitute for Dad. He was a one-off. He died too young. These past couple of years without him have been sad. My mother couldn't stay on Kooltar."

"I can understand that." She didn't say that having her difficult sister-in-law around all the time would make things hard, but instead asked, "Is your aunt still living with you?"

"Kooltar is her home." Clipped, ready to defend.

"She should have married. Gone away." Nicole sat in sober judgment.

"None of your business, Nicole. We couldn't all run."

That stung. "Now, *that* was cruel."

His hands on the controls clenched, knuckles whitening. "Yes, it was. Bloody cruel. I apologize. You suffered more than any of us."

"I found them. How many hundreds of times have I been back over that horrible day? It's like a video you don't know how to stop."

"I can understand that. The shock and the grief killed your grandfather. My own father was never the same after. The way the investigation ended! It as good as left everything up in the air."

She looked down at her locked hands. Didn't she live her own life on the brink, just waiting for someone to shove her off? "I'm sorry, too, Drake. But it was never my fault."

"Of course it wasn't!" He gave a grimace of dismay. "At the end of the day we were all betrayed. I've thought hard about this. As I said, I believe your father had nothing to do with what happened."

"Then you're the only one." She sighed. "If you're right, that leaves the glaring question of who did. What about Heath's alibi? What if the stockman was lying? He left the station not long after and conveniently got killed when his ute ran off an Outback track. That's like having a two-car crash in the middle of the Simpson Desert."

"It was reported, as well, he'd been drinking heavily for days."

"Probably had one hell of a guilty conscience. Does your aunt still hate me?"

Drake's features tightened. "She doesn't hate you, Nicole."

"Don't be daft. Of course she does! When it comes to intuition, men aren't half as smart as women."

"I'm not about to disagree," he answered.

"Good. Around you, Callista was always very careful. Brothers and nephews are sacred. To hell with the rest of us. She never shared your liking for me, even as a child."

He glanced at Nicole through narrowed eyes. "Can you imagine how difficult it was for her with you the living image of your mother?"

"There are differences," she declared. "I'm me. I'll never be unfaithful to my husband. I'll never abandon my child. Oh, God, Nicole, shut up," she bid herself, shocked at coming so close to condemning her mother.

"Let it out."

"I've had years of letting it out."

"Maybe the struggle has been too much. Maybe you have your own secrets you don't want to be known. At least you have a source of release through your paintings."

"Yes, maybe. Certainly mine aren't happy paintings, Drake, although critics seem to find them powerful."

"I hope I can see them."

"Sure, I'll bring some over to the house," she suggested with heavy irony. "I just know I'd be welcome. Dear Callista hated my mother long before she hated me. Even as a kid I saw glimpses of it."

"The devil you did! Cally was all set to be your mother's maid of honor."

"A piece of diplomacy."

"You know nothing about it. You weren't around."

"Well, you were only a toddler and I could have been already in the womb." Her voice was perfectly calm, accepting. "I was a premature baby. You'd almost believe it, except I was robust from day one. My mother and I talked a lot, you know. We were very close."

The gaze he turned briefly to her was piercing. "Are you trying to tell me your mother confessed to you that Heath Cavanagh wasn't your father?"

She stared back, hot color coming into her cheeks. "No need to look so intimidating. You don't scare me. She never said anything of the sort."

"I never believed for a minute she did," he retorted with complete conviction. "But you must have felt tormented. Did you ever ask?"

"Lord, no!" Nicole gave a violent shake of her head. "I wanted to believe it."

"What?" A single word delivered like a shot.

"That Heath was my father."

He gave a short laugh. "He *is* your father. Your mother would never have lied to you about that."

"She didn't lie, either, when she told me Callista hated her. Callista believed her brother's love for my mother threatened her own relationship with him. You've heard of envy, haven't you? It's one of the deadly sins. Even Siggy envied my mother, her own sister."

He shook his head wearily. "What else did you expect? It must have been very difficult for Sigrid to have a sister as beautiful and as fascinating as Corrinne. Poor Sigrid lacked those qualities.''

''And Heath Cavanagh never let her forget it.''

Hadn't he always thought there was something there? Drake pondered. Sigrid's unrequited desire for her brother-in-law? ''Corrinne besotted them all,'' he said finally. ''I know you don't want to hear it, but your relationship with Joel might have similarities.''

She shot him a horrified glance. ''You're insane!''

''I wish.'' His sidelong glance was deadly serious. ''I think your mother had a few concerns Joel was too much around you.''

Nicole couldn't restrain herself. She threw out a hand, clasping his strong wrist as hard as she could.

''Don't do that, Nicole.'' He shook her off, suddenly seeing a vision of his uncle behind the wheel, the beautiful woman beside him, striking out in anger, perhaps making a dangerous grab for—

''You make me so angry!''

''You always did have a temper,'' he observed grimly. Something she shared with her mother?

''Well, you arm yourself with your tongue, I think. You're making up all this business about Joel.''

''I don't make things up, Nicole. You should know better.''

''But Joel and I were reared together. He's my first cousin.''

''So he is. Maybe he finds that a problem. He can't focus on anyone else.''

She averted her head. ''Why do you hate Joel?''

''I don't hate him. I don't hate anyone. But even when we were kids, he was never harmless.''

''What do you mean?'' Oddly she half understood.

"You're never going to get your head out of the sand, are you."

"Are you implying something was wrong?" She found the whole subject too difficult to deal with.

"Of course not. But didn't your mother who spoke to you of so many things ever suggest to you Joel was too dependent on your company, your affection?"

"No, she didn't!" Nicole's answer was vehement. "What have you got Joel pegged as now? An incestuous psycho?" Had her mother ever mentioned something on the subject? If she had, Nicole was unwilling to open the door of her memories even a crack.

"First cousins can and do marry. Forgive me, it's just that I'm not comfortable with Joel. I never was. I remember him forever hovering, always wanting to know what we were talking about. He was right there at the race meeting in June. Hasn't changed a bit."

"Probably thinking he should break us up. Joel really cares about me."

"We all know that. Nevertheless, a word of warning won't go astray now you're back on Eden."

Her mind turned over his words, rejected them. "Why oh why do people get things so wrong?"

"I'm only trying to put you on guard. The protective streak I developed a very long time ago."

"If there's any threat to me, it could come from you," she said quietly. "We both know you'd like Eden. You'd like the Minareechi." She referred to Eden's largest, deepest, permanent stream that in flood turned into a tremendous sheet of water, the breeding ground for huge colonies of nomadic waterbirds.

He said nothing, so she continued, "You'd like to add it to the McClelland chain?"

Finally he spoke, his tone mild. "I'd be right there if Eden ever came on the market. Why not? If I didn't get it, someone else would. Has someone been dropping little hints in your ear, Nic?" He shocked her by using his childhood name for her. "Most probably Sigrid, while she was delivering the news that your father had returned."

"Siggy's no fool," Nicole said.

"I'll happily acknowledge that. But Eden has gone down, Nicole, you have to admit. It's no longer the same as it was in your grandfather's time. Sigrid does her best, but she's no replacement for Sir Giles. Her husband is little use to her. Alan's an odd bird, actually. You could know him for years and years and yet never really know him. And Joel isn't performing well as manager. You must have felt the weight of that when you were last here. He's arrogant. He has a harsh tongue on him. He's devoted to heavy arguments, instead of getting on with the job. Eden has had trouble holding on to good men. I'd say that was testament to Joel's style of management."

"No doubt you've poached them away," she accused him, perturbed by the truth of what he was saying.

"As it happens, three of your stockmen found work on Kooltar in the last couple of months. One of them said your cousin scared the hell out of him."

Color flew into her cheeks. "Is this an all-out attack on Joel?"

"If that's how you see it. Ask around, Nicole," he suggested grimly. "Joel has developed quite a reputation for violence. There was an incident in Koomera Crossing that left the locals pretty disturbed. A bar fight. Apparently unprovoked. It took four men to hold Joel down. He's been barred from Mick Donovan's."

Her whole body tensed. "So he crossed the line once. He's aggressive, just like all men are. Why are you telling me this?"

"For the obvious reason you need to know. Your cousin Joel isn't Eden's future."

"Eden belongs to me."

"Are you sure you want it?" His words were very direct.

"Of course I want it. Eden's my heritage. It's in my blood."

"But you prefer to live in New York?"

"You think that means I don't love and miss my home?" She stared at his strong profile. "New York has been my safe haven. It's a fabulous place. A city I've come to know and love. The city and its people. All the more so since September 11. I have wonderful friends there who've helped me rebuild my life. I take my painting seriously. I'm becoming known. I'm making an impression."

"So I've heard." His voice was filled with admiration.

"How? Through the family?"

His response was ironic. "I told you, I don't have casual conversations with any members of your family. I have my own sources."

Her tone was caustic. "They're usually called moles."

"We were all desperately concerned for your safety after we discovered the full extent of the destruction in New York. I was glad of my moles then. So, believe it or not, was Callista. Are you returning to the States?''

She took a deep breath, staring down at her locked hands. "Not for a while, Drake. There are things I need to address. Conflicts and identifications. Perspectives." Maybe even Joel's problematic impulsiveness.

"If solving once and for all who your biological father is, the answer is at hand. For all you say, Nicole, you have no real hope of moving forward until you face the truth.''

JOEL WAS THERE to greet her when they landed. Tall and lanky, broad shoulders, dressed in jeans and a bush shirt, high boots on his feet, a black akubra rammed on his sun-streaked blond head. No one who saw them together would recognize them as blood relatives, Nicole thought. She was a Cavanagh, while Joel took after his father, Alan. They both had narrow heads, narrow faces, and sharp regular features that could look foxy on occasions.

"Are you going to speak to Joel? Try to patch things between you?" Nicole asked Drake, her tone with a certain appeal in it.

"No chance! We've never really communicated.''

"Oh, please, Drake.''

Her look of anxiety weighed on him. "I can't see it doing much good, but okay.''

"God, what an honor! The great Drake McClelland!" Joel approached at a lope, glittery-eyed, confrontational, despite his lopsided grin. He opened his arms wide for Nicole to walk into them.

It was so much easier to do so than not, regardless

of what Drake had said about Joel. "The prodigal returns."

His kiss of greeting was startling, for it was not on the cheek as she'd expected but on the corner of her mouth.

"Nikki!" He gave a nervous laugh, hugging her so tightly she was afraid she'd have bruises. "Boy, is it good to see you!" His eyes shot sparks. "You can't know how I missed you." He drew back a little, searching her face.

"I missed you, too, Joel. I missed everyone. I miss my home."

"I hope you mean that." Joel's gaze turned still and serious before he brightened. "They're all waiting for you. Including your dad at death's door. Eden is like the dark side of the moon without you, Nikki."

His words sounded so extravagant that for a moment she didn't know what to say. "I needed space, Joel. Time. I never want to hurt anyone with my continuing absence."

"It's taken having your father back to bring you home again. Never mind. I don't care what the reason is, just the fact you're here. You look marvelous. More beautiful every time I see you."

"Molecules, Joel," she told him lightly. "The way they're arranged. You look great, too." Gently so as not to offend him, she withdrew from his embrace. For the first time ever she felt self-conscious with her cousin and she blamed Drake.

Joel's eyes moved briefly to Drake, who had never been his friend, preferring Nicole every time. "How you two managed to run into each other I'll never know.'' He eyed Drake closely as though he suspected it was no accident at all.

"The element of chance," Drake drawled. "Now that Nicole is safely delivered, I'll be on my way."

"Why rush off? Long time no see." Joel's tone was bright, but Nicole clearly saw the venom. Like his father, Joel had a giant chip on his shoulder.

"Things to do. Always things to do," Drake declined in an easy, casual voice.

"If what I hear is true, you're negotiating to buy out Vince Morrow."

Drake shrugged. "First rule of business, Joel. Don't give out advance information."

"You never change, do you." A definite sneer. "Always the big man. The big action hero. Or that's how everyone seems to view you. Not me."

"That seems certain," Drake responded. "I think I'll go before this gets nasty."

"Only fooling. Just testing," Joel said, and suddenly grinned. "Fact is, Drake, I've always admired you. You always were someone. Even as a kid. A kid destined to go places, according to my dear grandpa. 'Course, you had a head start, being your dad's heir."

"I think I'll skip the compliments, too," Drake said, secure in his ability to handle difficult customers like Joel Holt. He turned his head to Nicole, who was looking on in dismay, no doubt waiting for the right moment to intervene.

"Thank you so much for the flight, Drake," she said quickly. "You saved me a heap of trouble."

"My pleasure." He looked at her steadily, making up his mind. "I've done a lot of changes on Kooltar. Maybe you'd like to see it sometime?"

"My God, is that an invitation?" Joel cut in, his tone high and derisory.

"The invitation is extended only to Nicole." Something flickered in Drake's eyes, signaling he wasn't going to take much more.

"And I accept it." Nicole threw Joel a quelling look, which he promptly mimicked.

"Don't tell me you two have made up," Joel said incredulously.

"We're simply being civilized," Drake said. "We're neighbors. Our families were once close. Nothing can be accomplished when people are divided. I'll give you time to settle in, Nicole, before I ring you to set a time."

"Thanks again, Drake." Given Joel's aggressive attitude, she was on tenterhooks waiting for Drake to go.

"Be seeing you." He sketched a brief salute, then strode to the Beech Baron. He didn't so much as glance back.

"God, would you look at him!" Joel muttered, tanned skin stretched taut across his cheekbones. "Arrogant son of a bitch. Always did have that contemptuous air. Magnet for the women, though. A real stud. He's as good as engaged to Karen Stirling."

"Really? He never said." Nicole felt a betraying hot flush.

"What does it matter to you?" Joel asked, eyeing her closely. "For years now the two of you can't even look at each other without a fight starting. You launched right into an argument the last time you were here."

"You really saw it like that?"

"Are you telling me it wasn't like that?" Joel's gray-green eyes locked onto hers.

"I'm telling you I'm tired of the fighting. I'm tired of the hostility. As Drake said, our two families were close once. We still share a common bond. We love the land. I'm hoping with a little goodwill on both sides we can narrow the chasm that's divided us."

Joel guffawed. "I can't believe I'm hearing this! Are you hiding something from me, Nikki?"

"Don't be ridiculous. It's high time we buried the hatchet. Granddad's gone. So's Drake's father. The result of a single tragedy. It's so damn sad."

With a callused hand, Joel grasped her face and turned it to him. "You'd be the biggest fool in the world to trust Drake McClelland," he warned. "He's a devious bastard. He wants Eden."

"Well, he can't have it." Nicole considered her cousin squarely. "Let go of my face, Joel. You're getting much too aggressive. I want to go up to the house. I'm like they say in the song, I'm tired and I want to go home. I've done an awful lot of traveling. I'm not a good traveler."

"Sure, Nikki. I'm sorry. But I've been through a bad time, too."

"How exactly?" Nicole asked him quietly.

"I miss you so much when you go away. This coming and going is torture."

She exhaled. "That sounds so...oppressive. You don't depend on me for your happiness, Joel. If you do, there's something wrong."

He lifted his palms, dropped them again. "Is it wrong to miss you when you go away? God, Nikki, we grew up together. Under the same roof. Doesn't my missing you make sense?''

Unsure of herself, Nicole expressed regret. "Of course. I'm sorry.''

"But you're home now.'' Joel smiled, leaning forward to impulsively kiss her on the forehead. "I'm just so grateful.''

CHAPTER FOUR

SHE COULD SMELL the scents of her country. Feel its intense dry heat, bask in the radiant light so different from the light of the northern hemisphere.

Eden homestead faced her across a great downsweep of lawn, the broad stream of the Minareechi at its feet, meandering away to either side. Black swans sailed across its dark green glassy surface as they always had. There was a small island in the middle of the river, ringed by great clumps of white arum lilies, heavily funereal. A life-size white marble statue of a goddess stood on a marble plinth at its center, the base almost obscured by a purple mass of water iris. It should have been a romantic spot. In better days it had been. Her mother had loved it. Now the place bore a faintly haunted air.

Joel pulled up at the base of the semicircular flight of stone steps that led to the front entrance of the homestead. Eden was a departure from other historic homesteads. A large country house in the grand style, it showed more than a little of French influence with its great mansard roof and round viewing tower in the west wing. The first chatelaine of Eden, Adrienne, had been French. No expense had been spared to please her, uprooted as she was from a land of immense beauty and culture to a vast, arid, primitive wilderness, scarcely explored. Nevertheless, Adrienne had not only survived but flourished, bearing six living children. The French connection persisted. One of her great-aunts had married a distant French cousin and still lived in a beautiful house outside of Paris, Nicole's base when in Europe. A Cavanagh relative had brought a French bride home from the Great War.

Now Eden faced her with its proud tradition of service to its country. Her grandfather had been knighted for his services to the pastoral industry, as had his father before him. No such honor for Heath Cavanagh even if the queen's honor system hadn't been disbanded in favor of Australian honors. Drake McClelland would have been in line for that.

The great columns that formed the arcaded loggia were smothered not in the ubiquitous bougainvillea, but the starry white flowers of jasmine. The perfume was a potent blast from the past. Jasmine and its terrible associations. The day of the funeral... She tried to block its cloying scent, deciding then and there to have the whole lot pulled down and replaced with one of the gorgeous African clerodendrums.

"Welcome home," Joel declared, his hands on her shoulders possessively. "Let's go up. They'll all be waiting for you. Gran is nearly sick with excitement."

"I'm excited myself. I can't wait to see her." Neither of them mentioned Heath. Nicole looked around at her luggage.

"Barrett can take care of it."

"Who's Barrett?" she asked halfway up the stairs.

"The Barretts," Joel told her carelessly. "Mother hired them fairly recently."

"So what does Mrs. Barrett do? Help Dot?"

"Dot? Mum pensioned her off."

Nicole's first reaction was outrage. "Without speaking to me?" She heard the heat, the bewilderment, in her voice. "Dot's been with us forever." In fact, Dot had been born on Eden to a couple in service to the family. They'd lost Dot for a few years when she was married to an itinerant stockman who regularly beat her up and tried to sell her off to his friends. Afterward she'd returned to Eden penniless, defeated, permanently scarred, to ask for her job back. It was given to her gladly.

"Dot looked after us as kids, Joel," she reminded him. "She was our nanny. She was wonderfully kind and patient. Did she want to go?"

"Don't ask me." Joel shrugged the whole matter off. "I don't interfere in the domestic arrangements. She was getting on, you know. Hell, seventy or thereabouts."

"All the more reason to keep her. I thought you were fond of her."

"Nikki, the only person I've ever cared about is you." Joel gave her a strangely mirthless smile. "I thought you knew that. Don't worry about Dot. Mum would have looked after her."

"I should hope so," Nicole muttered, thinking this wasn't the end of it. Siggy had no business sending Dot on her way. Even if Dot had wanted to go, Siggy should have told her. Eden was hers, not Siggy's, wasn't it?

"Please don't be cross, Nikki," Joel begged with a quick glance at her face. "I just want you to be happy."

"Who's happy? Are you?" she asked briskly. "Occasional flashes of it are all we can expect."

"I need you to be happy," Joel said, putting much emphasis on *you*.

Once they were inside the huge entrance hall, the symbolic center of the house with its great chandelier, magnificent seventeenth-century tapestry and elaborate metalwork on the central staircase, a man and woman suddenly made their appearance. The woman was tall, rail thin, with short dark hair and deep-set eyes; the man was noticeably shorter. Neither of them looked particularly pleasant.

Joel introduced them briefly as Mr. and Mrs. Barrett. Dislike at first sight? Nicole wondered. It wasn't until she moved closer that she registered that the blankness of their expressions was actually shock. They looked the way people did when they saw a ghost.

Ah. It was her mother's portrait in the drawing room. Of course. She could have posed for it herself.

"Right, Robie, you can collect the luggage and take it up to Miss Cavanagh's room," Joel ordered sharply, irritated by the pair's demeanor. "Where's my mother?"

Mrs. Barrett was the first to recover. "Mrs. Holt will be here directly, sir. She asked to be told the minute you arrived. Lady Cavanagh is resting. I'll let her know you're here, Miss Cavanagh."

"Thank you, Mrs. Barrett. I'll see to that myself," Nicole was quick to answer.

Mrs. Barrett inclined her head respectfully, now a model of deference. "Mr. Holt is in his study."

In fact, Alan was coming down the central staircase

that very minute. Nicole looked up quickly, caught his expression before he had time to change it.

It wasn't welcome. It certainly wasn't joy as in, Darling Nicole's home! It was even possible he wasn't happy to see her at all. Uncle Alan had always played his cards close to the vest. No one ever knew what he was thinking, and he didn't even seem to have a past. Her mother had always said it was impossible to say what lay behind that bland exterior. Alan Holt escaped into his own world, but because of his fortuitous marriage lived exceedingly well.

Now around sixty Alan was still a handsome man, very elegant in his bearing. His full head of hair, once as blond as Joel's, was an eye-catching platinum. Did he enhance it? She wouldn't be in the least surprised, though Alan would keep them all in ignorance. His eyes behind his trendy rimless glasses were a frosty gray-green. "Fanatic's eyes," Heath Cavanagh once called them. Nicole thought that ridiculous. She'd never seen Uncle Alan get worked up about anything. Except after the tragedy, when he had sealed himself off in his own private tomb. Inside the extended Cavanagh family, some of them admittedly terrible snobs, no one could understand why Sigrid had married him. He wasn't "solid, one of us." He'd been an actor touring with an English repertory company when Sigrid, quite out of character, fell madly in love with him and married him before she'd had time to think about it; a quick private ceremony without benefit of family. Something she was never to live down. At least the marriage had lasted, though her grandfather had once remarked wryly, Alan would be terrified at the idea of going back to earning his own living.

Now he came down the steps holding his arms out to Nicole as though she was the nicest thing he'd seen in years. Pure theater. "Nicole, dearest girl!" An actor's good carrying voice, plummy accent, real? Religiously acquired? Who knew? That was privileged information.

"Uncle Alan! How wonderful to see you again." Hypocrisy was everything in polite society. Much as he had tried to win over her affections, Nicole had always found it difficult to get close to this man. Her grandmother, rather like Drake, was fond of saying, "One could live with Alan for fifty years and never know him."

As always he was impeccably groomed, a light jacket over his moleskins, smart open-neck yellow-and-white checked shirt. Pleasant whiff of cologne. A dandy. Useless around Eden. He didn't need to be busy. In the early days Siggy had been afraid that her sister's beauty would turn Alan's head. Of course, no such thing happened. David McClelland had been the center of her mother's life then, only there'd been no future for either of them.

They talked for a few moments about her long, exhausting journey getting there. "One would have to try covering the distances to know!" Amazement was expressed that Drake McClelland had elected to fly her home. How was he?

"As splendid as ever!" Nicole couldn't help saying, even though she knew Joel would take umbrage.

She excused herself to go to her room. Tidy herself up before she went in to see her grandmother. She didn't have a room exactly. She had almost an entire wing. Clear the furniture, and Joel and his friends

could have a polo match in her bedroom. Siggy had
arranged it all in a vain bid to keep her at home. A
leading decorator had been flown from Sydney to take
charge of extensive refurbishments. The upshot was a
suite of rooms that wouldn't have looked amiss at Ver-
sailles. All the rooms in Eden were huge by modern
standards, with lofty richly decorated ceilings. When
the decorator had seen the scope of his commission,
he had gone crazy with joy, muttering excitedly to his
sidekick about how much it would all cost. Normally
very thrifty for a rich woman, Siggy had given the
decorator and his team carte blanche.

It didn't add up to a decorating triumph. The de-
signer had gone right over the top, creating lavish
spaces only Marie Antoinette could have handled. Nicole would have to make a few changes even if Siggy
didn't like anyone to challenge her judgment. A lot
had changed since she'd grown up and Granddad had
died and left her Eden. Shifts in authority. Power.
Roles.

Dinner was always at eight. She knew they would
all meet downstairs in the library at half-past seven for
drinks. Inside the well-appointed bathroom, with far
too many mirrors—she wasn't that keen on an aerial
view of her bottom—she took a quick shower to
freshen up. Someone, probably the dour Mrs. Barrett,
had laid out soaps, body lotions, creams, potions, a
series of marvelously ornate bottles containing prod-
ucts for the bath. That was okay. Every woman liked
a bit of pampering. In a mirrored cupboard she found
a variety of over-the-counter painkillers of different
strengths, tubes of antiseptic cream, bandages—in case
she decided to slit her wrists? Everyone had heard her

story, knew she'd seen a psychiatrist for years. She remembered the time when even Siggy, the hardest-headed of all, had major concerns she might turn into, if not a nutter, a complete neurotic.

Satin-bound monogrammed pink towels had been set out, along with a pink toweling robe. She slipped into it, tying the belt, then opened her suitcases and put her clothes away. She spent several minutes deciding what to wear. Finally she dressed in a simple, white linen top and matching skirt, embellished with a fancy belt. She took two regular headache tablets, and only the thought of seeing her much-loved grandmother and not-so-much-loved aunt kept her from collapsing in a heap on the bed. Her hair had more life than she did in the summer heat. She brushed it back severely, twisting the curling masses into a heavy loop.

Her grandmother Louise and Aunt Siggy were waiting for her in her grandmother's sitting room, which adjoined the master-bedroom suite.

"My darling girl!"

The woman she loved most in all the world. "Gran." She flew to her, sending her aunt a sideways warm greeting. Her grandmother remained seated in her armchair, a sure sign of aching bones, graceful and amazingly youthful-looking for a woman approaching seventy. She was beautifully groomed from head to toe—Nicole had never seen her any other way—but frailer than the last time Nicole had seen her.

"I've been praying and praying you'd come home." Louise Cavanagh held her granddaughter's face between her hands. "If only for a little while,

Nikki. Just seeing you gives me so much joy and strength.''

Nicole blinked back smiling tears. ''I think of you every day, Gran. I dream of you when I sleep.''

''I love you so much, my darling.''

They were cheek to cheek. Hair touching. One a rich deep red, the other snow-white. When each drew back, their eyes glittered with tears.

The three women kept off the subject of Heath Cavanagh until all other questions had been raised and answered. Louise and Sigrid had long since heard about the Bradshaws—both from time to time had spoken on the phone to Carol, thanking her and her husband for looking out for Nicole. They were very grateful. They wanted to know all about her painting, her recent TV appearance, her continuing success. They wanted to know more about New Yorkers. And had Nicole met anyone—a man—she really liked? They knew of Carol's efforts, Nicole's few aborted relationships, the difficulty she had sustaining them. Most of all they wanted to know how she and Drake McClelland had got on. Just imagine, what were the chances of the two of them running into each other at Brisbane airport?

At one time her grandparents had lived for a happy union between the two families, planned a beautiful big wedding to be held on Eden. Their beloved daughter, Corrinne Louise to David Michael McClelland. It was to have been perfect. Only, scarcely a month before the wedding, Corrinne shocked and enraged both families by eloping with the devilishly handsome, hard-drinking, compulsive gambler Heath Cavanagh, a distant cousin. He not only stole Corrinne away. He stole the grand plan both families had laid down when Corrinne and David were little more than babies. Deprived them of the union of two pastoral dynasties. David was pitied. For a time he suffered severe withdrawal—there was a rumor, never substantiated, he had once attempted suicide—but the love of his family and the dynamic support of his older brother, Drake's father, saved his sanity.

Until he became involved with Corrinne again. The moth to the flame. Heath Cavanagh as a husband wasn't long in favor. David, her first and last lover, returned. After that it was only a question of time before tragedy overtook them. There was no way, given that particular triangle, they could escape their brutal destiny.

"So where is Heath?" Nicole asked finally, knowing there was no putting it off.

"He keeps to his room mostly," Sigrid said. "As I told you he's very ill."

"Shouldn't he be in hospital with the proper care?"

"It may come to that, but for now he desperately wants to stay here. He's come home to die."

"This isn't his home," Nicole said flatly.

"My darling, he is your father." Louise spoke in a near whisper. "He may have done lots of things to cause the family shame, but he's one of us. Our blood."

"Do you really believe that, Gran?"

"*I* certainly do," Sigrid suddenly barked. "Corrinne chose him. She had David, but she couldn't keep herself in line. She was a man-eater, and she looked like butter wouldn't melt in her mouth. You're not a cold person, Nicole. Just the opposite, but you're so bitter about your father. He suffered, too, you know.''

"What a lie." Nicole's blue-green eyes flashed.

"You were too young to see it," Sigrid said, her throat flushed with emotion. "Too much in shock. That man suffered.''

"That monster! I've never spoken of it, but he used to slap me.''

"I know nothing of this!" Louise said in amazement.

"I didn't want to start anything. Upset you or Granddad. He tried to throw a scare into me. It didn't work.''

"I'm not surprised," Sigrid said in a derisive voice. "You were just so…''

"What?"

"Spunky, I suppose. Cheeky. Too precocious.''

"She was adorable," Louise protested, never one to find fault in her even when she deserved it, Nicole knew.

"That man didn't love me. He didn't want me around.''

Sigrid snorted, loud as a horse. "That's not true, even if no one really rated beside Corrinne.''

"I don't understand how you can defend him, Siggy—when it suits you, that is," Nicole said.

This time Sigrid inhaled forcefully. "Because I feel sorry for him.''

"Well, I hate him. I mean, I really hate him. I could have had my mother—''

"You can't get off it, can you? You've got some incredible block.''

"Block, be damned!" Nicole saw red.

"My dears, please stop." Louise held a lavishly bejeweled hand to her head.

"I'm so sorry, Gran." Nicole broke off immediately. She and Siggy had always gone at it.

"There has to be hope for us," Louise said. "If Drake has asked you over to Kooltar, surely we can see that as a thawing, can't we?"

"Gracious me, who'd want to call on Callista?" Sigrid hooted. "You surely don't think you're going to fall into her outstretched arms, Mother. She bloody hates us, the cold bitch. She blames us all for the loss of her brother. She worshiped at his feet. Everyone knows that. If I'd have been her mother, I'd have sent her packing."

"To where?" Nicole asked. "That's hardly fair. She was the daughter of the house."

"They should have sent her to one of her relatives in Sydney or Melbourne," Siggy said sternly. "Opened up her life. Station living is too isolated. We're too much in one another's pockets. Callista was positively fixated on her brother. A byproduct of a lonely life. I tell you, if he hadn't been her brother, she'd have tried to bag him. She was too close. A bit kinky, I'd say."

"Like Joel is too close to me?" Nicole shocked her by saying.

Sigrid, on the voluptuous side when young, now bone thin, let out a swearword that made her mother wince. "That's the most preposterous thing I've ever heard. It's not at all the same. Tell her, Mother."

Louise sighed deeply, flapping her right hand helplessly. "I'm not sure if Nicole isn't right."

A worse swearword escaped Sigrid. "You've only

just come home, Nicole, and you're already stirring things up.''

"I'm trying to understand what's going on in my life, Siggy," Nicole responded hotly. "I don't want to upset you, especially when you let fly like a station hand. This may not be the time to ask, either, but why did you get rid of Dot?"

"Why talk about bloody Dot?" Sigrid made a gesture as though she was swatting a fly. "It was time she retired. She wanted to live on the coast."

"I never, ever heard her express that desire." Nicole lifted her eyebrows.

"It seems she did, darling," Louise intervened gently.

"She said that to you, Gran?" Nicole was amazed. "She said nothing to me and I was here in June. Why so sudden?"

"I don't know, darling, but she seemed quite happy to leave. I was most surprised. I thought Dot was a fixture on Eden."

"If you give me her address, Siggy, I'd like to contact her." Nicole turned to her aunt.

Sigrid nodded stiffly. "I'm sure I've got it somewhere. If you don't trust me, Nicole, to make decisions..."

"Of course I trust you, Siggy." Nicole felt free to lie. "You should have told me, all the same. Dot was devoted to Joel and me when we were children. How much severance did you give her?"

"Certainly not a blank check." Sigrid pulled a long face. "But enough to keep her comfortably for the rest of her life. That's if she's careful."

"If you don't want to say it, Siggy. Write it," Nicole suggested acidly.

"All right, twenty thousand." Sigrid compulsively smoothed her thick caramel-colored hair, her best feature for all her tendency to hack at it with nail scissors.

Nicole shook her head in dismay. "That was supposed to be generous? She could live for another twenty years unless she meets up with a bus."

"I don't think so," Sigrid replied briskly. "Dot smokes like a chimney. I thought anyone who smoked was a leper these days. No one could stop her, though she didn't dare smoke in the house. She'll probably finish up with lung cancer."

"Dot, poor Dot, what a vulnerable soul!" Nicole moaned. "This isn't the end of it, Siggy. I have to ensure Dot is secure. That's the least I can do. I suppose I can even meet Heath Cavanagh if I put my mind to it. If he's not as ill as you're saying, I'll put him on the first plane out of here."

"What about Zimbabwe?" Sigrid challenged. "Is that far enough?"

"You won't want to when you see him, my darling," Louise promised very quietly.

CHAPTER FIVE

WHERE WAS the handsome, rather bullish man she remembered? Where was the bulk of chest, the width of shoulder? The florid patches in darkly tanned cheeks? The voice like an erupting volcano? The intimidating demeanor? The glitter in large, mesmerizing, black eyes? Gone, all gone. His illness had reduced him to a haggard shell.

"Hello, Heath," she said softly, venturing into the large elegant room this man had once shared with her mother. Even with fresh air streaming through the open French doors, it had a sickly fug.

"Nicole." He moved to stand up, but fell back coughing into the deep leather armchair someone must have brought in for him. Siggy, probably. Nicole didn't remember its being there.

"You look ill." He looked far worse than ill. Despite herself she felt badly shaken.

"I *am* ill, bugger it, but the heart is still pumping." A faint echo of the bluster. "How beautiful you are, girl. Aren't you going to kiss your dear father?"

"That's one heck of a question to ask. No, I'm not. You're lucky I have such a sweet nature, otherwise I wouldn't have come to visit you." She didn't have the heart to say she half believed her real father was dead.

"Don't blame you," he mumbled. "Terrible father.

No skills for it. No skills for husbanding. The only bloody thing I was ever good at was bedding women. And on my good days backing the right nags. Please sit down. I hope you're going to stay a while.''

"So we can chat?" The animosity was unfolding. Nevertheless she did as he asked, taking a chair several feet away, facing the balcony.

"Sarcastic little bitch!" he grunted, his near-affectionate tone defusing the insult. "All right, so I'm a beast and a brute, but I care about you, Nicole. In my own miserable, insensitive way. Didn't have much to give after your mother— Adored her. The plain truth."

"I expect you've convinced yourself that's true."

"What do you know about passion, girl?" The sunken eyes flashed.

"Not much, but it's nice of you to be concerned. Most days I walk about frozen inside. That comes from finding the bloodied and smashed bodies of my mother and her lover in the desert with the carrion circling. Some people might call that a fairly seismic trauma. And the name's Nicole, by the way. I don't answer to *girl*. It's on my say-so that you'll be staying on Eden.''

He looked amused. "Pardon me, but is that a threat, my lady?"

"It sure is," she answered laconically.

"Even as a kid you knew how to crack the whip. Granddad's little princess."

"All destroyed."

"Yes." His sigh rattled. "I beg your pardon most humbly, Nicole, even if you were reared an uppity little madam. Not my doing."

"Maybe you never knew how to speak to me properly, you cruel man."

"When was I cruel to you?" He appeared genuinely taken aback.

"You used to take swings at me all the time."

"When did one land?"

"I was too quick."

He started to laugh, stopped, hand on chest, as though it pained him greatly. "You never told on me to your granddad. I admired that. I'd like to stay here, Nicole, if you can stand me. I haven't got a lot of time…"

Looking at him, listening to him, Nicole didn't doubt it. "Surely you should be in a hospital where they could give you the proper care. I'm willing to foot the bill if you can't."

"My dear," he said in a semblance of his once-deep, rich, whisky-and-smoke-laden voice, "I was hard-pressed just to buy a train ticket out here. After a lifetime of gambling, and I've had a few huge wins, I'm stone broke."

She looked away, more disturbed at seeing him like this than she could have imagined. "That's okay, you always were, until you married my mother. She must have been in one of her completely mad phases when she married you."

"My dear, we were both completely mad," he said almost cheerily. "But she loved me. For about ten minutes."

"Before you drifted back to all your little games?"

"Don't you bloody believe it!" he exclaimed loudly, then paid for it with a coughing fit during which Nicole passed him a glass of water. "Thank you." He drank, let her take the glass from him. "Can you believe it, all these years later and I still feel rage. Oh, that woman! I was the casualty, child. Your beloved mother was the one who was carrying on. I loved her."

"It was just that you didn't know how to show it." The sentence came out like a lament, which indeed it was.

"A tremendous handicap of mine. Look at me, Nicole, not out the bloody door."

She didn't know whether to laugh or weep, but instead said with stinging contempt, "I've already given you a complete once-over."

He cocked his dark head to one side as though making a judgment. "You know, sometimes you talk like me. Razor-sharp, but just a pose."

She shook her head in denial though it suddenly struck her forcibly that she did occasionally. Exposure to him, of course. Her mother never had a cutting tongue.

"I loved your mother like I've never loved anyone in my life," he said, clearing his throat. "I can't look in the mirror without seeing her head peeping out from behind my shoulder. She used to stand there, you know, when I shaved, her arms locked around my waist. She was such a seductive creature and she didn't even know. I can't walk down the street without spotting her ahead of me in the crowd. That marvelous hair. Your hair. Trick of the light, of course. No one's got your hair. You're not really the image of her. Everyone else might think so. I don't. Side by side you'd see the differences. You're taller, more willowy. You have a certain regal, albeit peppery, presence my

Corrinne couldn't match. She didn't have the sugges-
tion of a dimple in her chin, either.'' He put up a hand
to stroke his deeply dimpled jaw. ''Her eyes didn't
flash like yours or glitter with anger. I know you've
had a rough time, but you look like a fighter. You'll
be the kind of old lady no one wants to cross. Corrinne
was sweet and gentle like Louise. She never had your
kind of fearlessness. She bruised too easily.''

Nicole found these confidences very strange. ''I've
heard she had my temper.''

He guffawed, broke into another rasping cough.
''Nonsense! That's *my* temper,'' he said eventually.
''Corrinne was a pussycat compared to you. Even as
a little kid, you could work yourself into a fury.''

Nicole was flabbergasted. Is that the way he saw
her? ''Only with you,'' she burst out in defense. ''A
gentleman doesn't slap little girls. And ladies. I'd say
you enjoyed it.''

He shook his head, the once-springy black hair flat-
tened and thickly peppered with white. ''Girlie, you
were spoiled rotten. You really needed a firm hand,
but you didn't get one. Your antics only served to
entertain. Your grandfather in particular. He under-
mined every effort to put a curb on you. You were the
grandchild he wanted. The sweet little firebrand with
the Shirley Temple curls. Poor difficult little Joel
missed out with the old hypocrite!''

She stared at Heath, shocked. ''That's not true!''

''Of course it is.'' His breathing wheezed. ''But we
can keep that between you and me. Siggy loves her
boy without liking him. She's always trying to protect
him, but Joel has been a big disappointment. He really
needs to get out before it's too late. I don't know why

he doesn't pack up and leave like I did. He's got the consolation prize—plenty of money—even if he didn't get Eden. He doesn't want it, anyway. Hell, I was a better cattleman than him. He's not even a good horseman. Too hard on 'em. Give a horse what he wants, food and affection, and he'll do anything for you. You know that. You're the horse lover. Joel would give anything to possess the skills of someone like Drake McClelland. It always seemed to me you had a bit of a crush on Drake, for all the sparks that flew between you.''

She felt as if a deep dark secret had been ripped from her. ''I'm afraid you're way behind the times,'' she said coolly. ''We were friends, but that was a very long time ago when we were kids. Any adult relationship was damned.''

''Yet I suspect some part of you craves one all the same.'' He pulled out a handkerchief and pressed it to his mouth.

Nicole shook her head. ''I'm sure neither of us has given the other much thought these past years. I'm not into obsession and neither is Drake.''

''But neither of you can exorcise your demons any more than I can. I want my name wiped clean before I die, Nicole. I've had to live all these years like a murderer who somehow got off. I've lost so much— my friends, my wife, my daughter, a future. My health.''

''I don't blame you for feeling sorry for yourself.'' She sat farther back in her chair as though to ward him off. He was reaching her and she wanted to shut her heart on him.

''What would you know?'' he asked sadly. ''My

heart was torn from me. I would never have harmed a hair of your mother's head, though God knows she had it coming to her.''

''What about David McClelland?'' she asked tightly.

''That bastard! I hated him. I could have happily killed him with my bare hands. I certainly wished him dead. Maybe it would have gotten around to that.''

''I'm sure he returned the strong feelings,'' Nicole said. ''Only, he wasn't homicidal. You took his fiancée from him.''

Cavanagh sighed loudly. ''Ah yes, of course, of course. How can anyone take someone from the person they truly love? How did I find it so easy to sweep Corrinne off her feet? I swear, I didn't kidnap her. Corrinne was like a child. She did what her family wanted. She lived to please her father. Good old Sir Giles! Always the perfect gentleman, twinkling blue eyes and the patrician demeanor. A benevolent tyrant all the same.''

Nicole stared at him. ''Then what drove you apart? If my mother loved you enough to run off and marry you—defy everyone, two families—what went wrong?''

He studied his trembling hands. ''She got pregnant.''

''So? You didn't believe I was yours?'' Nicole tried unsuccessfully to keep painful emotion from choking her. At long last they were getting to it.

He fixed her with his sunken black eyes. ''You're like me, girl. I might seem vile to you, but I had my good points. I realize I was rotten in the role of father, but you're like the best of me. What I once was.''

"How absolutely dreadful!" Nicole shuddered. "You can't imagine what effect that news has on me."

"Please don't talk like that. I wasn't so bad before I fell in with your lot. I never had the security of money like you, Nicole. No one gave me everything I wanted. No one doted on my every word. My poor old dad, your grandfather, was a gambler like me. I lost my mother. Dad lost a wife early. We were an odd pair, my dad and I. It wasn't long before he became a rock-bottom case. Like I am now. But when I was young, I was very popular. Especially with the ladies. It seemed to me before I met your mother I was making something of my life. After Corrinne, it all blew straight to hell. Our marriage was all I needed to run completely off the rails. Another woman might have thought I was worth saving. She might have offered me loyalty and support. That's very important, you know. I might have made something of myself with a little help. Instead I walked straight into a minefield. I didn't have you. I was nothing and no one on Eden. Just the feller who supplied the sperm. Your grandfather reigned supreme. A colossus striding around his desert kingdom. Charming. Well bred. Greatly respected. So quietly spoken but everyone fell over backward to listen. Wife and daughters adored him."

"Maybe he looked at you and saw nothing," she said. "I adored my grandfather, too, might I remind you. In all my life he never said a cross word to me."

"More's the pity!" Heath barked, causing a bout of coughing that left him wheezing. "Those twinkling blue eyes could look very intimidating. The white

smile could turn to icy contempt. You didn't know
your grandfather in his glory days. A bloody tyrant!''

"Who tolerated you and Uncle Alan.''

"Please, do me a little favor. Don't lump me in with
that poor fish Alan. He's loaded with neuroses.''

"And don't you speak ill of my grandfather. He
offered you both sanctuary.''

"What was at the heart of it, do you think?''

"What do you mean?''

"Alan was tolerated because he's Joel's father and
Siggy's husband, though she wanted him as long as
Corrinne wanted me—five minutes. Your grandfather
vowed to get rid of me. I was trouble. He may even
have set out to bring Corrinne and McClelland back
together, only, I hung in there. I really enjoyed thwart-
ing the old bastard.''

"Hung in there?'' Nicole's voice rose in mockery.
"You couldn't wait to make your escapes. For years
you were rarely home.''

"I could never persuade your mother to escape with
me. She was only sensitive to what Papa wanted. He
made no spoken demands. Plenty of unspoken demands. Besides, she could never escape and take you.
If your grandfather loved your mother, he positively
doted on you from your first yell, and you did yell—
at the top of your lungs. I was there, though it was a
wonder I was let in. Dear old Sir Giles completely
forgot he already had a grandchild. Cranky little Joel,
who couldn't measure up. The sins of the fathers are
visited on the sons. You were his little angel when
you were no angel at all. Watch Joel, by the way. As
a kid he was too bloody clingy. I used to say to your

mother—'That boy's got to go!' I thought she understood."

"Understood what?"

Heath's head fell back wearily. "Your cousin, my dear, has always been inordinately fond of you. It aroused a bit of anxiety. Joel never did obey the rules."

She felt wary and vulnerable like a woman under attack. "You make it sound like Joel is deeply disturbed. He had to get love from somewhere. We spent our entire childhood and adolescence together."

"Maybe that set the stage," Heath suggested carefully. "Human sexuality is a very strange thing. Monkeys don't get worked up about it. But humans! It's not only undesirable but I understand illegal in some countries for first cousins to marry."

"Rave on," she said angrily. "It's not illegal here. Kings and queens did it all the time. Maybe you're the kind of man who sees something sinister beneath everything. Just tell me this—am I your child?"

He studied her gravely, perhaps the one person who could see the contrasts with Corrinne clearly. "Is that so awful? You don't see that miserable wimp Mc-Clelland as your father, do you? I don't recall having a breakdown afterward. No one pitied me. They put me into the position of murderer."

"You had motive and a violent temper. It made for pointing the finger. And you've had your doubts about me—don't deny it, because you've expressed them."

He shook his head. "That's grief talking. Are you asking me to give a DNA sample to decide paternity." He breathed laboriously.

"No, I'm not."

"Thank God, because I still have some pride left. What are you frightened of, anyway?"

"Who said I was frightened?"

"You're emitting your fear to me, my dear. Or maybe it's because I know all about fear. Are you sick at heart you might be Drake's first cousin? You're not! I blamed your mother for a lot, but I never seriously doubted you're my child. McClelland was such a wuss he was probably impotent."

"Do impotent men carry on affairs with another man's wife? I'm sorry, but there must have been plenty of sex. Drake doesn't believe we could possibly be related. We once had a furious row about the whole subject. He doesn't believe you had anything to do with the tragedy, either."

"Because, my dear, he's got a brain. The McClellands needed a target at the time. Especially that silly neurotic bitch Callista, who regarded her younger brother as some sort of god. Sickening! I mean, no one should regard a brother like that. Feelings ran so high I could have been lynched. It's been very hard for me getting through life, Nicole. I'm almost glad it's nearly over."

"Is there nothing to be done?" Her voice faintly trembled as she spoke. His frailty had taken away her rage.

"Nothing. Say it's my own fault." He lifted his hand and for a moment looked into her eyes.

She could feel her heart beating painfully. "My anger seems to be draining away. I've fed on it for years. I can't feel any affection for you, Heath, even if you are my father. You did that to me."

His mouth twisted. "Your grandfather would relish hearing that from his grave. I wasn't allowed to love you, Nicole. I know you don't want to believe it, but it's true. Your grandfather and his kind know how to rule."

"How much better all our lives would have been had you left my mother alone."

He gave a strange rasping laugh. "But then you wouldn't have been here. You're my daughter, Nicole. Make no mistake."

She stood up abruptly, feeling she couldn't deal with any more right then. "Is there anything you need?"

"Just a little bit of respect. Am I allowed to stay?"

She wanted to passionately shake her head, but instead answered gently, "There's no need whatever to confine yourself to this room. You may treat Eden as your home. If there's anything you need, you have only to ask. Professional care can be arranged when you feel the need for it. Anything to improve the quality of your life. Come down to meals whenever you feel up to it. Or meals can be brought up. As you choose."

"Thank you, Nicole." A broken man, his vigorous good health gone, Heath Cavanagh bowed his head.

"It has little to do with love, Heath." Although her eyes stung with unshed tears, she couldn't find it in herself to keep up her nearly lifelong hostility.

"Ah yes, but then, you're a good girl at heart," he said, staring away across the room to where a lovely smiling photograph of her mother stood atop a cabinet. "You don't want for compassion."

NICOLE SLIPPED BACK into station life with the ease of someone who'd never really been away. She'd half expected sore muscles from the demands of being back in the saddle after long layoffs, her finely honed instincts blunted by disuse, but the moment Joel gave her a leg up into the saddle everything came right. Of course there were the initial protests in her legs and thighs and once or twice in her shoulder handling a strong and frisky chestnut colt, but she took it all in her stride.

It didn't take long to find out what Drake had told her was true. Joel wasn't running Eden with anywhere near the degree of efficiency her grandfather had. Where her grandfather with his fine reputation had given his quiet orders, always obeyed to the letter, Joel delivered them in a manner that often rankled with the men. She could see it on their faces. Everyone on the station—stockmen, their wives and children, the accountant in the office—had always referred to her tall, distinguished grandfather as Sir Giles. Joel, however, didn't seem to rate a name at all.

The situation wasn't good. In fact, she was very disappointed but scarcely knew how to put it to Joel. He had the tendency to be defensive, despite Siggy's best efforts to lend him support.

"How are you finding things on the station?" Siggy asked her after a week or so of settling in.

"I have some concerns, Siggy." Nicole decided to play it straight. "I need to look at the books."

"Of course. Whenever you like. What's bothering you?"

"One thing in particular. I suspect it must have been bothering you for some time. Things aren't going as smoothly as they should. There's a different atmosphere on Eden. It's worse every time I visit."

Siggy slumped wearily, sipping her tea. "No one could replace Father."

"No. It doesn't give me any pleasure to say this, Siggy, I know how much you love him, but Joel isn't on top of the job. God knows he's had the training. He doesn't seem to know how to relate to the staff. He gets their backs up without even trying. The sooner we get a good overseer, the better."

"Hang on!" Siggy's tea went down the wrong way and she spluttered. "You'd put an outsider over your own cousin?"

"It can't be totally unexpected, Siggy. Surely you didn't think you were going to hoodwink me. I toured Eden with Granddad all my life. We're talking business here. This is a working station. Eden has always had a wonderful reputation. I'm not going to allow that to slide away."

"So you're blaming Joel?" Motherly indignation was in Siggy's blue eyes. "What the hell!"

"Please don't take that attitude, Siggy." Nicole touched her aunt's arm in a conciliatory manner. "I'm not blaming Joel exactly, but in that, I'm being kind. I suppose the crux of the matter is he isn't in the right job. He uses a kind of force to get things done. No force should be necessary."

Siggy bit her lip, frowning ferociously. "He works very hard long hours. Eden is his life."

"I'm not about to sack him on the spot!" Nicole tried an element of humor. "Eden isn't Joel's life, Siggy. He tries to measure up, but let's face it, it's *your* life."

"Fat good it did me," Siggy said bitterly. "I should have been a man."

"Why? Is being a woman too much for you?" Nicole again tried to joke.

"I'm saying no woman could run this place. It's not a little farm with a few cows. It's a vast cattle station. I can't easily see you doing it for all your smarts. You're an artist, for God's sake. I know the men would do anything for you, but you have to be able to tell them what to do. You know as well as I do this is a man's world. A hard, tough man's world."

"I agree. Regardless, I'm going to give it a go. We'll get a hard, tough man to run it. A man who understands power and how to use it. I retain my position as owner. Whoever that man is he'll work for us."

"And where are you going to get such a man?" Siggy demanded as though there was no possibility of finding one. "It's not as if they're thick on the ground. The good ones are taken. A lot fail. The qualities you're talking about are bred in the bone. They belong to people with a whole background on the land, like Drake McClelland. Drake is already a force in the industry, and he's not yet thirty. The McQueens, to the north, the Claydons. The latest addition while you've been away, Brock Tyson. He's back. He inherited Mulgaree from his grandfather. The cousin, Philip, missed out. Brock's going to marry that little Logan girl, the nice one, what's her name again? I should remember. You were friends. A redhead like you, only her hair is titian."

"Shelley!" Nicole exclaimed in delight. "Indeed we were friends, though she's younger. I must get in touch with her again. I didn't see her when I was here in June. I must let her know I'm home."

"Well, she's found her man," Siggy said, a touch of snideness surfacing. "Fell right on her feet."

"Good for her!" Nicole said stoutly. "Life hasn't been easy for Shelley. I remember Brock, of course. He was absolutely wild, but so handsome and dashing. Shelley will make him the perfect wife. Help him settle down. I'm so glad his grandfather came to his senses. What happened to Philip? I always found him a pain in the neck."

"He's running another station in the Kingsley chain," Siggy answered brusquely. "It's what I'm saying, young men like that are born and bred to the job. They know how to handle the demands instinctively."

"So what, then, went wrong with Joel?" Nicole asked, staring across the table. "He's not on top of it, Siggy."

"He wasn't the grandson Father wanted," Siggy said as though that answered it.

"Oh, Siggy!" Nicole felt pained.

"It's true." Siggy drummed her fingers on the table. "Father was very special, but he broke a lot of hearts. Emotional deprivation it's called. He never gave Joel a sense of confidence like he gave you. No, that's not right. You were born a holy terror with chunks of charm. Joel was different. An introverted boy who didn't bond easily with anyone but you. Father never treated him in the right way. His attention was always focused on you. He admired your spunky ways. The way you used to stand up to your father. Even when Heath was right, your grandfather always took your part. It had the effect of undermining your father. Maybe Alan and I didn't handle Joel properly, either. I've spent my life trying to push Joel. I had to give up on Alan. We've all agreed Alan is at his best doing nothing. But Joel! It's awful trying to act as a partner. He won't cooperate, but he does a reasonable job.''

''Not reasonable enough, Siggy.'' Nicole shook her head sadly. ''We don't just want to keep afloat. We need to lead. It isn't as if we couldn't be gobbled up. Drake admitted he'd make it his business to acquire Eden if it ever came on the market.''

''I can promise you that.'' Siggy laughed harshly. ''In my opinion he's determined on it. As a family they can't find closure with us on their border. He must be feeling he has a good chance. What interest have you shown in Eden these past years, Nikki? The grand inheritance Father left you. Five years in all. Five years is a long time.''

''Not when you're fighting your way out of a terrible trauma, it isn't.'' Nicole's response was equally fervent. ''I needed that time, Siggy. Obviously what happened affected me far more deeply than you. I was a child. It was my mother. Finding her was horrendous.''

Siggy looked away abruptly, her vision blurred. ''I know that. I'm sorry. But I haven't been able to count on you. You left me carrying the ball.''

''Isn't that what you wanted? I wouldn't hear a peep out of you if Joel was up to speed.''

''I didn't get Eden,'' Siggy wailed. ''I got big bucks, instead.''

''So when do you intend to spend it?'' Nicole challenged so swiftly her aunt blinked. ''Most people would consider big bucks enough. You needn't sound so outraged."

"Eden is worth more than money," Siggy declared passionately, giving Nicole a shocked glance. "It's the land. I love my desert home. I have no place else to go."

"So who's pushing you out?" Nicole demanded. "Look, no offense, but there's a big wide beautiful world out there, Siggy."

"It's not Eden." Siggy stuffed her hands deep in her pockets.

"Perhaps not, but wouldn't you and Alan like to spend some time in the great capitals of the world? The best hotels—no need to be tight."

"Are you saying I'm tight?" Siggy asked very coolly.

"Aren't you?"

"Maybe," Siggy admitted grudgingly. "I was never in your league, floating around in all your beautiful clothes. By the way, you're too skinny."

"*Slender's* the word, Siggy," Nicole corrected. "Let's get off me. I expected you to keep Joel on his toes."

"Ah, God, Nikki! I told you, Joel doesn't want direction from me. He'll do anything but take it. Every time I try to talk to him, he tunes me out and just waits for me to leave. Sometimes I think he doesn't have the balls for the job."

"Well—" Nicole gulped and waited a moment "—he's fairly desperate to convince people he does. Have you been checking on what he's doing?"

"Of course I have!" Siggy retorted in a voice that suggested she was mortally offended. "I'm not as young as I used to be. Not as limber in the saddle, either.''

''I'll have to speak to him.''

''Go ahead!'' Siggy invited. ''He'll take it from you. He's thrilled out of his mind you're home. Talks to you constantly. Honestly, I'm his mother and all I get out of him is grunts. It doesn't make sense. Any of it. He has never been jealous of you and he had every right to be. The sun rose out of your arse— excuse the language. I've deteriorated dreadfully. Joel always looked on you as his gorgeous little sister when you stole all of Father's affection. Father wasn't fair to my boy.''

''Why swipe at Granddad?'' Nicole finished off her cold cup of tea, grimaced. ''I just don't buy it. I never saw Granddad being anything but kind and tolerant with Joel. It was always Joel who had problems.''

''Joel's way of trying to get some attention,'' Siggy said moodily. ''No, Nicole, Father wasn't fair to my boy. Or me. First it was Corrinne, so beautiful! Father was a collector. He loved beautiful things. Corrinne was perfect even when she messed up. I was just the frumpy one with the abrasive tongue. Then you turned up, the *premature* baby.''

Nicole's quick intake of breath made a hissing sound. ''Ouch! You're saying I wasn't? Swell! Thanks a lot, Siggy.''

Siggy shrugged. ''Sorry about that,'' she said, but didn't sound sorry at all. ''You were the bonniest, most robust little premie I've ever seen.'' She shifted the subject. ''Corrinne was just so bedable. You can bet your life she and the oh-so-gallant, that really superior gentleman, David, were lovers. Corrinne was so sexy she should have been tied up. Then you arrived. Who needed to start counting? Father devoted his entire life to you from that moment on. It was really sweet except it was a giant pain in the ar—neck. The rest of us missed the attention. He left you Eden and most of the loot. The irony is, you won't keep it.''

"I'd just love to prove you wrong.'' Nicole tossed out the challenge briskly, well aware of her aunt's accumulated resentments. Eden, not money, was the thread that ran through everything.

Siggy sighed deeply. ''Your friends the Bradshaws mean a lot to you. You've rung them two or three times since you've been home. You've settled into New York. You've changed your whole way of life. Your career is there. And that's great. New York is the center of the world. Eventually you'll go back. You won't want to keep Eden going. Drake Mc-Clelland has brought himself right back into the picture for a very good reason. Hasn't it crossed your mind it might all be an act asking you to Kooltar? I can't believe he's sincere. He needs to learn of your plans. It would be a perfect time to try and talk you into selling.''

"It's a possibility.'' Nicole frowned for a moment, considering. Manipulation was certainly in Drake's line.

Siggy lowered her voice as though he was right outside the door. ''Just so long as you know. Drake can be extremely persuasive, as many have discovered before they quite knew what was happening. It's not friendship, believe me. I know. He's being a bloody hypocrite. They'll never invite us to rejoin the circle. They'll always hate us. They'll never forget about David, the guy that was cuckolding your father. Callista especially. The tragedy sent her off the deep end.''

"In my opinion she was in the deep end before that," Nicole said crisply. She leaned forward, speaking as gently as she could. "Siggy, what's all this about Joel gaining a reputation for violence?"

Siggy looked mortally offended. She'd been sitting slumped, now she came as grim-faced and erect as an Easter Island statue. She didn't reply for a very long moment, either. "Where did you hear that?"

"A reliable source."

"Yeah, the mighty Drake McClelland," Siggy intoned. "You should have told him to mind his own ruddy business."

"Look, just answer me. Is it true?"

"Okay, one incident," Siggy threw up a hand, suggesting it was all a wild exaggeration. "I'd appreciate it if you didn't mention the fight to Mother. Lord only knows how she's kept that sweet innocence. Joel had a few drinks, and some guy at the Koomera pub made him furious."

"What did this guy say? Any idea?"

"No." Siggy looked down at her weathered hands with their blunt nails. "I asked, but he wasn't interested in telling me."

"Maybe the guy made a pass at him. Asked him if he wanted to move in." Bemused, Nicole attempted black humor. "It had to be something really untoward to start a fight. I hear they don't want Joel at the pub anymore, and Mick's pretty easygoing."

"Nothing to it!" Siggy said. "They'll let him back in soon." She didn't sound confident.

"Joel can't do this." Nicole looked directly into her

aunt's eyes. "I won't have it. Had he been an ordinary employee, he'd have been told to pack up and leave. Granddad was very proud of the station's good name."

"Sure. That's what got Heath off the hook. The Cavanagh name."

Nicole reached out and gripped her aunt's wrist.

"Ouch, that hurts! For a featherweight, you're strong." Siggy sounded very hard done by.

"I'm not releasing you until you tell me exactly what you mean by that."

"Don't take any notice of me." Siggy's shoulders drooped. "The older I get the more garbage I spout. I'm a bit like you, Nikki. The way we lost your mother and that prize dope, David, pushed me over the edge. Poor old Heath had nothing to do with it. He was miles away."

"Only one person could vouch for that and he's dead."

"That was the man's third accident on his motorbike. He was no Evel Knievel. Away from Eden he drank heavily. He once came back from Darwin wearing a big silver hoop earring in one ear and a really weird headband made out of crocodile skin. Alan liked it so much he actually sent for one. But the man didn't lie about your father. Actually, I'm very proud of you for giving your father refuge. The way you strode off from our first meeting last week had Mother and I really worried. We thought you were determined to throw him out. Maybe by yourself."

"No one could throw him out the way he looks," Nicole said, her expression bleak. "I think he should be hospitalized."

"Would you want to die in a hospital when you could die at home?"

"I guess not." Nicole sighed deeply.

"Just thought I'd ask."

"I don't know what it is, but you've always had a crazy soft spot for Heath." Nicole sought her aunt's eyes.

Siggy flashed a wry grin. "If I did, it was a big mistake. People were having it off all around me. I missed all the action."

"Oh, Siggy," Nicole breathed, "what lives we've led! It might come to hospital for Heath all the same. I can't believe the change in him. The way he used to look, the way he looks now."

"He was the handsomest man I'd ever seen," Siggy reflected. "So macho. Those eyes of his would have lured any woman into his bed. No wonder Corrinne went temporarily insane. That was your father in those days."

"Were you in love with him?"

"As if I would tell you," Siggy said, brushing the question off.

"He was never very kind to you."

"Well, who cares! That in itself doesn't mean a great deal." Siggy's thin cheeks grew flushed. "Things being what they were, Heath was married to my sister. I kept my wild fantasies to myself."

"Absolutely wise, considering you were married to Uncle Alan. By the same token, I have the unsettling feeling you're not telling the truth."

Siggy started to haul herself up. "Bless you, you should have been a detective. It's all long ago, Nikki.

No one cares anymore. Are you really going over to Kooltar?''

"Not yet. There's too much I want to see here, but maybe toward the end of next week, if it suits Drake."

"It'll suit him," Siggy observed very dryly. "You're aware he's got a girlfriend?"

"I'm not planning to seduce him."

"You probably will, anyhow. It's something over which you've no control. Just don't eat any pancakes for breakfast if Callista offers them to you. They could be laced with the weedkiller she picked up at the Koomera store."

CHAPTER SIX

JOEL WAS UTTERLY DISMAYED when she asked him to ferry her over to Kooltar in the helicopter. His narrow features drew together, giving him a curiously pinched look.

"I can't for the life of me understand why you want to go." He turned hard, reproachful eyes on her.

"Look at it this way. Wouldn't it be better if we stopped the feud?" Recent comments about Joel had done funny things to her. She almost felt as if she didn't know him at all. "We mightn't ever get back to being friends exactly, but I think it's about time we all tried to put the past behind us."

"Oh, cut it out!" Joel began to pace the terrace where they'd been sitting. "You'll have me in tears next. It's McClelland, isn't it? You're attracted to him." Joel came closer, looking as if he was about to grasp her arms.

She leaned back in reaction. "You think so?" She made her voice distant. His pronouncement was far too close to the truth.

"It's my gut feeling. He always had a powerful effect on you. What happened to all those hostile angry feelings?"

Good question. "I expect they'll resurface from

time to time." She sat straighter, ready to get up and leave.

"We can never forget the past," Joel said with fierce certainty. "It's cemented in place. Mum's right for once. They hate us. They truly hate us. He wants to absorb Eden into Kooltar. We've got a tremendous asset in the Minareechi."

"That could well be it," Nicole agreed tightly. "There are a lot of wild guesses, half-baked rumors, ideas I have to track down. I'd like to sort them out first. It might all come to nothing."

Joel glared at her. "I have to tell you I'm dead set against this." He shook a fist in anger. "I don't trust McClelland. He's a guy who goes about acquiring things. He's already got a foot in the door. Who's to know what's going on in his arrogant head? He's a man of dangerous ambitions. A man of power. They reckon he's increased his father's fortune several times over. He might be set on acquiring you. Wouldn't that be a tremendous coup? At the same time he'd get Eden. Everything would come together. Aren't you troubled by this?"

"Dammit, he's got a girlfriend! Karen Stirling." Nicole was really on edge now. She didn't want to listen to Joel's ranting. "You told me yourself."

Joel stared at her, his hands jammed into his pockets. "He's been mixed up with a string of girlfriends all begging for him to marry them. It's so easy to get women when you're rich and high on the social register."

"Why feel so sorry for yourself? What's holding you up?"

He gave a faint smile. "No one will measure up to you, Nikki."

Some shade of expression in his eyes left her shaken. "Don't be ridiculous. I'm your cousin. We're family. Remoteness does have its drawbacks. It's very difficult for you to meet eligible women except at the functions that mercifully get organized so the opposite sexes can come together."

His moody face lost its smile. "Don't start trying to marry me off." He turned away, visibly ruffled. "I get enough of that from Mum. I have a sex life, Nikki. I've bedded my fair share. But you're my goddess."

Nothing could have dismayed her more. "Goddess? Good grief, I hope that's a joke." She braced herself.

Suddenly he was laughing. "When I look at you, goddess comes to mind. You can melt men to honey."

"Oh, stop it." Nicole was disgusted. She rose from her chair, looking out over the garden with its magnificent date palms and desert oaks.

"If we weren't first cousins, would you marry me?" Joel followed her. She stood beside a white column that looked bare, stripped of its thick veil of jasmine.

"What sort of question is that?" She was aghast. "We are cousins. Produced by sisters. We're close family. It's the only way I love you."

"Do you think I don't know that?" He lifted a hand and stroked her smooth cheek, a gentle caress. "Only joking, Nikki. You're such a special person. I badly need to find someone like you, but I figure that's impossible. I can't hide my emotional attachment, but it's a mystical thing. Don't you feel it, too? Growing up together, sharing experiences, a little boy and a little girl. It's an intimate thing."

Only, intimate was unthinkable.

DRAKE WAS WAITING for them by his four-wheel drive as they taxied in.

"You're not getting out?" Overnight bag in hand, Nicole looked back at her cousin, who made no move to leave the cockpit.

"Say hello to him for me if you have to," Joel said flatly, making no bones about the way he felt. "I just hope to God he treats you well. Him and that bloody bitch Callista. Talk about attachments! Boy, did she have a problem with her brother."

"Who's now dead," Nicole reminded him quietly. "Callista never created a life for herself unfortunately. Her life was her family. Thanks, Joel. I'll let you know when I want to come home."

"You said tomorrow?" he inquired sharply.

"I mean what time tomorrow. See you." She gave a little wave. "Drake's coming."

He looked out briefly. "He'd better not try to prolong your visit. Take care, Nikki. If you can't put up with more than a day, I'll be back in a flash for you."

"See you then," she said.

"Tomorrow or earlier," he corrected.

"JOEL IN A HURRY to get away?" Drake's expression was sardonic.

"He said to say hello. He's pretty busy. He's following up on a few of my suggestions."

"That's gutsy, confronting Joel. He's so darn belligerent." Drake looked down at her, absorbing her beauty. Her abundant hair was up in some sort of knot except for a couple of long locks that curled forward onto her cheeks. She looked exquisite, but a little pale, he thought. He hoped that cousin of hers hadn't been acting threatening in any way.

"Sometimes I think I am gutsy." She laughed. "I could have gone under, but I chose not to. Anyway, Eden is mine."

"So you can say exactly as you please."

"Well…within limits. Siggy didn't like that I had all the jasmine pulled down from the columns. She couldn't make sense of it and I didn't explain."

"Bad memories. Perfume has an astonishing ability to remind us of people and places. When we were kids, you had the fragrance of boronia all over you."

"How extraordinary you remember. I can explain it. Dot always tucked sachets of it into my clothes and the bed linen."

"Nowadays you wear Chanel's Gardenia."

"You're too good."

"Maybe I had a girlfriend who wore it."

"I assume a girlfriend no longer," she parried lightly. "I left Siggy and Joel holding the fort. You're right—Eden has deteriorated with the passing of time, but I intend turning it around."

"So you're planning on staying?" His glance was keen.

"I'm going to make life interesting for you, Drake. I'm not going to tell you my exact plans."

"You don't trust me?"

"Not for years and years. The family's amazed on two counts. One, you issued an invitation to Kooltar. Two, I accepted. Heath actually laughed when I told him."

"How is he?" Drake opened up the passenger door, before stowing her overnight bag.

"Dying," she said bluntly.

"That could well have been preventable, but after your mother he simply didn't care. It's suicide in a way."

"I agree, but he was always self-destructive."

"Rumor has it he had a hard early life," Drake remarked when he was behind the wheel. "Most of our troubles start in childhood. You're allowing him to stay?"

"No one with any heart could send him away. I was shocked at the change in him. Worse than I ever imagined. Sadly, I feel no love for him, but I'll still do everything I can."

"He is your father, after all." He set the vehicle in motion.

Nicole left her window open, preferring to breathe in the dry aromatic air. The scents of the bush were wonderful to her. Better than anything that came out of a bottle. "It's been years since I've been on Kooltar," she said eventually.

"Sir Giles's auburn-haired princess."

"Your mother once told me she'd longed to have a daughter."

"Instead, she only had me."

"Maybe you were too hard an act to follow."

He smiled. "Thank you for coming, Nicole," he said quietly, giving her a sidelong look.

"It's time for us to ease back into a normal life. How did Callista react to my being invited here?"

"My aunt is far more sensible than you think. Any guest of mine is made welcome."

"Do you invite your girlfriends over? Of course you

do. Why not? Rumor has it you're all but engaged to Karen Stirling.''

"Would that upset you?" he retorted.

"I'd rather die than admit it.''

He gave a low attractive laugh. "Karen and I have a thing going. I don't know that you could interpret it as a serious commitment.''

"Not on your part," she said dryly. "As I recall, Karen carried a torch for you from her teens.''

He swung his head. "Who told you all this? It had to come from home.''

"Come to think of it, it was Joel.''

"He needs to find himself a good woman and marry her," he said firmly.

"One could say the same about you.''

"It's not my most urgent quest at the moment.''

"What is? Acquiring property?''

"Certainly that's part of it. Running a cattle chain efficiently and at a profit takes total commitment. At the moment, as you said yourself, you have a bit of a crisis on your hands.''

She brought her chin up. "I see it as a challenge.''

"You'll have to bring in someone with a diversity of skills to run Eden if you're going to survive.''

"I realize that. But surely finding someone isn't an insurmountable problem, is it?''

He glanced at her. "I wouldn't make too light of the magnitude of the undertaking, Nicole. There's so much to learn. So much to know. Do you think I'd be as effective if I hadn't been bred to it? I don't think so. For that matter, how would Joel take to having a man put in charge over him?''

She felt a chill. "I don't imagine he'd like it, but I have broached the subject with Siggy."

"And?"

"She's fully aware Joel needs help, but of course he's her son and she wants to see him remain as boss."

He groaned softly. "I don't envy you your task. What do you suppose will happen after you return to New York?"

"Let me settle in here first," she said wryly.

"What about your painting? Don't you want to continue to show your work?"

"There are any number of first-class galleries in Australia, Drake. Surely I don't have to tell you that."

"But I thought you'd embraced your new lifestyle. The glamour and excitement, the feeling of being at the center of things. It would be hard to beat New York."

"Are you trying to get rid of me? Be honest."

She might have been laying down a challenge. "I want you to stay," he said.

A WOMAN IN RIDING DRESS, cream silk shirt, beige jodhpurs, polished boots, stood on the first landing of the finely joined cedar staircase that ran to the left of the spacious entrance hall. Tiny and dolllike, she had large dark eyes and hair black and sleek as ebony wrapped around her head in a braid.

Callista McClelland.

Nicole looked at her, apprehensive despite herself. Even at that distance she could sense the lack of welcome. "Miss McClelland!" She didn't forget to sound respectful. There had never been a time in her life she hadn't addressed Callista formally. Callista McClelland was that sort of person. Meeting her was like being on the receiving end of a jug of ice water.

"Nicole, so you're here." Callista seemed to have a struggle finding words. Nevertheless, she continued gracefully down the stairs, extending her small hand as if it demanded a deferential kiss rather than be shaken. "How are you settling into being home?"

Dark, thickly lashed eyes, glittering like metal, drilled into Nicole.

"As if I'd never been away." Nicole accepted the cool, dry hand that was offered, finding the touch unwelcome, even embarrassing, given the hostility she had encountered from Callista during her childhood and adolescence. "How are you?"

"Oh, much the same, Nicole, though I see you're even more like your mother."

Well, she hadn't expected Callista to envelop her in a hug, had she? "In looks, perhaps," Nicole said pleasantly. "I have my own identity. My father doesn't even agree about the looks. He says apart from the coloring there are differences."

"Only he can see." Callista gave a cool little smile. "You must be furious he's back on Eden."

Nicole, who had labored all her life to feel affection for Heath Cavanagh, now felt positively filial. "Let me say I hope *you're* not, Miss McClelland. I simply don't have the heart to be furious. He's a very sick man."

"Ah well, at least he's had a life." The bitterness spurted like a geyser, for all Callista's attempt at civility.

"Callista, please." Drake lifted a staying hand, his handsome features tightening in protest.

"Forgive me, dear." Callista's smooth cheeks colored. She laid a conciliatory hand on his sleeve. "Sometimes my feelings get the better of me. I know you said it's important we all be friends." She turned her head to smile bravely at Nicole. "Let me show you to your room, Nicole. I know you'll like it. It faces the garden. And please, do call me Callista. Miss McClelland makes me feel quite ancient."

"When you look ridiculously young," Nicole said.

"I try to look after myself," Callista replied, dismissing her amazingly youthful good looks as if she had far more important issues to consider.

The truth probably was that Callista McClelland in her mid-forties didn't want to grow old, Nicole thought. She steeled herself to follow the woman up the stairs.

"Would you like coffee, Nicole?" Drake called after her.

"Lovely." She paused to look back at him. Why was she really here? To suit his ambitions? However wary she felt, her heart gave an involuntary buck at the sight of him. He was a marvelous-looking man; one arm leaning on the banister, those vivid chiseled features, eyes glimmering against his tanned skin, little flames at their center.

Beware, Nicole. Be very careful around this man. Don't fall under his spell. It would be so easy.

"Settle in, then I'll take you on a tour of the house," he promised.

"I'm looking forward to it. Everything looks great."

"Callista must take the credit for that."

"I do it out of love, darling," Callista said smugly. "I was very privileged to grow up in a beautiful house. I can't imagine how I'll cope when you marry, Drake, and I'm no longer chatelaine."

Now there's a thought! Nicole wondered if the future Mrs. Drake McClelland should be warned.

The bedroom was large, bright and airy, a mix of modern and antique pieces, the color scheme sunshine yellow and pristine white. Two lovely flower paintings decorated the walls. A nice change from the over-the-top sumptuous bedroom Siggy's decorator had created for her, Nicole thought in relief. Sunlight streamed in across the broad veranda, giving the room a welcoming glow. On a small console table that held a charming silver-gilt bust of a young girl was a bowl filled with lilies and trails of a silver-gray native vine. Nicole approached and touched a white petal. "How lovely! Your arrangement?"

"Of course. Arranging flowers is quite beyond Annie." Callista dismissed Kooltar's housekeeper's creative abilities with a wave of her hand. "I love beautiful things. I had the flower paintings hung in here. I hope you enjoy them."

"French." Nicole moved closer. "I'd say that one is by Jacques-Emile Blanche." She was too far away to read the signature. "The other—"

Callista butted in, apparently not pleased by Nicole's ability to identify the works of famous artists. "Louis Gaillard. Signed and dated 1888. You're right, the other is a Blanche. I forgot you were an artist."

"*Am* an artist, Callista. I still paint." Nicole sent Callista one of her own looks of feigned sweetness.

"I've had two successful showings in New York. As tough an art scene as you'll find. But I don't paint beautiful flowers like these."

"What do you paint?" Callista's eyes gleamed with an odd challenge.

"Journeys of my mind." Nicole's mouth twisted a little as she said it. "Visions."

"I take it they're not happy paintings full of light?"

"Some of them, in fact, are rather monstrous, but certain people lock into the emotion. They sell. Every trace of cheerfulness was knocked out of me years ago."

"You still see a psychiatrist?" Callista looked at her guest with anything but sympathy.

"Not for a long time, but it's helpful to sit on a couch and have a highly trained professional listen to your problems. I credit Dr. Rosendahl with helping me to face life. I'll always be grateful to him. Actually I'd like to see him now that I'm home. Perhaps I'll invite him to Eden if he has the time."

Something flickered in Callista's metallic gaze. "Unfortunately for him, he has all the time in the world. Don't you know, Nicole? Rosendahl is dead. He was killed in a hit-and-run accident leaving his Sydney office."

Shock blocked Nicole's throat. She could see the doctor's kindly distinguished face as clearly as if he stood before her. "No one told me."

"Your aunt should have known." Callista shrugged. "It was in the papers. We do manage to get them, if a bit late."

"When was this?" Nicole felt sick.

"Oh, six or eight months ago. It was a small item.

I expect Sigrid missed it, or else she didn't want to upset you. I mean, you can't have many emotional resources.''

Briefly Nicole debated how best to answer. Spirit won out. ''On the contrary, I think I've met the challenge of facing up to my daunting past, Callista. What about you? Have you successfully mastered your pain?''

Callista bristled. ''Never. I'm a woman who feels very deeply.'' She gripped her throat in a dramatic gesture that struck Nicole as playacting. Callista was the perennial young girl trapped in a middle-aged woman's body.

''So what you're saying is you wish to cling to the unhappy past?''

Dislike was written all over Callista's unlined face. ''Don't be so naive, Nicole. The past is always with us. We can't just shed it.''

''You don't want me here, do you?'' Nicole spoke quietly, prepared for Callista's reaction.

''Why so melodramatic? This is Drake's house. He invites whom he pleases. I would never go against him. You and I can work something out between us. We're both adults, but you know as well as I do we can never be close. You are your mother's daughter. You even have her voice. Extraordinary thing, genetics. Because of Corrinne I suffered a terrible loss.''

Nicole looked back urgently. ''I know that and I'm deeply sorry. But I know all about loss, too. It makes me want to weep. The difference could be I'm trying to deal with it. Feeling such terrible resentments can only be a burden to you, Callista. Don't you want to lay them down?''

Callista's dark eyes were unblinking. "Then I'd be breaking my emotional connection with my brother. I adored him."

Nicole lowered her head. "I acknowledge that, but he's gone beyond human adoring, Callista. He's passed on."

"Which doesn't mean I won't see him again." Callista hugged her body tightly. "I don't expect you to understand."

"Why not? Can't you allow my heart is broken, too? In my case, it was a mother." She turned away to compose herself. "I think we should stop there, don't you? Before anything else is said."

"I agree. Life is hard. It really doesn't matter, anyway. Soon you'll go back to New York, get on with your life, as will I. Of course, I may have to rethink my situation after Drake marries."

"You think he has someone in mind?"

"My dear, it's an open secret. Karen Stirling. You know her. Lovely girl! Simply stunning. We get on extremely well. We have long talks when she visits."

"Does she have this beautiful room?"

"No." Callista gave a highly suggestive little laugh. "She prefers to be closer to Drake, if you follow my meaning. I expect they'll announce their engagement very soon."

"That's curious. Drake didn't mention a word about any engagement. I imagine a man on the brink of proposing to the woman he loves would want to tell the world."

Callista ran her fingers over the smooth surface of the little antique writing table. "Even as a child you thought Drake was your property.'' Her smile was nastiness in full flight.

"We were friends, Callista. We hope to be friends again. Forgive me, Callista, but I can't think Drake is truly in love with Karen. I do remember her as warm and friendly. Perhaps you simply want him to be.''

Callista's exhalation was sharp. "I knew it would be impossible for us to have a normal conversation. You're like your mother. One of those women who can't let a man go. Possessive to the end. Make no mistake—Drake is serious about Karen. He wants to marry a woman of good family, not someone with a tainted past.'' She spat out the words, choking with the bitterness she didn't seem able to transcend.

"You never let go, do you?'' Nicole retorted. "Well, better to have it out in the open, I suppose. I've only stepped across your threshold and already I'm a threat. Would you be brave enough to repeat the 'tainted past' bit in front of Drake, I wonder?''

Callista closed her eyes briefly, holding a hand to her throat. "I'd deny I said it. You might remember, my nephew is very loyal to me. I've devoted my life to him.''

"Forgive me, but it seems you've devoted your life to your own private hell. I don't appreciate being told I'm a member of a tainted family, Callista.''

"I didn't say that.'' Callista backed off.

"But you did. Please don't underestimate me. I'm no longer a child you can taunt and push over the edge. I'm a woman. I've taken my life in hand. I'm only here for a visit. I don't want unpleasantness. We can be civil to each other, surely?''

"Why not?" Callista gave a peculiar laugh. "I've found I can do anything if I put my mind to it."

Nicole didn't doubt it. Unbidden came the sickening image of her mother's battered body sprawled over a desert boulder.

CHAPTER SEVEN

CALLISTA EXCUSED herself from sharing coffee, saying it was time for her afternoon ride.

"I'm sure you have lots to catch up on!" She bestowed a gleaming smile on Nicole. She had small white pearly teeth she was obviously careful to look after.

Round one to Callista. Nicole had long since learned that Callista chose her moments to release her venom.

"Enjoy yourself," Nicole called cheerily, not to be outdone.

All would have gone according to plan had the housekeeper, Annie Prentice, not picked that particular moment to enter the garden room carrying a laden tray.

"Here, let me take that from you," Nicole offered, rising. Annie was of the same vintage as Dot.

The housekeeper, whose eyes had been on the tray, looked up to respond.

When she saw Nicole, she let out a disbelieving wail, and the tray fell from her hands.

Such clumsiness might have happened on a regular basis, given Callista's furious response. "Watch out!" she cried, moving as deftly as a prima ballerina out of harm's way. The coffeepot went over, splashing hot liquid all over the tray and onto the floor. Big spatters reached Nicole's legs, mercifully protected by her blue cotton slacks, but for seconds she keenly felt the heat. The two coffee cups and saucers flew through the air to crash on the unyielding terra-cotta floor tiles.

"Annie, I'd have sworn you could handle just about anything!" Drake shook his dark head in mock amazement. "But I'll need a double brandy after that."

"I'm so sorry." The housekeeper was the picture of despair, shoulders shaking, tears in her eyes as if she'd just pulled out of a triathlon.

"Settle down, Annie. No real harm done," Drake soothed. "What about you, Nicole? That coffee was hot. Did it burn you?"

Her legs were smarting a little. "I'm fine. I'll pop upstairs and change in a minute." She looked at the housekeeper with a sympathetic smile. "Did I startle you, Annie?" Hadn't she shocked the Barretts when they'd first caught sight of her?

Annie, a sturdy woman, put a hand to the comfort of her large bosom. "For a minute there, I thought you was a ghost. What was I going to do?"

"Turn and run?" Drake asked thoughtfully.

"Then I realized, it's you, Miss Nicole, all grown up."

"How are you, Annie?" Nicole's smile widened.

Whatever Annie's answer was to be, Callista wasn't in the mood to hear it. "Don't just stand there gawping, Annie. Clean this mess up."

Whatever happened to niceness? Nicole wondered, resenting Callista's attitude on Annie's behalf.

"Yes, ma'am. I'm on my way."

Annie seemed to have all the attributes of that dying breed the faithful retainer.

"Take your time, Annie," Drake said, coming to the besieged housekeeper's defense. "You're out of breath."

"Shock, sir, and my rackety old ticker. Miss Nicole is the spitting image of her mother, that beautiful creature. I'm just horrified I dropped the tray. I wasn't prepared."

Again Callista displayed her anger and impatience. "Okay, so you were surprised, Annie. Nicole is the image of her mother. Would you please clean this up and make fresh coffee? Leave that, Nicole." She eyed Nicole, who was busy picking up the broken pieces of fine china, with disapproval. "Annie will attend to that. It needs a dustpan and brush."

"I've got most of it, anyway," Nicole said mildly, thinking she wouldn't speak to a feral camel the way Callista was speaking to the housekeeper. "I'll change out of these slacks. Won't be long."

"Let me have them and I'll make sure there's no stain," Annie called after her.

Nicole turned. "I'd appreciate that, Annie. I'm not exactly sure what you use to treat coffee stains."

"I do," Annie responded with relief. "I'm so sorry, dear."

"We're all agreed you're sorry, Annie," Callista said in the same sharp voice. "Go get the mop," she ordered. "You've broken the set. Those coffee cups are very expensive."

It was a wonder she didn't say she was going to deduct the cost from Annie's wages, Nicole thought, moving off.

Pausing on the stairs—she overheard Callista say crossly it was high time they traded Annie in.

Oh, well, why bother about loyalty? Nicole stood stock-still waiting for Drake's reply. If he agreed with his absolutely awful aunt, she'd be back on Eden before midafternoon.

Mercifully his answer came with calm authority. "Annie stays, Callista. I'm not about to lower the boom on her. She's always been a good worker and very loyal. You shouldn't have been so harsh with her."

"If you ask me, her shock at seeing Nicole was far less than mine," Callista answered. "I wonder you can ignore this thing, Drake."

"What thing?" Drake sounded exasperated.

"What a mistake it is having Nicole here."

Nicole knew she should go on her way, but she didn't want to miss anything. She gripped the banister with one hand. Obviously she hadn't changed much since she was a child trying to catch the grown-ups' hushed conversations.

"We've already discussed this, Cally," Drake said in a voice that should have given his aunt pause. "Don't fall apart on me. It's my decision. I don't like you to be upset, but I don't answer to anybody."

"But there's a potential for trouble here, dear. More and more trouble." Callista was back to her dramatic mode. "Can you blame me for worrying about you?"

"What hurt could Nicole inflict?" Drake's tone was soft, but there was little doubt about the steel beneath it.

A long silence, then Callista's tense reply. "We'll see."

Heed the warning, Drake, Nicole thought, shaking her head. Not a chance she could ever win over Callista.

IN HER BEDROOM she changed her coffee-stained slacks for a turquoise skirt printed with hibiscus. The garment was light and cool and went well with the white tank top she already wore.

I've only myself to blame for coming here. Siggy had warned her. So had Joel. Within a mere ten minutes of their meeting, Callista had revealed her hostility. Callista was a woman frozen in time. She had even made it clear to Drake she didn't want Nicole on Kooltar. Not that Callista had much say. Drake would do exactly as he pleased. It shamed Nicole slightly to realize she'd only agreed to come because the thought of spending time alone with Drake was irresistible. Despite everything that had happened between their families, she found herself more drawn to him than to any other man she'd ever met. And she'd met quite a few through Carol, all of them interesting, attractive, eligible. Yet in so many ways, now as in the past, he was her ideal.

When she returned to the garden room, made sensuous by the profusion of plants, the furnishings and the collection of huge Javanese glazed pots, fresh coffee had already been set out on a low marble-topped table.

"No scalds I hope?" Drake asked, rising to his feet, his eyes moving over her pretty skirt.

"A little pinkness that will fade. I'm ready for that coffee. Shall I pour?"

"Be my guest." Amusement played around his handsome mouth.

"Callista was a little harsh with Annie," she ventured, passing him a cup.

He sighed. "Callista always overreacts. It's the way she lives her life. I guess most people would call her emotional. She seems to be hurting all the time, but I don't have the answers."

"It's a lonely life, Drake. Frontier life. She doesn't have the support of a marriage."

"She's had her admirers," he said, shrugging. "They never seemed to come up to her standards. As for me, I'm all for frontier life. I don't covet life in the big cities. Even New York, which I've visited a few times, as you know. Like everyone I found it very stimulating, but the desert is my home. No better place on earth. Callista, too, is tied to it. She's still a very attractive woman. It's not impossible she could find the right man."

He'd have to be a very tolerant individual, Nicole thought but didn't say. "Perhaps she's too anchored in the past. This house, however grand, must reinforce her sense of separateness. She mentioned to me that she'd face changes when you marry. She's lived dependent on you. Dependent on Kooltar."

He took another long sip of his coffee, then set the elegant coffee cup, a lucky survivor of the broken set, back in its saucer. "Callista is financially independent. She is, in fact, a rich woman."

"I know that. But money, for once, is not the problem. I mean she's emotionally dependent. Are you happy with your role?"

For a moment he was silent, his striking face somber. "My aunt is an especially vulnerable woman. I would expect you to understand that."

"Believe me, I do. But she doesn't want to get better." She recognized they were getting into the familiar series of thrusts and parries.

"I've tried strategies, Nicole. I've failed. Callista is harboring all manner of resentments and guilty feelings. Most of the time she's sweet and gentle. Then she has short lapses into suppressed rage. As I expect you do."

"Okay, I admit it, but I'm not as rude as she is. But you won't hear any criticism of Callista, will you?"

He shook his head slightly. "She's family."

"You had no hesitation attacking Joel. He's my family."

"I didn't exactly attack him. I just thought a few things needed to be brought to your attention."

She sighed in exasperation. "But, isn't that interference?" A pause. "I couldn't help overhearing Callista say I can only bring trouble."

His gaze was very direct. "So you're back to your old trick of listening on the stairs, are you?"

"It wasn't often I heard anything good."

He laughed. "It never stopped you. You know darn well what Callista means. She's afraid I'll fall in love with you."

Nicole tried not to let her reaction to that show. "Who knows your intentions, outside yourself?" she said breezily. "Aren't you and Karen Stirling almost ready to announce your engagement?"

His eyes came up to hers. "I've already told you that's not true. Callista continues to cherish hopes. She and Karen get on well."

"An absolute necessity if they're going to cohabitate," she said. "Or maybe after the marriage the position might alter. It wouldn't be the first or the last time. It would be fairly easy for a charming young woman like Karen to butter up Callista."

"Something you're not likely to do," he retorted.

"Not when she feels such enmity toward me."

"You're overstating it."

"Not at all! You're too smart not to see it."

"I can handle it, Nic. Can you?"

She tossed back her auburn hair, suddenly feeling caged. She ignored the question and said, "Look. I'm desperate for answers. Do you believe what happened was murder-suicide or just plain murder? You said yourself the coroner did a poor job. No one believed it was an accident. Dr. Rosendahl didn't. He had theories that, as they were just theories, he wasn't prepared to discuss. He's dead, did you know?" She swallowed, trying to rid herself of the throb in her voice.

He looked genuinely shocked. "Good God, when did this happen? He can't have been all that old."

"Apparently there was a piece in the papers, but it was very hard to find. Or the breeze blew that particular page away."

"Try to stay with the facts, Nic. Sigrid told you?"

"Callista told me," she said flatly. "She seemed quite pleased to. One might be forgiven for thinking she would have told you, as well, but she must have thought you wouldn't be interested. Anyway, he and I lost touch over the years, but I thought the world of Jacob Rosendahl."

"As well you might. He was a fine man. Highly respected. What did he die of? Heart?"

"A hit-and-run accident some six or more months ago. I intend to follow it up."

"It's the sort of thing one would want to follow up. I'm really sorry, Nicole."

"There could be a killer out there," she said slowly. "It's almost liberating to say it. I want that person caught and punished."

"If there is such a person. The official finding was an accident."

"You fear my investigation?" She looked at him.

"I fear for you is more like it."

She shrugged. "I can look after myself. I can't afford to be soft. It was suggested they fought. Let's consider it. *We* fight."

"You look for it more than I do. My uncle suffered a breakdown. He was never the same after your mother married Heath Cavanagh."

"Are you suggesting he decided to end both their lives?"

His face contorted with pain. "In regard to your mother and no one else, my uncle was slightly mad."

"When you all had Heath Cavanagh as the villain?"

"Nic, I was fourteen years old. Just a boy. I'm no expert on human relationships all these years later. But I've had plenty of time to think."

She set down her cup carefully. "We all withdrew, instead of being open."

"Being open calls for great wisdom and understanding. Terrible grief disrupts those abilities. The inner rage and the hopelessness take precedence. The shock was so great no one was acting rationally. Violent death has a horrible way of tainting the innocent families. We all carried the burden.''

"Don't you want to know, Drake?'' She knew she was almost pleading. ''This is an unresolved conflict. The theory that my mother grasped the wheel and caused the accident is at odds with what Heath told me. He said she was a pussycat compared to me.''

In response, Drake made a deep mocking sound in his throat. ''I distinctly remember a little tiger.''

"I have a temper,'' she acknowledged. ''God knows I've got the red hair. Who else do we have as a suspect? Some psychopath passing through? It has happened. Men on the run make for the Outback. Somewhere they can easily hide. But then, why and how could a man like that do such a thing?''

Drake's wide shoulders slumped a little. ''My uncle could have been disabled in some way. Both of them taken unawares.''

"Or maybe they knew the person. Judged him harmless.''

"This person who couldn't control murderous impulses?'' Drake asked in a taut, incredulous voice.

"People do things they believed they never could. We read it in the papers. See it on television. All it takes is a single moment of unpremeditated, ungovernable rage. Which brings us to Heath. The culprit had to be Heath. He had the motive. A crime of passion.''

"Maybe he'll tell us on his deathbed,'' Drake said in a splintered voice.

"Which can't be far off.'' She moved restlessly, rising to her feet. ''Show me the house, Drake. I can remember playing here. Your parents didn't blame me for my mother's actions.'' Or had Drake's mother and father believed it possible she could have been David's child? That would have accounted for their softening attitude toward her. They never did forgive Corrinne.

"How could they, Nicole? You were the innocent victim.''

She nodded. "Yes, but the family secrets! So many that are not to be spoken about, just lived with,'' she lamented.

"Well, I, for one, want to compensate for lost time. Only a week ago I never imagined you'd be here with me. Now the unimaginable.'' For a long moment they traded looks, intense and searching, both aware of their growing intimacy as they let down their guard. They had bonded so well as children, and now they were brushed by very real adult desire.

It seemed to Drake her fragrance was all around him, so intoxicating it made him feel reckless. Her masses of curls were a rosy cloud around her face, tiny tendrils damp in the heat around her forehead. How easy it was for a woman like her to bewitch a man. He was filled with a mad impulse to wrap skeins of her hair around his hands. He stared at her lovely mouth, the upper lip so finely cut, the lower as full and ripe as a peach. Passion was a whirlpool that caught a man before it sucked him under. It had happened to David. Yet staring into her beautiful questioning eyes that seemed to mirror his own recklessness, he realized he wanted her with a fierceness that startled and even appalled him. Despite all his talk about making up for lost time, his uncle's tragic past was never distant. David had gone down into the vortex, never to fully return.

"Don't look at me that way," she said, feeling distinctly uncomfortable.

"How is that?"

"A little bit of everything. Attraction. Rejection."

"Rejection, no. I'm just giving us a chance to get our bearings."

"Is that so?" She raised an eyebrow. "How perfectly you, Drake. You always like to be in control."

"Agreed." There was a glint of wry humor in his eyes. "Let's see the house, then."

"I have memories of your father's study," she said as they moved out of the garden room.

"My study now."

"Have you kept all the trophies? Those wonderful paintings of horses, the huge mahogany partners desk?"

"I have. I've hardly changed a thing."

"And the smoking room with all the artifacts and curios? The fascinating things your family gathered. I especially loved the huge Indian paintings on cotton."

"They're still there. Most of the guns have gone, except the antiques which are under lock and key. No smoking allowed anymore. Callista has done quite a bit to the main rooms of the house. It keeps her happy shifting things round, constantly refurbishing."

"That happens with people who love houses," she murmured. "Why do we love houses so much?"

"Because they're our castles. We want to keep them intact for our children."

They moved into the formal drawing room with its series of double-hung windows and four sets of French doors, allowing light to flood in. Whatever Callista's failings, she had mastered the art of decorating, Nicole thought. Hanging above the fireplace was a magnificent painting, a landscape-skyscape she'd never seen before.

"That's amazing!" She was irresistibly drawn to it.

"I bought it in Melbourne. It spoke to me across two rooms. A new artist, Nick Osbourne."

"He'll be going places." With her trained eye she was impressed.

"He already is. His prices have jumped accordingly. There's a lovely portrait of a young woman in the dining room, I'd like you to see. I found it on one of my trips. It keeps my male guests at the table."

"I can't wait to see it."

As they entered the spacious dining room, which had in the old days hosted many a party, Drake switched on the overhead chandelier for additional light. A huge antique mirror over the long sideboard reflected the painting on the opposite wall. "Why, she's a redhead." Nicole spun around, thoroughly intrigued. It was an oil-on-canvas portrait of a beautiful young woman in a satin evening gown that showed off her lustrous skin and the upper curves of her breasts. She was half sitting, half reclining on a deep wingback chair upholstered in a rich ruby silk brocade, slender arms extended, one lovely hand adorned with a huge diamond-set emerald.

"That's another Blanche," she said, referring to the turn-of-the-century French artist.

"It is. He certainly knew how to paint women."

"She looks a little bit like me." Nicole moved in for a closer inspection.

"She's a lot like you," he answered dryly. "I wasn't immune to the fact when I bought it."

"Surely it's not why you bought the painting. That's unreal."

"You're a bit unreal yourself."

"I'll take that as a compliment, Drake. Callista can't like the painting much."

"Well, I love it. Wherever you go, her eyes follow you, and look at those beautiful hands."

"Hands are very difficult to paint. She's a sexy little wench. I'm awfully flattered, but surely I'm not that seductive-looking?"

He glanced at her. "You have your moments."

"I don't see myself that way," she said, faintly surprised by his words.

"I know you don't. That's what makes the appeal more potent."

"Well I've no wish to be a femme fatale," she said tightly, and turned away.

"I guess you have no say in the matter."

THE LIBRARY like Eden's library, was a grand room at the heart of the homestead. Nicole knew the magnificently carved bookcases that rose almost to the high ceiling were the work of the gifted cabinetmaker George Wingate. Wingate had been transported to Botany Bay as a convict for what today would be a misdemeanor. Once there, however, his career didn't suffer. He found plenty of work in the homesteads of the rich "squattocracy." As well as the huge collection of beautifully bound books in all their jewel colors, the shelves held curios and dozens of small sculptures of horses. The McClellands, like the Cavanaghs and other Outback dynasties, had always been horse crazy.

In Drake's study she discovered he'd added another large painting of a splendid palomino, its coat a rich dark gold, its flowing mane and tail platinum white.

"I love this!" She gazed into the large liquid-brown eye the palomino presented in profile.

"You wouldn't be an Outback woman if you didn't," he said.

"Such beautiful creatures! Remember our journeys on horseback over desert sand, tangled scrub and all those rocky creek beds? When Joel rode along, he did a lot of complaining—I never did know why. I've missed a fast gallop, I can tell you."

"I bet." He smiled. "You're a natural in the saddle. Straight from the crib onto a pony's back. Sir Giles saw to that. You never had the least fear."

"You're right. I must have started before I knew fear. I had so much faith in Granddad. He would never have allowed anything to hurt me. Besides, horses have always known what I'm saying to them."

"It's a gift."

She moved to a wall covered in photographs that chronicled moments in McClelland family life. Friends, too, and the many celebrities who'd visited the station over the years. There were numerous photographs of Drake, an unqualified photographer's dream especially when he smiled—as a boy, as a young man, action shots playing polo, others beside the twin-engine Beech Baron, many shots with his father. Invariably his father's arm was slung proudly around his shoulders. There were other shots of Drake's father with various VIPs, photographs of extended family at celebrations; the young Callista in evening dress looking not unlike the elfin actress Winona Ryder. She was smiling brilliantly, a study in happiness and excitement. Sitting on a couch beside her was her brother, David, young and remarkably handsome in black tie. There were more photos of David farther up the wall. Full of life, smiling. It was difficult to look at them without feeling a great sadness for the loss of life, the loss of a future.

"It must be hard looking at these," she said, a knot in her throat.

"They came down for a long while," he answered quietly. "Callista especially couldn't bear to look at them. Now I think she's desperate to find his image anywhere."

An idol to be worshiped! "Poor Callista!" Nicole, a woman of sensibility, recognized the extremes of love. "The loss of love embittered her."

Drake stared at the photograph fixedly. "That happens to a lot of people."

"Hopefully not beyond repair."

"They were great pals, you know. You see her there. What was she? Twenty? So happy, dazzling in her unusual way. Princess for the night. Joy is written all over her. They were at a ball."

"This must have been before David succumbed to my mother."

"And Callista lost her role. The world was her oyster before Corrinne came on the scene. David shifted his attention entirely to Corrinne. That must have hurt Cally. She's always been extravagant with her joys and her sorrows."

"Do you suppose she could have gone off the deep

end?'' Nicole looked away from the photograph and met his eyes.

''We can all go off the deep end, given the right circumstances. What are you saying, Nic?'' A vertical line appeared between his black eyebrows.

''The unacceptable, apparently.'' Nevertheless, Nicole forged on. ''Maybe it was an abortive attempt to break up the lovers—my mother and her brother. Maybe something went drastically wrong. A horrific accident just waiting to happen. You said yourself you're familiar with Callista's big mood shifts. She can work herself into a rage over a dropped tray.''

Drake turned away from her, overcome by his own complex thoughts. ''Callista is excitable, not flagrantly mad. What about Joel? Let's turn the tables on you. Isn't he overly demanding of your time and attention? Your mother had concerns about him. Maybe she threatened to send him away from you. Callista isn't the only one with a capacity for self-dramatization. He couldn't imagine life without you. How's that for an alternative scenario?''

The green of her eyes was intensified by strong emotion, he'd always noticed. ''That's coming from a skewed viewpoint,'' she said calmly.

He shrugged. ''Well, I'm supposed to allow yours.'' How easy she found it to rouse him. He didn't enjoy the sensation. ''Would you even recognize the truth when you heard it, do you think?''

''God knows.'' She sighed, baffled, confused. ''I'm sorry, Drake. Talking about the past only seems to tear us apart.''

''Because we're chasing phantoms. Chasing secrets. What you need is a strong dose of reality. Get your father to give a DNA sample. Living with doubt is disturbing your mind. I don't know how much longer I can tolerate it. I really don't want you as a cousin.''

''I don't want you that way, either,'' she retorted. ''But we can't count out the possibility yet.''

''The devil we can't!'' he said emphatically. ''This is the age of great scientific advances. The way you persist with this, Nic, you're flaying us both. I'm just frustrated enough to try something. A little experiment.''

''What?''

Something she saw in his eyes made her inwardly quake. Her heart knocked a loud warning. She knew if she showed the slightest vulnerability, he could exploit it. ''Not a good idea, Drake.''

''Why?''

''I'm unsettled enough.'' Indeed, she felt curiously fragile, acutely conscious of being a woman.

''So you're going to stop me?''

''Knowing you, I probably can't. You've got a lot of nerve.''

''My successes have been determined by nerve. It seems you've lost yours.'' He reached for her slowly, drawing her into his arms.

''I won't let you do it.''

''I think you will. This is it, Nic. An experiment or only folly? Either way, it's been a long time coming.''

CHAPTER EIGHT

SHE CLOSED her eyes as his mouth covered hers. *You have no power over me,* she thought dazedly. Determined to keep a cool head, she was immediately lost.

Sensation after sensation unfolded. She had anticipated an element of vengeance; instead the feelings were so voluptuous she felt herself go limp against him, almost desperate to lie down. A strange weakness was in her legs, yet she had never felt more sensually alive.

This is something I can't fight.

She felt his arm encircle her body, near the hip, taking her weight. She might have been a woman abandoned in the desert only to stumble upon a crystalline pool overflowing with sweetness. She could feel the contractions start up in her body, the tight pull of her breasts, the vibrations deep in her womb. Sexual excitement took control.

With her eyes tightly shut in an attempt to hold all sensation in, she gave him her open mouth, allowed his tongue entry. The kiss was unbearably pleasurable, inexpressible. It was a tremendous effort to contain her rising excitement. Soon the last shreds of pretense would be torn away.

Passion was a glory or a curse. She had never experienced such delirious want, and never from a kiss.

This shivery, shuddering excitement, her whole body curiously heavy and languid with desire.

As if from a distance, she heard him murmur her name. Her senses were reeling. She should stop now, she thought, while she could...

Then he released her, and she almost cried out, grasping the front of his shirt, her fingers unconsciously clawing his chest.

"Lord God!" he breathed, exhaling a long breath. "It's not often reality exceeds imagining." He looked down at her, unaware that his voice, strangely harsh, projected his inner turbulence. He wanted to peel that pretty little top from her, put his mouth to her breasts, catch the budded nipples; feel them like succulent berries between his teeth.

She stared up at him as though hypnotized. "I'm sorry. I have to sit down or fall down."

He quickly moved, assisting her to the sofa where she lay back, legs outstretched.

"Is it hot in here?" she asked vaguely. Her body felt damp with sweat.

"No. It's the heat inside you. But you have lost color."

"That's because of what you've done to me."

"What have I done?" He smiled, but he, too, had taken long moments to collect himself.

"Kissed me like I've never been kissed before. I'm twenty-four. No innocent, but..." She felt robbed of words.

He lowered himself into a leather armchair, leaning forward, resting his elbows on his knees. "Nic?"

"I've known you all my life, but that's the first time you've ever kissed me."

"It isn't the first time I've *wanted* to kiss you," he said sardonically. "Only you've been too ready to slice me up with your scalpel tongue."

"I wanted to hurt you," she admitted almost sadly. "I don't understand why. If I did, I'm sorry."

"You didn't believe we'd ever kiss?" he asked in a highly skeptical voice.

"Maybe I did. Women should be warned about men like you."

"Now you know what to expect. You're getting your color back. That's good."

She realized her right hand was clenched. Slowly she unbent her fingers, still waiting for her heart rate to return to normal. "Odd how sexual excitement makes one lose color."

He moved to the couch to sit beside her. "So you admit to feeling pleasure?"

She made more room for him. "Some kind of pleasure. Hard to describe it." Her hand fumbled with the dense masses of her hair. "You don't play fair. I didn't expect what just happened. Or maybe I did."

"Ah, the truth at last. You don't do a bad job of kissing."

"What's kissing—pressing lips?"

"A lot more than that, don't you think?"

She sank her head into a cushion. "It could be the beginning of a chain of something. Strategy. I don't altogether trust you, Drake."

"I don't trust you, either." His eyes traveled the slender length of her, while he wrestled with the idea of pulling her back into his arms. "Would you like me to massage your hands?"

"No, thank you. The kiss was quite enough."

"Not for me. I couldn't function exclusively on your kisses." He didn't add that already an unbearable ache had begun because of the kiss.

"One thing I have to get perfectly straight. You're not in love with Karen?"

"I've already told you." He met her eyes.

"Tell me again."

"Unlike your kisses, once is enough. Is there anyone in your life you want to go back to? Some man?"

She looked away. "Half a dozen. Intelligent, good-looking, well connected."

"Who of course know nothing about your trauma because you haven't told them."

She turned her face back to him. "How did you guess?"

"I don't talk about mine, either."

"I bet you don't suffer horribly from nightmares."

He stared into her eyes. Crystal clear, blue-green like the sea.

"You need someone to sleep with you," he said, aware that with the one kiss they had redefined their relationship. "Someone who can dominate your dreams."

"You?"

He shrugged. "It's going to happen."

"Is it now!" She made a determined effort to sit up. "You're too sure of yourself, Drake. I don't like that. Weren't we arguing about our relationship only ten minutes ago?"

"Don't bring that up again," he warned. "I thought we'd settled it. You've only used it for self-protection, anyway."

"I've never thought about our relationship that

way." She grasped his elbow, offering him her white brow. "I think I must have a fever. Feel."

He slid his fingers back and forth across her forehead. It was warm, but not feverish. "What about a swim to cool off?" he suggested in a mocking voice.

"Have your fun. Are you going to let me up?"

"I don't know. I rather like having you in my power."

Maybe you've always had me in your power, she thought. Happy memories began to surface, and she found herself leaning against him. "Remember when Granddad used to have those big weekend gatherings? Everyone used to come from near and far. When the adults were talking, a group of us used to find the best lagoon to swim. I was just at the stage when I thought you were wonderful, and didn't Joel hate it."

"That hasn't changed. As for you, we'll make allowances for your age." He was loath to disturb her mood, the near-affectionate attitude that was a relic of the days they'd both been young and carefree.

"We're carved into one another's lives, Drake."

"It seems like it."

She brought her head up abruptly, as some thought struck her. "As I recall, you were very much interested in the Minareechi even then."

"Nothing remarkable about that. The Minareechi is the finest deep-water, permanent stream in a vast area."

She maneuvered herself gracefully to a sitting position beside him. "Just think, you could have it if you have me."

His tone was sardonic. "It has occurred to me. Are you offering yourself?"

Her heart fluttered like a bird caught in the hand. "If I were, wouldn't it be too good an opportunity for you to pass up?"

"Not if you're more trouble than any other woman in the world."

"I wouldn't be a problem to a man like you." She gave him a sidelong smile.

"I wish I could believe you."

"So the idea's crossed your mind. Why wouldn't it? You're great at making arrangements. That's what's bothering Callista, who has her hopes set on Karen. The Stirlings have a very nice property, but they're relative newcomers and they couldn't compete with Eden." She waved the obvious taunt like a flag.

He looked directly into her eyes. "You're safe enough. Unless you'd rather you weren't?"

She stood up. "What happened today was a mistake. Think again if you think I'm going to bed with you." Despite her strong words, she saw herself poised at the brink of a chasm.

"I'm as interested in your soul as your body, Nicole. So don't worry. You're my guest. I'll be the perfect gentleman."

So why didn't that give her a lot of joy?

THE AFTERNOON WAS SPENT outdoors where the air was as sweet and heavy as syrup. Inside the Toyota it was mercifully cool, the air-conditioning pouring into the vehicle full blast. Drake drove to various parts of the station, pointing out all the improvements to the giant operation. Along the way there were conversations with colorful characters; mostly trackers and stockmen. Also a man called Boris, an exile from

"Mother Russia" who could speak five languages fluently, mend any piece of machinery and restore it to full running order, but wanted nothing more out of life than the peace and freedom of Outback station life. Nicole had Drake stop frequently so she could take photographs. They even fitted in billy tea and fresh scones with the brumby hunters when they rode in. These highly experienced stockmen—two she acknowledged as ex–Eden employees—had spent much of the previous day scouring the vast station for wild brumbies that could be successfully trained as useful workhorses. Afterward they continued their leisurely drive surprisingly in accord. It was the land, Nicole reasoned, its calming effect on them both.

The spinifex plains marched their countless miles to the Larkspur ranges, which ran in a series of east-west parallel lines to the horizon. Not high as mountain ranges went, the Larkspurs nevertheless presented a spectacular outline, deep ragged indentations and long, inviting valleylike chasms against the brilliant cobalt-blue sky. Their purplish hue was the same dry-pottery purple used by Namatjira, the famous Aboriginal painter. It contrasted wonderfully with the orange-red of the desert soil, the burnt gold of the spinifex and the patches of gray-green of the extraordinarily hardy desert vegetation.

Nicole viewed the natural terrain in all its drama and brilliance with her painter's eye. She wondered if there was ever going to be a time when her work reflected her spirit at peace with itself. Surely that spirit was starting to emerge. She knew she was feeling stronger.

Majestic river-red gums lined the white sandy banks

of the innumerable watercourses—billabongs, lagoons, remote swamps where pelicans built their nests—that crisscrossed all Channel Country stations and allowed the raising of giant herds. Despite the drought, there was quite a lot of water in most lagoons, with splendid water lilies of cerulean blue, deep pink, cream, standing aloft, turning their lovely smooth faces to the sun.

As always the birds were out in their teeming millions. Nicole viewed them with the greatest pleasure; the great winged formations of budgerigars passing overhead like bolts of emerald- and gold-shot silk, the clatter of flocks of whistling duck, the white sulfur-crested cockatoos that completely covered trees like huge white flowers, the chattering pink and pearl-gray galahs, the countless little finches and chats of the plain. The great wedge-tailed eagles and the falcons dominated the skies, no other birds a match for them.

She would never forget the falcons, wings spread, coming closer and closer to the sprawled, defenseless body of her mother.

"What's the matter?" Drake asked perceptively, registering the abrupt change in her.

"I never see falcons without thinking of that terrible day," she said in a pained, low voice. "The way I ran about crazily trying to frighten them off. The way Granddad was trying to hold me while we both died inside. I wasn't going to let them come anywhere near my mother."

Recognition of her terrible trauma was in his eyes. "It was a ghastly experience for you, Nic."

"I'll never forget it no matter how long I live. I've never been able to go back there. The escarpment used to be a favorite resting place, remember? A marvelous vantage point, the best on Eden, though it isn't high, a couple of hundred feet. It's amazing how hills and ranges seem to tower when everything else is so flat. It's the way Uluru astounds, rising so abruptly from the desert floor. It appears mighty. Remember how we used to go to the escarpment after the rains to see the miracle of the wildflowers? Miles and miles of flowers shimmering away on all sides, clear to the horizon. And the heavenly perfume! The desert Aboriginals used the escarpment as a resting place on their walk-abouts.'' She suddenly seized his wrist.

"For God's sake, Nic, be careful," he warned, the muscles of his arm flexing.

"I'm sorry. Stupid of me. But what if some of the desert nomads were in the area that day? They could have seen something."

He sighed heavily. "Many people asked that question, Nic. There was no sighting of any Aboriginal party."

"That doesn't mean a thing. They move like shadows. They could have been there and feared to come forward."

"You're only torturing yourself."

"Okay, then. But so many odd things have been happening lately. I've only recently heard that Siggy paid Dot off without a word to me."

"She shouldn't have done that." He swung his head to her in surprise. "I would have thought Dot would die on Eden. Or die if she had to leave it."

She nodded with a small frown. "I have to follow up on that, as well as what happened to Dr. Rosendahl. Hit-and-run driver? It doesn't sound right to me. I know that street. Narrow. Cars lining both sides. An unlikely street for a hit-and-run. What I don't know is if anyone was caught.''

"Don't go thinking there's a connection. I can't believe Rosendahl's death had anything to do with the old tragedy, Nic.''

"Don't dismiss the idea out of hand," she said slowly. "Dr. Rosendahl knew an awful lot about us.''

"If he was murdered, surely you're not suggesting the person responsible could have been someone we know," he asked incredulously.

"It's damned odd." She swung her binoculars up to watch two brolgas dancing on the flats of a lagoon. "Slow up, would you?" she murmured. "There's a ballet in progress.''

Drake not only slowed, he cruised in gently to the shade of the blossoming orchid trees, the bauhinias.

It was a familiar vision but one that always enchanted her. A bush ballet. The long-legged cranes, their plumage pale gray, their heads swathed in a broad band of red almost like scarves tied around them for the dance were well into their fascinating ritual—lifting up and down excitedly, bowing, pirouetting. One of the great sights of the Outback.

They were both silent, watching. "How beautiful!" Nicole breathed. "I'm so glad I've seen that." She lowered the binoculars, her expression soft.

"The small wonders around us," Drake observed as he reversed the vehicle. The heat of the afternoon had built up swiftly. Far off in the distance, a mirage shimmered before them like swinging curtains of crystal beads, creating optical illusions of wondrous forms, misty-blue pinnacles and domes guarding phantom lakes that had lured many an early explorer deeper into the desert with the promise of life-giving water.

It was Drake's keen eyes that first discerned the speck in the blue sky.

"A plane." He peered through the windshield. "Unless I'm very much mistaken, the Stirlings' Cessna."

"You're joking!" Nicole shook her head in mock surprise. Callista hadn't wasted a moment.

"I'm seriously considering it's Karen."

Nicole made a little derisive sound. "It didn't take Callista long to call for help."

"What the devil could she want?"

"Be your age. She wants you. Kooltar. Do you want me to go on? Callista has got her here for security and comfort. That bad girl, Nicole Cavanagh, is back on the scene."

"It could be her father," Drake said, not very hopefully. "He could have a cattle buyer with him. One's working the area."

"Want to bet?" Nicole asked, thinking she wasn't going to get the chance to be alone with Drake for long.

"How much?" he grunted, his eyes still on the sky.

"Five hundred thousand? I'll take a check."

He gave her a gleaming glance. "We can continue our trip."

"Suit yourself." She shrugged, not giving protest or encouragement. "She's *your* friend and, I guess, your sometime bed pal. Don't worry. I'm not jealous, even though Callista was thoughtful enough to point out that Karen's bedroom is close to yours. So easy to pop in."

"Do you have a problem with that?" he asked lightly. "We're both single."

"Anything that makes you happy. But is the affair incendiary enough for you? Why not pepper it up with a little competition?"

His voice sounded edgy. "I just hope Cally hasn't engineered this."

Nicole looked off to the right to where a palisade of papyrus met the shining water of the river. "You think she'd ever admit to such a cunning plan?"

His eyes glittered. "I promise you I'll find out."

CHAPTER NINE

THEY ARRIVED BACK at the homestead toward sundown, having continued their leisurely exploration of the station. Neither had made any further effort to debate whether they should return to greet Karen. They had simply gone on their way, Nicole climbing out of the vehicle now and then to examine some feature more closely. Once she'd stopped to talk with an old friend, Judah, a full-blooded Aboriginal. Judah had once been Kooltar's finest tracker, but he was now old and physically diminished, the black liquid eyes not as good or as bright but as wise as ever. Judah had been part of the search party for her mother and David McClelland, coming upon her and her grandfather as they huddled on the sand in grief. Even through her shocking trauma, she'd been aware of how kind and sensitive Judah had been with her.

"We old spirits, missy," he'd told her, his dark eyes tragic. "We survive. Your mama fly up to the sky. Understand? After longa while, you'll see her in the stars."

So far she never had, but the idea still gave her comfort.

When they arrived back at the homestead, seated on the broad veranda were Callista, expression as inscrutable as ever, and a tall, good-looking brunette dressed in a tight strawberry-red T-shirt—she had eye-catching full breasts—with knee-length navy shorts, a sparkling white smile on her face.

"Hi!" she called in a bright, friendly fashion, pushing out of the rattan armchair. She moved to the top of the steps. "I was in the area—over at Mount Myora actually, an errand for Dad—I just had to call in. Hope you don't mind?" She'd been addressing Drake, and now her golden-brown eyes shifted to Nicole. "Nicole, how lovely to see you again. It's been such a long time. How are you?"

"I'm fine, Karen." Nicole walked up the steps, extending her hand. "You look wonderful."

"So do you. Like a model on safari in one of those glossy magazines." Her dark eyes swept appraisingly over Nicole's willowy figure. Nicole was dressed in a black T-shirt with khaki cargo pants. She'd woven her long hair into a thick braid. It hung between her shoulder blades, a carefree style that showed off the elegant column of her throat and the shape of her head. Her cheeks were flushed from the heat. Her eyes glowed an iridescent blue-green.

Inspection over, Karen linked her arm through Nicole's in friendly fashion. "You have to tell me all you've been up to. It's really good to see you. I was in Singapore when you were here for your grandmother's birthday. Callista very kindly invited me to stay to dinner and overnight."

"You might as well spend the night with us as fly in the dark," Callista said, giving Karen a fond smile. "I'm sure you two young women have lots to catch up on. How did the afternoon go?" Callista's glance slid to her nephew, who was lounging against the wrought-iron balustrade.

"Fine," he replied casually. "We managed to see a lot."

"That's splendid. I thought you might have returned earlier."

He shrugged. "The idea was to have Nic see as much of the station as she could."

Callista appeared disconcerted by the nickname. She gave Nicole a glinting look. "Why don't you both sit down. What would you like, dear?" She addressed her nephew.

"A nice cold beer." Drake held out a chair for Nicole, who slipped into it. He sat down beside her with Callista and Karen in their original positions on the opposite side of the glass-topped table. "What about you, Nic?"

"A gin and tonic would be lovely. I've thoroughly enjoyed our little sight-seeing trip, but it was thirsty work!"

"Not so little," Callista cut in. "You've been gone for hours." She said this as though she thought they'd been astoundingly rude.

Nicole barely stopped herself from laughing aloud. "The time passed so quickly. Kooltar is in remarkably good condition, given the drought."

"Drake takes the trophy as a cattleman." Karen beamed at him, reaching across Nicole's body to touch his hand. "Running a big operation takes very special skills. My dad says Drake is the best in the business."

"One of the best," Drake amended. "It'll be quite a while before I can touch Kyall McQueen, for one. He's a truly formidable businessman."

"So are you," Karen maintained loyally.

"I imagine nothing is the same for Kyall with his grandmother gone." Nicole gave a tiny involuntary shudder. "I was terrified of Ruth McQueen when I was a child and I didn't scare easily. I remember once we were at a wedding getting overexcited and noisy. One look from her silenced the lot of us. She was positively awful to Christine, her own granddaughter. Christine was so sweet and beautiful. She tried so hard to please. Oh, I do want to see all of my old friends again. Shelley Logan was special—very brave! I understand she's marrying Brock Tyson. Kyall married his one true love, Sarah Dempsey, at long last."

"Dr. Sarah McQueen, head of the Koomera Crossing Bush Hospital," Karen said. "Sarah is much loved and respected. She's a fine doctor. The far-flung community is lucky to have her. She's expecting another baby, did you know? It's only just become official."

"I'm quite sure Nicole hasn't heard Sarah's extraordinary story," Callista said, more than a tinge of disapproval in her voice.

"Actually, my grandmother told me," Nicole said quietly. "Gran has always had a soft spot for Sarah. Sarah was there for my grandfather. Gran will never forget that. When you think about it, Sarah's story is not so unexpected. She had a baby when she was fifteen. She's not the first and she's not the last. She and Kyall loved each other. The miracle is they found their daughter Fiona even though she'd been adopted."

"You'd know Fiona anywhere, Nicole," Karen said. "She's Sarah's mirror image, just as you're your

mother's. I expect you'll meet up with everyone at
Shelley's wedding. We're all going.''

"Alas, I don't have an invitation.''

"That's easily attended to,'' Drake said lightly.
"Brock has already asked me to be best man. He has
Philip of course, but they've never been close. Shelley
will be delighted you're home, Nic. Every time I run
into her in town, she asks after you.''

"As if you'd know.'' Callista stood up as if at a
signal. "I'll go attend to the drinks. Anything else for
you, Karen dear?''

Karen leaned back comfortably in her armchair.
"I'll join Drake in a long cold beer.''

NICOLE HAD BROUGHT something pretty so she could
dress up a little for dinner. She brushed her hair until
it crackled, then allowed it to hang full and loose the
way the men in her life had always liked it.

What men? They paled into insignificance beside
Drake. She had all but broken away from this man,
but look how effortlessly he had reeled her back in.
Something inside her, some niggling little voice, suggested he could have been the real reason she'd found
it difficult to make a lasting commitment to any other
man.

Under the shower she'd felt herself reliving that
kiss. The kiss she couldn't deal with. It was more like
a revelation with the potential to disturb her life. All
that long hot afternoon, they'd been acutely aware of
each other, the hot air sexually charged, but he'd made
no further move to touch her.

It could be his plan. His eyes watching her, like a
big cat with its prey. Despite what Karen had said, she

still believed Callista had called the young woman to come, but Callista was the only one with claws. Karen's manner was friendly, her attractive smile at the ready, but Nicole knew there had to be a great deal of wondering going on behind the pleasant facade. Maybe their relationship hadn't arrived at the point of commitment, but Karen obviously held to her high hopes. Her golden-brown eyes were constantly on Drake, her expression a dead giveaway. She listened attentively when he spoke. She was obviously madly in love with Drake, but he chose in his male arrogance not to heed it.

Men!

It was nice to get out of slacks and a T-shirt and into a dress, this one silk, in an iridescent shade of blue, cut like a slip. Her only jewelery was a pair of silver and enamel art nouveau pendant earrings set with amethysts given to her by her grandmother. They were right back in fashion. A light spray of Chanel's Gardenia and she was ready to go. She couldn't allow herself to be upset by Callista's deeply ingrained hostility. Some things never changed. Callista had never been kind to her. Drake was the reason she was here.

She was ready to go downstairs, when someone tapped on the door. She knew it wasn't Drake from the light, rather hesitant tap. Not Callista, either, she thought.

Opening the door, she looked into Karen's glossy-lipped face. "Hi, Karen, have you come to get me?"

"I wondered if we might have a word." Karen looked beyond Nicole into the large bedroom.

"Sure. Come in."

"This is a beautiful room." Karen advanced, staring around her. "Those paintings! Aren't they lovely?"

"Haven't you been in here before?"

Karen looked almost shocked. "Gosh, Nicole, Callista doesn't give me the run of the house."

"How extraordinary! I thought you were good friends. Please, sit down."

"Thanks." Karen, looking very sexy in a black halter-necked number she would have to have begged, borrowed or stolen from Callista if her story of "popping in on her way home" was to be believed, sank into a comfortable armchair, crossing her long legs and staring down at her strappy sandals. The sandals, at least, couldn't have been borrowed from Callista. Callista's feet were so small they might have been a child's. Obviously the two conspirators were playing little games.

Surprisingly, Karen said, "I suppose you've cottoned on to the fact Callista got in touch with me." She gave Nicole a rueful smile. "Anyone can see you're no fool."

Nicole let her laugh ripple. "Not all the time, I hope. It wasn't difficult to figure out, unless you carry a little black dress with you at all times. Callista has always had a struggle liking me. Even before the old tragedy happened."

"I wonder you plucked up the courage to come here," Karen said, as though Callista, like Lucretia Borgia, had a reputation for poisoning troublesome guests. "I've never found her an easy person at the best of times. She's madly intense. She loves to control everyone and everything."

"Fortunately she can't control Drake."

"Oh, I know that. She knows it, too. Her whole life revolves around him. He's very kind to her. You can bet your bottom dollar lots of other nephews would have asked her to move out." Karen grimaced thoughtfully. "I expect I would," she confessed. "It's not as if she can't make a life for herself. She's still young. She's got plenty of money. What is there for her here? Everything points to Drake marrying soon."

Nicole considered. "You sound very confident of that, Karen. How do you know?"

"Believe me, I know." Karen nodded her head wisely several times.

"You're in love with him, right?" Nicole decided not to beat about the bush.

Karen started kneading her hands. "I can't remember a time when I wasn't. I've taken a big gamble on Drake even when I know I mightn't win. He has far too many concerns. He's just so ambitious! Excessive, in my opinion. It's not money. He's got enough money. It's not even power."

Nicole held up her hand. "Karen, Drake has a hard-headed determination to accomplish as much as he can in his lifetime. If you don't understand that, you understand nothing about him. He wouldn't be happy if he didn't lead a highly constructive life. To him that means coming out top of the class. Making his mark. He was reared on the principle that hard work is greatly to be valued. The job comes first."

"That's just the trouble," Karen groaned. "The job is Kooltar around the clock, and don't let anyone forget it. I don't think any woman will mean as much to him as the job. He's a great businessman. A mover and shaker. Dad says he's an even better operator than his father. It doesn't seem to occur to Drake to enjoy life. Travel. He wants to build on everything here.''

"And you think that's crazy?'' For half a second Nicole wondered if Karen knew Drake at all.

"Life should be much more fun.''

"So what you're saying is you resent Drake's strong commitment to his obligations?'' Nicole asked.

"I suppose I do.'' Karen pursed her mouth. "I want him to have time for me. We could do lots of things together. Not always be looking for new fields to conquer. He's taken over Opal Springs in Central Queensland, did you know that? He might have his eye on Eden.''

"Did he tell you that?'' Nicole couldn't keep the sharpness out of her tone.

"He may have.'' Karen wrinkled her forehead as though trying hard to recall. "Is that important?''

"It is to me,'' Nicole acknowledged bluntly. "I'd say it was far more likely you got that information from Callista.''

Karen shifted in her chair. "She could have said it. I can't be sure. But you must find holding on to Eden a burden now that your grandfather has passed on, don't you?''

Nicole felt slightly nonplussed. "Karen, you don't understand any of this. I come from a pioneering family who just happened to open up this country for the pastoral industry. Eden is my ancestral home. My inheritance. I would fight to the death to keep it. And incidentally, I'm not hurting for money, before you go thinking I might have to sell.''

"I had the impression you were going back to the States. Aren't you?'' Karen asked, pink with fluster.

"Is this why you're here?" Nicole asked. "Your job is to sound me out?"

Karen slumped forward, revealing a spectacular cleavage. "Honestly, can you blame me? You're beautiful, Nicole, and sexy. You're an interesting person, too. I hear you paint. Well enough to give an exhibition in New York. You must surely want to return there. It must be a fabulous lifestyle, the hub of the world. We're so dreadfully isolated."

"Yes, we are. It sounds like you're at war with your environment, Karen. I know you weren't born to it. Perhaps you should have made a life for yourself in the city."

"I want Drake. I've got to have him."

"Drake will never leave Kooltar, Karen. I've benefited greatly from my time overseas, but love of my own country runs through my veins, too. Love of the land doesn't appear to have touched you, but it has me. Of course I'll see New York again. I have dear friends there. But I've made no immediate decision on my future. I've barely touched base here. In any case, my family is running Eden."

Karen looked up quickly, her expression sympathetic but with a touch of triumph. "Nicole, everyone knows Joel is finding running Eden after your grandfather a huge challenge. He's certainly not in Sir Giles's league."

"Who is?" Nicole retorted crisply. "Do you mind my asking, Karen, is this Callista keeping her hand in? Did she put you up to all this, or is that utterly preposterous?"

Karen flushed violently. "No need to be sarcastic. Callista knows how much I love Drake. I have to know, Nicole. Forgive me if I offend." She gave Nicole a humble glance. "Do you have any romantic interest in him? It would make it very hard for me if you did. I've put in so much effort I can't just walk away. You're quite right about Callista, of course. She doesn't like you. She thinks you and Drake would be a disaster."

"Like the old disaster?"

Karen bit her lip. "It was horrendous, though, wasn't it? A scandal that won't go away."

"Not that your knowledge of it would be good. You simply weren't around."

"But the way your mother and Drake's uncle died goes a long way toward explaining Callista's point of view," Karen persisted.

"She needs to blame someone. Me. I don't want to offend you, either, Karen, but you may have a few things wrong. I've known Drake all my life. We grew up together. Our families were once very close. If he were planning on getting married, I think he would have told me."

Karen's attractive face turned stubborn. "It's a loving friendship. At least it has been to date. I've hung around longer than the others, at any rate. Having a family, an heir, will become increasingly important to Drake. I love children. I'd make a great wife and mother. I'm not getting any younger, either. The biological clock is ticking away."

"Karen, I can't help you on this," Nicole said. "You should ask Drake to confirm his feelings for you." Not fantasize about becoming Mrs. Drake McClelland. It looked very much as if Callista was using Karen for her own ends, Nicole thought.

"You don't sound as if you think my chances are good." There was a tiny flash of hostility in Karen's eyes.

"Drake is the one to talk to, not me," Nicole repeated, making a determined move toward the door.

"He's very, very fond of me." Karen rose to follow her.

"You'd better get cracking, then."

They moved down the corridor, hung with lovely paintings. "Have you ever slept with Drake?" Karen asked boldly.

"I can't believe you're asking me that, Karen," Nicole replied lightly.

"But you're here…" Karen looked at her with a worried smile.

"Drake and I have decided to patch up the old feud. It's only civilized."

"Nothing more? Be honest." The golden-brown eyes focused on Nicole expectantly. Heartwarming girl talk.

Nicole didn't oblige. "My private life is just that. Private."

"I have offended you, haven't I?" Karen moaned.

"No, no!" Nicole shook her head. What she really meant was a firm *Yes, yes!*

"You're not going to confront Callista about our conversation, are you?" Karen asked with a note of genuine alarm.

"Lord, no. My lips are sealed."

Apparently greatly relieved, Karen grasped Nicole's hand, locking fingers like good friends. "I just don't believe how nice you are."

ANNIE HEADED OFF another tongue-lashing by producing an excellent three-course meal. Even though there were only four of them at a table that could accommodate six times that number, they were eating in the hushed elegance of the homestead's formal dining room. Dining in such grand style obviously made Callista happy.

They started with a clear consommé, followed by wonderfully tender fillet of beef in a potato coat served with asparagus and a mustard-grain brown sauce. The dessert was chocolate and cherry mousse "domes" garnished with brandy snaps.

"That was a terrific meal, Annie," Nicole complimented the housekeeper as she deftly removed plates. No fumbles this time, though she was sure Annie was fated to recount the story of "the time she saw a ghost" for years to come.

"We have our standards." Callista gave a tiny delicate sniff, small hands fluttering like butterflies over the expanse of pristine white damask, fine china, sterling-silver cutlery, sparkling crystal wineglasses. Tonight she had looped her glossy dark hair into a thick crescent that curved around the nape of her neck, a style that suited her beautifully. In fact, it was so flattering to long thick hair Nicole thought she might try it herself. With the overhead chandelier on a dimmer and candelabra on the table lending their flattering golden light, Callista looked as lovely and exotic as a young Merle Oberon, a film star of yesteryear. For the umpteenth time Nicole wondered why Callista had never married, sitting there so small but regal, sipping her splendid dessert wine. She would ornament any man's table, but all her love seemed to have been given to a brother who was gone.

That same sense of loss started to bear down on Nicole as though David McClelland was all around them. His spirit hadn't been put to rest, she thought dismally. He was still in the house, just as Corrinne was woven into the fabric of Eden.

Afterward they moved with their coffee into the drawing room, where Callista went immediately to the grand piano, a nine-foot Steinway, its lid already up.

"Oh, lovely! You're going to play for us!" Karen stated the obvious with delight, then curled into a wing chair, looking as though she wished for nothing more than to hear Callista play. "Callista is a marvelous pianist," she said, injecting a lot of respect and flattery into her voice.

"I'm out of practice," Callista demurred modestly, though Nicole sensed this was far from true.

"Come and sit beside me," Drake said quietly, taking Nicole's hand. They both settled on the sofa.

Callista took her seat on the long ebony bench, the light burnishing her hair. "A little Schumann to start…"

It was a ritual from the past. The young Callista playing to her brother, David, who adored music. Who had loved her. Before Corrinne Cavanagh had changed her golden days to darkness.

Music poured into the room, Schumann, Brahms, Chopin, a very difficult Liszt prelude taken at a cracking pace without a slump. Callista became a funnel of energy and passion. Each note was crystal clear, perfectly precise, the big chords splendid. For a small woman Callista had a lot of power. The all-important

"singing tone," as opposed to sheer technique, testi-
fied to a real gift. Had she not been rich, she could
have earned a comfortable living as a pianist.

After twenty minutes or so, Karen was so lulled by
the music she fell asleep in her comfortable chair,
emitting the gentlest of snores. That didn't disturb Callista in the least. The woman seemed utterly oblivious
to her audience now.

Drake very firmly regained Nicole's hand and without speaking, inclined his head toward the open
French doors.

"Gosh, should we have walked away?" Nicole
asked in a doubtful whisper when they were out beneath the glittering canopy of stars. Callista, like Joel,
was always apt to explode.

"She won't notice for a good hour. I've seen all
this a thousand times before. Callista loses herself
when she plays. Sadly, not a lot of people get to hear
her."

"But she must get great pleasure out of her accom-
plishment. I don't paint because I need people to see
my work. I paint because I have to. It must be like
that with Callista. If only she could be a happier person."

Drake sighed. "It comes down to choice, doesn't
it? Some people elect to go through life unhappy, making their partners unhappy, as well. We do have a
choice. Callista has chosen this way to live. I know
my grandparents were very concerned for her mental
health. She's very highly strung, rather like her Steinway. She toppled into some kind of a psychic void
after David died, then made the decision it was fairly
comfortable to stay there, a splendid martyr. My uncle

more than anyone used to love to hear her play. Sometimes I can't take it, the sound of the piano at night. I don't mean the beautiful music she makes, it's the…'' Words seemed to fail him.

''I know.'' Nicole gently squeezed his arm. ''When you're trying to cure yourself, you don't want the wounds continually ripped open. There've been too many tears. Too much loss. Let's forget it for a while.'' She paused for a moment to look up. The great constellation of the Southern Cross was right above their heads. To the desert tribes, the Southern Cross was the footmark of the great wedge-tailed eagle Waluwara. The Milky Way spread its diamond-encrusted glory across the center of the sky; a river with many Dreamtime legends connected to it.

''Such a beautiful night.'' The dense heat of the day had gone. The desert sands cooled down quickly.

''Let's walk.'' He linked his arm through hers, the fingers on her bare skin trailing flames. He had only to touch her and all her senses came alive.

I'm falling in love, she thought. *And I can't stop it.* It was a kind of bliss tempered by too many serious concerns. Yet being with him was so exciting. It vibrated through her.

''What will they think when they realize we've gone?'' she asked, acutely aware of the touch of his gently moving hand. It thrilled her right through to the bone.

His laugh was rueful. ''Callista will go on like that until she gets it out of her system. It's much like going to a gym for a strenuous workout. Karen's had one glass too many.''

"Actually I did, too." Her blood seemed full of sparkling bubbles. "Be gentle with her, Drake."

"What is that supposed to mean?" He pulled her a little closer to his side.

"Don't play dumb. You know exactly what it means." She waited a few beats before changing the subject. "Karen seems to think you have your eye on Eden."

There was a ringing pause. "Would you like me to make you an offer?" His tone was suave.

"You couldn't afford it if you were one of the Rockefellers. We're a tenacious lot. Would you sell your inheritance?"

"Of course not. I hold it in trust for my children and my children's children. But I'm here working it, Nicole, not far away in another country. Kooltar is the flagship around which my life revolves."

"Think you could ever love a woman that way?"

He glanced down at her. "How do you know I don't worship at *your* feet?" In the moon's radiance her skin bloomed, smooth and creamy like a water lily, the Aboriginal symbol of a star.

"You're not that sort of man," she scoffed. "I can't see you in any submissive role. I can't see you acting as I imagine your poor uncle David did with my mother."

"What do either of us know about that? We were too young."

"Well, he did let Heath take her from him," Nicole said, a shade wretchedly. "Whereas you, like Heath at least in that respect, are definitely a man of action."

"I'd like to see a little action with you." A faint

smile creased his face. "I took an awful risk kissing you. As it's turned out, it was instantly addictive."

"You should have considered that before you started."

"Some things you don't think about. You just do."

"Here I was thinking it might have been part of the plan. Me, with Eden thrown in."

"Is it so impossible?" His voice, deep and hypnotic, caught her like a hook.

She held her windblown hair with one hand. "You told me yourself you're a risk taker."

"Maybe I've been blinded by your charms."

"I don't think so. You're very clever."

He pushed back a long curving frond that blocked their path. "I've been waiting all my life for a woman to appreciate my mind."

"Brains and brawn. You have both."

"Just as well. I'd be no good at my job." He halted for a moment as a bat soared out of a tree, its silhouette eerie against the moon.

"I don't think the nightmare is over, Drake. I wish I could believe it, but I can't."

"Oh, Nic!" He took hold of her shoulders. "Are you ever going to leave this alone?"

She shivered. "I want to, but there's a voice inside me telling me there's more. You know as well as I do there are too many loose ends. They need to be tied up."

His fingers tightened, a delectable pain. "I don't want to see you put yourself in a position of danger. If there's someone still out there, your stirring things up could make you the next victim."

She gave a shaky laugh. "But I have to learn who

that someone is so that I can take revenge. My own revenge.''

"Revenge is bad.''

"I'm sorry. That's the way I am. If someone killed my mother, I want them brought to justice. You weren't there, Drake. Granddad and I found them.'' She turned to move on. "It's a strange thing to be asking you, but do you think you could find me a good overseer for Eden? Joel needs help.''

"You're seriously contemplating putting someone above him?''

"I can be ruthless when the situation demands. The job is too big for Joel.''

"The consequence would be crushing. Joel has always battled a low self-image. Even as a boy.''

She felt a flare of anger. "Are you implying that Granddad was forever finding fault with him?''

"No. I'm saying he couldn't get your grandfather's attention. He might have, had he been able to cope with your grandfather's expectations, which were that he needed to turn into a carbon copy of Sir Giles. Impossible for him, and the result was alienation.''

"That's not true.'' She focused on the path in front of her, which stretched into a dark perfumed infinity.

"I'm afraid it is. You've got your head firmly stuck in the sand. The only one Joel was free to love was you. Siggy angered him with all her rules, and his father leads some interior life of his own. Who the hell knows Alan? He's a dark horse if ever there was one.''

Nicole gave a dismissive shrug; she was never interested in Alan. "He's simply a man who was corrupted by money, marrying into a moneyed family. It could be the reason he rushed Siggy into marriage. He certainly doesn't work. He fools around in the office, mostly for appearances. At this stage, it's easier to leave him alone.''

''In short, he's a man behind a mask.''

''Pretty harmless, I'd say. He's never given anyone any trouble.''

''Did your grandfather never run a background check on him?''

''Good grief, no!'' She was appalled. ''At least I never heard about it. He's Siggy's husband.''

''They're hardly a loving couple.''

''You think you know everything about my family?'' Her temper rose again.

''I saw more than enough.''

''You didn't see everything.'' Her voice quivered with outrage.

''I saw more than you. I'm older. I was always very observant.''

''Can we stop?'' she asked, thinking an all-out argument was quite possible. ''So many things I remember too vividly. Others perhaps I don't want to remember. Feeling helpless, impotent, is a dreadful situation. Can't you understand that, Drake?''

''Of course. But if we're trying to pin this on someone, it has to be someone with the strongest motive. To many, that's your father.''

''Yes. More than just on the face of it. I believe he's a murderer.''

Drake threw her a look of angry exasperation. ''Nicole, I'm not going to listen to this. Your father is dying. You want him to make a full confession before he goes?''

"He said he's come back to Eden to clear his name."

"Why can't you believe him?"

"I've despised him for most of my life," she blurted out.

"It never crossed your mind he might have had a raw deal?"

"You must be joking! For years he lived the good life."

"You call the good life being marginalized? Your grandfather shoved him into the background. He wasn't even allowed to be a father to you."

"That's not true!" Her hostility burned and burned. She threw up an agitated hand and he caught it in midair.

"It is true." He held her wrist, knowing she would push each stage as far as she could. Push him. "Your grandfather didn't want you to see anyone as the dominant male figure in your life but him. Surely you realize that!"

"I won't be drawn into this. Don't turn Granddad into a villain, Drake. He loved me. Heath didn't. He could have been a father to me if he'd wanted to, but he didn't. He was a drunk and a gambler. He had a violent temper."

"Things might have been different if your mother had really loved him," he said. "But it all went wrong."

"It must have been right for a while. I mean, they got married. My mother rushed headlong into his arms, but it must have been over by the time they got back from church."

"God knows," he said, sighing. "They had you."

"So you keep saying."

"Please don't push it, Nic."

She stared down at their locked hands. "I can't seem to breathe when you touch me." The confession was forced out of her.

"You're afraid of yourself."

"I'm wise to be."

He turned, realizing suddenly that the piano had stopped. For how long? Arms encircling her, Drake drew Nicole off the path, not stopping until they were lost in a thicket of towering shrubs.

CHAPTER TEN

ALL THEY HEARD at first was silence. Then Callista's voice like a downpour of icy hailstones. "Where on earth did they go?"

"They're probably up ahead. Why are you so angry, Callista?" This from Karen, high heels clattering on the path as if she was trying to keep up.

"I really don't have to explain myself." Callista was at her most regal and withering. "So rude! I find it absolutely incredible you should fall asleep, Karen. I thought you had a little bit of culture."

"I'm so sorry. I apologize." Karen's voice cracked. She sounded on the verge of tears. "I don't normally have more than two glasses of wine, but we were having such a good time and the wine was so delicious. What are we supposed to do when we catch up with them?"

"We're simply out for an evening stroll." Callista's tone was positively menacing.

"Then you'd better slow down. Oh, look at those stars, they're glorious!"

"Do shut up, Karen. Haven't I convinced you she's out to steal Drake? She's even more like her mother than I thought. She stole my brother."

"Well, someone was going to steal him," Karen

said in a perfectly reasonable tone. "He was your brother, after all, not your boyfriend, Callista."

Callista obviously treated that remark with the contempt she thought it deserved. "Why don't you go back to the house, Karen," she snapped.

"I think I will." Karen showed some spirit. "This isn't the way to do it, Callista. Spying on your own nephew. Especially a man like Drake."

"The best of men are putty in a beautiful woman's hands," Callista responded, her normal cut-glass tone almost rough.

"Well, I'm not bad-looking and I've never had that experience," Karen said. "I'll leave you to it."

In the shelter of the grove Nicole drew a shaky breath. Every nerve in her body was jumping. It should have been comical, this game of hide-and-seek, but it wasn't. How much did anyone really know about Callista's dark side? She stepped back in alarm, which caused her to collide with Drake, and she was instantly aware of the powerful angles of his body, his unique scent she found so arousing.

They retreated farther into the deep shadows, cocooned in sweet-smelling darkness.

"She'll never find us." Drake's lips skimmed her ear. His palms were running up and down her arms.

"Of course she will." His caressing hands made her feel defenseless. Desire was consuming her like a slow-burning fire. Even the air around them had gone molten.

"She won't," he promised, dipping his head and kissing her neck. Desire had encompassed him, too, an exquisite form of torture. Compulsively his hands moved to her breasts, draped in liquid blue silk. All evening he'd ached to touch them, his eyes drawn to the low cut of her dress, the creamy perfection of her skin.

Her head fell back against his shoulder, her voice unashamedly desperate, as though she feared losing her restraint. "Wait. This scares me a little."

"Me, too." His forefingers and thumbs teased her hardened nipples, a ministration that unraveled so many physical sensations that Nicole felt the strong pull right through her body, as the tide feels the pull of the moon. All previous experience seemed trivial by comparison. The passion rising in her now was thrilling—and dangerous.

But she didn't care, didn't wish to retreat. Just as before, she worried her legs wouldn't hold her, but he had her strongly about the waist, the lean fingers of one hand splayed across her stomach, the tips only inches from her pulsating mound. She could feel herself turn damp, grateful for the darkness that obscured the yearning expression she knew must be on her face. For all the deep-seated fears that stirred her brain, her body never doubted him at all.

Time condensed. When he turned her in his arms to close his mouth over hers, such intensity engulfed her she became entirely what he wanted, not pausing for a second to weigh the outcome of her ardent response. If she'd thought she could control herself, control him, an aspect of intimacy with her past lovers, she swiftly found she'd been deluding herself. He was too bold. Too demanding. It was an erotic experience on a completely different level. She had never felt such physical identification with a man's body. The total loss of autonomy. To her cost?

The night swallowed them up.

CALLISTA, EYES ADJUSTED to the darkness, kept to the path, looking frantically from left to right through the towering trees and banks of shrubs.

How easily they had concealed themselves, she fumed. Drake and Nicole, a cruel echo of David and Corrinne. Just so had David and Corrinne, with her mesmerizing beauty, melted into the darkness of the garden, returning to the house with Corrinne's face radiant, David with his arm around her as though he'd never let her go.

Damn you to hell, Corrinne, Callista breathed. Life wouldn't be long enough for her to forget that bitch's treachery.

AT SUNRISE he came for her. They had a date to go riding.

"Ready?" Drake asked, so vivid and vital he almost crackled with electricity.

"I've been ready for ages." Nicole had hardly slept. She'd tossed this way and that, racked by physical frustration, wondering what it would be like to have him there in her bed. God knows he might have been, except by the time they'd returned to the house, she had recovered sufficiently to resurrect her guard. For every rash action there were consequences. She had almost gone over the brink. Falling in love with Drake could be her downfall. Sleeping with him would increase her vulnerability to an intolerable level. She had to cling to the illusion she was still in control.

When they'd returned to the house—trying to appear normal was quite impossible—Karen was waiting for them on the veranda looking lonely and forlorn,

vivacity quite gone, asking fretfully where they'd disappeared to. Nicole was acutely aware Karen was
looking more coldly on her than she had till then. Callista, it seemed, had gone off to bed citing the onset
of a migraine that promised to blow her head off.

It was the opportunity for Nicole to excuse herself—save herself, whatever—leaving Drake and
Karen to stay on and maybe fight it out.

Not the sort of evening Karen had intended, Nicole
had no doubt, but it didn't pay for a woman on a
mission to fall asleep.

She and Drake had agreed on a dawn ride while
they were walking back. Dawn was an ideal time,
blessedly cool. Nicole rode a chestnut gelding, sweet-
tempered and even-gaited; Drake a majestic stallion,
black as coal. All the signs indicated the animal
wouldn't be easy to handle, but Nicole didn't worry.
Drake was a superb horseman.

Twenty minutes later they were galloping across the
enormous spinifex plains, giving the horses their head.
All the old emotions came flooding back. She hadn't
lost her riding skills. She was rediscovering the great
thrill of feeling the powerful animal beneath her. The
wind in her face bore the lovely familiar scent of the
wild boronia that grew thickly near the countless ar-
teries of watercourses, stirring memories of when she
was a child and had ridden with her grandfather.

The sun was climbing. The pale blue of the sky deepened to cobalt with every passing moment, flooding the
vast splendor with dazzling light. With the sun came
the birds, an airborne explosion of glorious enam-
eled colors, the tranquillity of the dawn broken by

their loud and brilliant orchestrations. There seemed little evidence of human intrusion save for the two of them. A distant dust cloud gave evidence of a moving mob of cattle.

With the arrival of the sun, the desert country began to change color, always an incredible phenomenon even when one was born to it. The earth and the rocks, the low eroded hills, a soft salmon pink, started to burn with a fiery brilliance. The trunks of the desert ghost gums stood out starkly white against the glittering blue of the sky.

They reined in their mounts and walked them in companionable silence to Deep Water Billabong, a smooth sheet of dark emerald water in a wonderful half-moon shape. The billabong issued a compelling invitation to dive into its cool depths; it was the perfect swimming hole and few could resist.

They tethered the horses and moved down to the water, a milky apple green in the shallows.

"Lord knows how I didn't visit you last night," he confided. "I came close."

"What stopped you?" She picked up a pebble and sent it skimming across the water. The movement startled a flock of little white corellas that exploded into the air in protest.

"I have to let you decide what you want." He glanced down at her. She wasn't wearing makeup—she didn't need any with her skin—not even lipstick, which he found strangely erotic. "Which isn't to say I'm going to wait a long time."

"For me to decide to sleep with you?" Her head tilted, her eyes more green than blue in the shade of her wide-brimmed akubra.

"You will, whenever, wherever. We both know it."

She looked back at the peaceful, unspoiled scene. "It could be a mistake. Neither of us is exactly reconciled to the past."

"I'm trying, Nic. You find it very hard to trust."

"I'm concentrating on getting my life right."

"You think increasing intimacy with me will only interfere with that?" His tone was deeply serious.

She nodded. "I can't deal with you like I've dealt with other men in my life, Drake."

"How many?"

"Fewer lovers than you," she answered tartly, suddenly finding the idea of him with other women unbearable.

"How would you know about that?" He bent forward and picked up a small glittery stone, like fool's gold.

"I've heard."

"Ah, yes, your ears. They've never failed you."

She shrugged, her eyes on a sacred kingfisher, its plumage a glorious azure against the textured trunk of the tree where it had its nest. "Because no one ever told me anything, I had to eavesdrop to keep up with what was going on. It was a house of secrets. Even as a child I recognized that. I probably wouldn't have gone with Granddad that day, only I was listening on the stairs. Heath was shouting, filling the house with his rage. I was so frightened. Not of him. I was never frightened of him. I had an awful feeling something dreadful had happened to my mother. I knew she was never coming home. Not alive, anyway."

"Poor little Nic." He looked at her with enormous sympathy.

"For years I thought I hated the McClellands, David's family. Even you."

"You didn't really."

She shook her head sadly. "I flew off to escape the mess. Now I'm home." She moved restlessly. "And I'm hot. I'd love to go for a swim. The water is far too enticing."

"Who's stopping you?" he asked mildly.

She held her head the way she did as a child when she was about to challenge him. "I'm wearing a swimsuit."

"I know." He gave her a lazy smile. "I can see the top through your shirt."

He moved back to sit on a large rock that protruded from the white sand.

"You're not going to watch me, are you?"

"Why so nervous?"

"Because you make me nervous, damn you. I like sensitive subtle men, not men who look like they're about to swoop me up and carry me off to their cave."

"You're getting quite chickenhearted! I won't touch you, Nic, I promise. I might, however, join you when I'm ready."

"Please yourself," she tossed at him carelessly, though her heart rocked.

Under the canopy of the trees, her back turned to him, she kicked off her riding boots, peeled off her cotton shirt and stepped out of her jeans—in so much of a hurry she almost tripped over them. She was wearing a navy-and-turquoise two-piece that didn't go a long way toward covering her, but normally she was quite unselfconscious about her body.

When she finally turned around, his appreciative

eyes were on her, and she thought she might as well discard her swimsuit altogether, so naked did she feel. Without another word, she ran swiftly to the billabong, wading out a little before she slid into the surprisingly cold water, kicking out in a crawl. Her thick braid would get soaked, but she didn't care. It was wonderfully invigorating to be in the water after the rigors of the gallop.

The lagoon spread around her, stands of trees like sentinels around its banks. She swam a distance downstream in a smooth rhythmic crawl.

As Drake watched her stylish stroke, his yearning for her became a physical ache in his groin. He yearned, too, for that carefree closeness they'd once shared. He knew—in the deepest recesses of his heart he realized he'd known for years—that Nicole Cavanagh was very special to him. Now he was in up to his neck, even with the wretched issue of her parentage that had caused such deep division in the past still unresolved. At least for her. What was she backing away from? Dangerous love? He understood she didn't want to complicate her life, when she'd fought hard to get herself together. Wounded psyches didn't heal overnight. She said she liked sensitive subtle men, which he took to mean men she could control. He was sensitive and subtle enough when he had to be. Obviously something about him threatened her. Or was the threat the power of passion?

He'd been thinking lately of making the pilgrimage to Eden's escarpment and the desert floor where her mother and his uncle had died. He knew—not certain how he knew—that Heath Cavanagh had played no part in the final tragedy.

SHE WATCHED HIM get to his feet and cross the sand to the water's edge. From lifetime habit he'd come prepared for a swim, too.

"Oh, man!" she breathed silently, realizing how beautifully he was built. Superbly fit, he wore royal-blue hipsters, no part of his body not darkly tanned. He was a man in perfect condition, every single ounce of superfluous flesh run off by hard work. She took in the wide shoulders, broad chest tapering to a narrow waist and lean flanks. Despite the coolness of the water, she could feel heat mount inside her like a furnace being stoked....

"Ah, that feels good," he said when he reached her, throwing back his dark head and smoothing his wet hair off his forehead. Droplets of water glistened on his skin. In the dazzling sunlight it bore a dark golden luster, his beard a faint outline. The thick black lashes fringing his eyes were long enough for any woman to envy.

I want you for my lover, she thought. *I want you badly.* However carefully one prepared to protect oneself in a relationship, there was always someone who broke through the barriers. That was the dangerous thing about overwhelming attraction. Not with anyone else had she laid herself so candidly open. Yet how did a single kiss give him possession? Whatever the answer, she felt anxious about her ability to withstand him, even when she had the constant reminder of her own mother's fate. In her mind since the tender age of twelve, adult passion had been linked to disastrous consequences. She realized that was an extreme view, but sadly it had become deeply ingrained.

As for Drake? He was looking utterly carefree, rev-

eling in the uncomplicated pleasure of swimming in
crystal-clear water, cooling his sun-drenched skin. As
she treaded water, she couldn't seem to take her eyes
off him, her mind conjuring up countless occasions
like this in the distant happy past.

Then, as if by mutual consent, they started swimming together, not a race, but a slow languorous progress down the deep lagoon with its galleries of riverine
trees—the twisted trunks of the river red gums
streaked and mottled with yellow, gray and white, the
native cypress pines, the salmon gums with their tall
umbrellas of dark green glossy leaves. Pushing their
way between these trees was a variety of acacia,
shock-headed with yellow blossom, the stunted inland
mallees, their branches and leaves dusted with silver.
Small aromatic shrubs abounded, some hung with inviting cherry-red berries Nicole knew were hallucin-
ogenic. It was a lovely oasis in the middle of the desert's aridity, a green corridor that cut through the
fiery-red terrain.

Again by mutual consent they veered away from the
deep center of the pool with all its glittering incandescence toward the shelter of a leafy arbor. One of a
series along the curving watercourse, it was deeply
shaded by the branches of the overhanging gums, the
leaves hanging in long pendant crescents. Their re-
flections lay upon the dark emerald waters, smooth as
glass, gradually breaking up under their advance, little
wavelets radiating out. Masses of sun-dappled water
reeds and wild purple lilies, perfect gems of the wilderness, thickly screened the white sandy banks. Their
sweet pungent fragrance released on the hot air suggested a combination of gardenia and passion fruit.

The peace and beauty of the billabong was remarkable. The small chirruping sounds from the birds in the trees only served to enhance the extraordinary peace and quiet.

For a little while Nicole stayed beneath the water that bobbed at her chin. If she stood up, the surface of the water would barely skim her breasts.

"You look so young," he said in a voice that was unnervingly tender. Her long hair had worked its way out of its thick braid and now floated around her like a mermaid's. The beautiful rich auburn was sleek and dark with water, but nothing could subdue the highlights that glinted in the chinks of sunlight.

He stood up, the water lapping at his waist, his eyes never leaving her. He held out his hand to her.

"Drake, I don't know…" To take his hand was the forerunner to giving herself completely. Giving herself to wild splendor. She saw this in his eyes.

"Don't be afraid," he said. "I'm the same guy you knew as a child." He pulled her from the water, watching it stream off her, revealing the perfection of her shoulders and breasts, the luminous quality of her flesh.

"What are we doing?" Desire was beating at her like wings, yet her voice was melancholy, as though she expected psychic injury.

"What comes naturally, I guess. Like the song says, it had to be you, Nic, even if I don't know what goes on inside your head." He reached out to cup her face between his hands, holding it still while he studied her familiar features. They'd always seemed stronger to him than her mother's. "You fight it from long habit, yet I've never met a woman so in need of love."

There was painful truth in that, yet she answered defiantly as pride welled in her. "Surely you don't think I can't get it, do you?"

"I'm absolutely certain you can. You could have as many lovers as you like. But you need real love. Up until now, it seems you've just had sex."

"Which for the most part I found considerably overrated. What about you with your vast experience?" She shook his hands free. "Karen looked very tearful last night when we came back."

"She was hurt. I'm sorry about that, but I didn't invite her. I like Karen. She's a friend. She was never a casual one-night stand, but there's been no fervent avowal of love or even passion. Just a man and a woman treating one another with affection."

"You'd better tell her that," she advised.

"Forget Karen," he said, drawing her closer. "Forget your defenses."

"I need them to protect me," she said in a light brittle voice. "This could be a maneuver of yours, Drake. A way of gaining control."

"Oh, for God's sake!" His voice was terse. "You sound neurotic."

"Perhaps I am. I seem to have been suffering emotionally all my life. My mother was wrenched from me in the most horrific circumstances. No child should be separated from its mother. And never like that."

Something had to be done and now, he decided. He folded her into his arms with utter thoroughness, the sound of lapping water all around them, warm little perfumed breezes, dazzling light. "Losing her has dictated your entire history," he said, smoothing her long hair. "Just be quiet now."

They stood in an embrace for long moments in that enchanted place, then irresistibly his mouth began to move. It trailed down over her temples and cheeks, skirting her mouth to find the arc of her throat. This woman haunted his heart. She was so unlike anyone else.

Nicole stood motionless, head turning this way and that to accommodate his kisses, her eyes closed. For all her genuine anxieties, her habit of suppression, once she was in his arms, her body, not her mind, articulated her needs. Romantic love was a profound kind of magic. It was able to dissolve conflict at a touch.

He seemed to be breathing in the scent of her like much-needed oxygen. He teased her, his mouth stopping just a shiver from hers so that in the end, ravished by sensation, she was driven to set her mouth on his.

"Stop being so cruel," she said against his teeth.

He laughed and kissed her more deeply. "Is this really you, Nic?" he drew back to ask. "I thought you said you wanted me to leave you alone."

She kissed him feverishly. "I accept that you won't."

His hands moved with a kind of reverence to her breasts, the Lycra of her bra top slick and wet. Her little gasps came into his mouth as he undid the clasp, sliding the straps from her shoulders. Feeling startlingly exposed, she tried to snatch the top back, but with one expert throw he hooked it onto a low branch. "Your breasts are exquisite. I want to feel their weight." He began to fondle them, molding his hands to the creamy, dusky-tipped globes.

Her knees dissolved. The pleasure was too intense.

She arched backward as the sweet pleasure grew. They went under. Even there he embraced her, the cold water turning steamy. They surfaced, him holding her above him while she leaned into yet another voluptuous kiss that took them back under the shimmering surface. She was tired of grief. So tired. This was rapture. Her hands began to move over him, deriving knife-keen satisfaction from the slow exploration of his body. He was so familiar, yet so achingly unfamiliar. She felt his powerful arousal, knowing her yearning matched his own.

Emboldened, she locked her legs around him as their bodies strained together, her naked breasts cool and sleek against his chest.

Drake, in the grip of sexual desperation, hauled her with him into the shallows, shaking back his hair so the water flew in a diamond spray. "I can't take any more of this, Nic," he muttered, barely recognizing his own voice. "I want you too much. Do you want me?"

"You know I do," she cried. "I wonder why you even ask."

She might have been weightless he lifted her so easily, finding a path through the lilies and the soaring reeds to the white sand. "Are you protected?" he asked urgently, kneeling to face her as she lay on the sand.

Her heart stumbled, nearly stopped. "The truth?"

"Of course the truth." His handsome features were hawkish with tension.

"It's a safe time for me, but one never knows."

"Then I'll just have to marry you." He stared directly into her eyes.

"I'd make a bad wife."

"I'd prefer you to a good one." His hand moved from the perfect dimple of her navel down to her pubic mound and her secret crease, her most intimate flesh. He lowered himself over her, bending his dark head, kissing her through the slick Lycra so her thighs involuntarily widened and her legs parted. She gave a curious little cry that resonated like a bird's in that quiet scented grove.

Pure sensation. Her body seemed to be subtly levitating, rising to him as though it desired his touch above all else.

"My Nicole," he whispered, touching his mouth to her lips.

"A prize?" Some contrary imp showed itself.

"Of course." She picked up the faintest lick of triumph in his voice.

"I can't control my body, I'm afraid." Not with her flesh melting like wax.

His hand began a sensuous circling of her nipples. "You're like me. Both of us have become accustomed to standing at a distance from our emotions."

"It doesn't appear to be working today."

"Are you sorry?"

"No."

He cupped one lustrous breast, with its tightly puckered nipple. "I can feel your heart pumping madly under my palm."

Her body was rippling now to his every stroke. "This could be a very reckless thing we're doing."

"When it's been unspoken between us for years?" He turned to kissing her as though he would never stop, kissing her until she was breathless and her blood was suffused with heat.

She twined her legs around his, her slender arms endeavoring to hold him fast. "I want you inside me. Now." She was carried away by sensations so powerful they hurt.

The desperation in her voice, her trembling state, pushed his desire for her deliriously, dangerously high. For one long exquisite moment he pressed against her swollen mound, letting her feel his powerful erection, then in one swift movement he stripped the bottom half of her bikini down her legs, and she helped by kicking it away.

"You're beautiful, so beautiful!" He levered himself over her, the muscles of his shoulders bunched.

"So are you." Her hands, evoking exquisite pleasure, gently worked the velvety shaft of his engorged penis, guiding him to her entrance.

It flowered open to him, filling him with a tremendous rush. The driving power of a passion such as he had never known. He bore down slowly, in perfect control, going deeper, deeper, feeling her multiple contractions as she gripped him. One part of him hungered for her so badly he could have plunged into her there and then and erupted, but he wanted to imprint this experience not only on her body but on her soul. He wanted, needed, to take his lovemaking to its intense trembling peak. It required discipline, control. He wasn't going to rob her of a single moment of this heart-stopping coming together.

He let the sweet pressure grow…ripple after ripple…wave upon wave, and on to the gathering climax.

She would remember him. Only him. It was that simple.

CHAPTER ELEVEN

HER OLD FRIEND Shelley Logan was waiting for her when Nicole arrived in Koomera Crossing. Joel had ferried her in by helicopter, saying it was no bother. He had errands to run around town. They arranged to meet up again in two hours for the return trip to Eden. That would give Nicole ample time to have coffee and a long chat with Shelley and say hello to various people in town.

Eden and Kooltar were the farthest flung of all the stations, but the advent of helicopters had made covering the distance into the town quick and easy, a far cry from the long haul overland.

Shelley was already seated in the coffee shop looking out the window when Nicole arrived. The instant Shelley spotted her friend, she stood up, her face breaking into the sweetest of smiles. The two young women embraced warmly.

"How wonderful to see you again!" Shelley said excitedly, once more resuming her seat on the banquette with Nicole sitting opposite her. "You're more beautiful than ever!"

"I couldn't possibly look more radiant than you." Nicole studied her friend's expressive face and lovely hair. "Let's have a look at that rock," she said admiringly, indicating Shelley's engagement ring.

Shelley presented her left hand for Nicole's inspection. "An emerald to match your eyes," Nicole said. "It's absolutely beautiful, Shelley, and it suits you so well. How is Brock these days?"

"Working very hard," Shelley said proudly, looking relaxed and confident. "He inherited Mulgaree from his grandfather, did you know?"

"My aunt told me. I'm so glad for you, Shelley. You deserve every happiness. Your mother and father, your sister, Amanda, how are they?"

"Far more settled, though my parents aren't entirely over their depression. I suppose they never will be, but they're delighted I'm marrying Brock. You're invited to the wedding, of course. I have an invitation for you right here." She turned to rummage in her shoulder bag.

"Nothing would keep me away. I'll have to get an outfit organized."

"A gorgeous outfit is imperative." Shelley laughed. "Here it is." She passed the invitation to Nicole, who took it out of its embossed envelope to read it. "I found an old photograph of the two of us I thought you might like to see."

"Show me!" Nicole held out her hand. "Oh, would you look at us!" The colored photograph showed two little girls arm in arm. They were wearing some sort of fancy dress with feathers in their hair. Both were smiling at the camera, Shelley about six, looking like a mischievous elf, Nicole a couple of years older, taller, auburn hair cascading around her shoulders and down her back, her head resting sideways on the top of Shelley's short bubble of red-gold curls.

"We were playing dress-up," Nicole said. "I remember it well. We cut up a feather boa Gran gave us.'' Quietly she added, ''Us before disaster struck.''

Shelley nodded. ''A few weeks later Sean drowned.''

''Your darling brother. The pain never goes away, does it?'' Nicole reached out to squeeze her friend's hand.

''I've come to the conclusion it never will. I'm sure the same goes for you. But I've found the man of my dreams. Brock is my miracle. How about you? Anything to relate?''

Nicole felt herself flush. ''I'm enmeshed in something that could be very risky,'' she confided. ''I'll let you know how it turns out.''

''It sounds exciting,'' Shelley said.

''It is.'' Conscious of the heat in her cheeks, Nicole paused to slip her invitation into her handbag. ''Could I possibly keep the photograph? I love it.''

''It's for you,'' Shelley said. ''By the way, I'm getting in early with the news. Brock has asked Drake McClelland to be his best man. Brock thinks the world of him. How does that sit with you, given the shift in relationships?''

Nicole smiled. ''Actually, I've spoken to Drake. He told me he was going to be Brock's best man. We've decided it would be a mistake to keep up the old feud. Bitterness never gets anyone anywhere. I met up with him of all places at Brisbane airport. He gave me a ride home, which was an enormous help. I was thoroughly jet-lagged. Last week he invited me over to see what he's done on Kooltar.''

''That's wonderful!'' Shelley looked up as the waitress came to their table. ''Here I was worried about fireworks and you've made up. You and Drake friends again, just as you were meant to be. That makes me very happy. Brock will be, too. Now, what are you going to have?''

Nicole consulted the menu. ''Vienna coffee, gourmet sandwiches, paper-thin roast beef with Roquefort and cream cheese, lots of black pepper. A sliver of orange and almond cake. How about you?'' She smiled at Shelley, feeling happy they were together.

''Cappuccino, and I'll have the buffet sandwiches, too. Chicken, avocado, peppers, lots of herbs. A slice of old-fashioned lemon pie. It's always good.''

''Homemade,'' the waitress piped up.

''How did you get on with Callista McClelland?'' Shelley asked after the waitress had gone.

''Oh, splendidly,'' Nicole offered, deadpan. ''She thought it a marvelous idea we all be friends.''

''That'd be nice if it were true.''

''Not much better than usual,'' Nicole confessed. ''She's never liked me.''

''Gosh, is she capable of liking anyone outside her own family?'' Shelley put up her hand and whispered behind it. ''Between the two of us, she called Amanda a slut.''

''Good grief! What brought that on?''

''Mandy is a flirt. You know that. She wears sexy clothes and she still giggles a lot. Miss McClelland thought that all added up to slut.''

Nicole grimaced. ''There is a certain prudish aspect to her. Apparently she's quite fond of Karen Stirling.''

''Not a chance!'' Shelley said, shaking her head. ''Though I like Karen myself. She'll have a hard time trying to land Drake. She's been frantically in love with him for years."

Nicole looked up to see Shelley looking closely at her. "Be that as it may, the differences between them are many," she offered laconically. "Now, are you still keeping up your drawing?" she asked, shifting the subject away from Drake. It was all too new, too overwhelming. "You were always filling sketchbooks with wildflowers. They were beautiful, with great botanical accuracy. Do you still do that?"

Shelley sat back a little, smiling. "Not much time lately, with all the excitement of the wedding, but I'll get back to it. What about your painting? You're the one with the real gift. SoHo showings I heard. A glowing review in the *New York Times*. I want to see it. My work is just very pleasing."

"Don't put yourself down," Nicole advised. "I'd like to catch up with what you've done. I wouldn't have been in the fortunate position to have a showing, but for influential friends. Wonderful friends who treat me like family. There's always a market for good flower paintings, Shell. They have enormous appeal. With me my painting is therapy. Dr. Rosendahl first suggested it. He died, you know. He was killed in a hit-and-run accident in Sydney."

"When was this?" Shelley seemed appalled by the news.

"Maybe six months ago. I fully intend to get the full story."

"Did the police find the culprit?"

Nicole shook her head. "Another one who got away."

Shelley's intuitive green eyes didn't move from Nicole's face. She reached out and touched her hand. "You never did accept your mother's death was an accident."

"I wasn't the only one. Someone had a hand in it."

"You can't say that with certainty. You were a frightened child. I remember how traumatized you were for years and years."

"No one found the coroner's report satisfactory. Something very odd happened on that escarpment for them to hurtle down into Shadow Valley."

"You're determined to find out? That's scary." Shelley thought for a moment. "You don't think there's a connection with Dr. Rosendahl's death, do you?"

Time for Nicole seemed to slow down. "All these years later? It seems unlikely there can be, unless he uncovered some new piece of evidence."

"Didn't Joel go to him for a time?" Shelley sent Nicole a quizzical look.

Nicole's head snapped up. "What do you mean? I was the one who had the ongoing counseling, not Joel, though there was a time Dr. Rosendahl spoke in depth to the whole family. He had to. Joel was only sixteen when it happened."

"I don't mean then, Nic, I mean more recently. I take it you didn't know…"

"How do *you* know, more to the point?" Nicole asked, greatly surprised.

"Joel let it slip talking to Brock. He wasn't confiding in Brock or anything like that. They don't have that kind of relationship. Apparently Joel got agitated about something and mentioned going to see Dr. Rosendahl. Brock's very quick. He figured out Joel meant professionally. Afterward he told me.'' Shelley's voice grew anxious. ''I hope this isn't going to make a difference, Nic, but Joel hasn't been invited to the wedding. He and Brock don't get on at all. I guess that's why Brock took a stand against inviting him.''

Nicole put her hands on the table. ''What did Brock say exactly?''

Shelley gave a slight shake of her head. ''Only that Joel had problems and was under a lot of strain. He had been for years. Brock believes that's why Joel breaks out from time to time.''

''You mean acting up in town? Joel always did have a problem with his temper.'' Nicole swept back a long curling strand of her hair.

''The only person I ever saw Joel interact with is you.'' Shelley rearranged the salt and pepper shakers. ''He must miss you dreadfully when you go away.''

Nicole's eyes clouded with bewilderment. ''Do you know, Shelley, I've never really thought about Joel's affection for me. It was just there. You seem faintly troubled by it.'

Shelley flushed. ''I have absolutely no business embarrassing you. All I'm saying is how much Joel is devoted to you.''

''Is that so unusual? We were reared together. He's my first cousin. We were inseparable.''

''Of course. He talks about you such a lot. Quite a lot.'' Shelley folded her hands.

''Did you discuss that with Brock?''

''Inasmuch as both of us regard you as our friend.'' Shelley's gaze was steady.

''And both of you truly dislike Joel?''

''Not me, Nikki.'' Shelley caught Nicole's hand and

held it. "I don't know him well. Does anyone know Joel well? But I do accept what Brock told me."

"You think I need a word of warning?" Nicole asked quietly.

Shelley contemplated her friend. "I can't know what's in Joel's mind, but I can say this to you. Friends are protective of one another. What are Joel's feelings for you, really? Maybe you're so close to him you don't recognize them."

Nicole gave Shelley a look of doubt. This was so strange. First Drake, now Shelley. "You're saying that as if Joel might in some way harm me."

"Oh, no, no! Why did I start out on this?" Shelley looked to the ceiling for an answer.

"It's perfectly obvious why. You have concerns."

Shelley's flush deepened. "That sounds terrible. I never meant to imply—"

Nicole cut her off. "Something Brock said to you gave you a reason for speaking. I should tell you Joel brought me into town. He's taking me home."

"Does he know you're meeting me?" Shelley raised anxious green eyes.

"Of course. He knows of our long-standing friendship. Gosh, we were kids together. He bears absolutely no ill will toward you, Shell." As soon as she said it, Nicole realized she didn't actually know.

"I'm glad." Shelley gave a faint shudder. "I don't want him to feel bad about not being invited to the wedding, but Brock was inflexible on that point."

"Don't worry about it," Nicole advised. "There is a possibility Brock got that bit about Joel seeing Dr. Rosendahl wrong. He would have had to travel to Sydney. Dr. Rosendahl found time for me, but that was different. I was a child in deep trouble and Granddad paid for him to fly in and out of Eden. Seeing a psychiatrist wouldn't be Joel's way. In fact, given Joel's opinion of shrinks—his word—I think it highly unlikely.''

''Who knows what strains he's been under,'' Shelley countered, glancing up as the waitress approached their table. ''You can't ask him.''

''Why not?'' Nicole was wondering in what circumstances she could.

''He'll conclude it was Brock who told you. Or more likely me.''

''And that would worry you?'' Nicole studied her friend.

''Nicole, Joel may have many good points, but he does have an ungovernable temper when provoked.''

Nicole lowered her voice. ''So who is he going to inflict it upon, you or me? I'm not in the least intimidated by my cousin.''

Shelley paused again, looking stressed. ''I'm sorry, Nic, I wouldn't worry you for the world, but in my opinion maybe you should be.''

''You've thought this through, haven't you,'' Nicole said, appraising her friend.

Shelley's gaze was steady now. ''It was a pretty hard decision to come here telling you things you wouldn't want to hear—I've so been looking forward to seeing you, talking about happy things—but not telling smacks a little too much of dodging my obligation to my friend. Am I really telling you something you didn't know, Nic?'' The seriousness of Shelley's expression lent her words special emphasis.

"About Joel?" Nicole gave her friend a curious little smile.

Shelley nodded.

"The answer's yes."

IT WAS A LITTLE after two when both young women walked out into the sunlit street.

"You have to find the time to spend a day with me on Eden," Nicole suggested. "It's been so good to see you. Thank you so much for the wedding invitation and the photograph. I'll treasure it. Say hello to Brock and your family for me."

"I will. I hope I haven't upset you, Nic," Shelley said quietly, giving Nicole a hug. "I value our friendship."

"Friends stick together," Nicole said, noticing the lanky young man watching them from across the street, his black akubra tilted way down over his eyes.

Shelley followed the direction of her gaze. "That's Joel now," she said, her smiling face turning sober.

"If you don't want to meet up with him, go now," Nicole urged her softly.

Too late. Joel dodged a dusty four-wheel drive to join them on the sidewalk.

He moved close to Nicole, took her arm in a gesture that anyone would have interpreted as possessive. "Hi, Shelley Logan. How's it goin'?"

"Fine, thank you, Joel." Shelley gave him a pleasant smile.

"And how's that handsome dog of a fiancé of yours?"

A little pause. "He's well, Joel. Working hard."

"Seems he doesn't want me at your wedding?" Joel's voice held challenge. "How about you?"

A longer pause while Shelley began to edge away a little. "We had to keep the numbers down, Joel. I hope you understand."

"I bet you gave my beautiful Nikki here an invitation." Joel shifted his gaze to his cousin.

"Of course I did," Shelley answered in a different voice. Crisp and cool. "She's my friend."

"Now that *is* being candid." Joel looked amused. "Obviously I'm not."

"Can't you leave this, Joel," Nicole broke in, not knowing where it would end. Shelley Logan was no marshmallow. She had a temper. "Shelley and I have had a very enjoyable meeting. Don't spoil things."

"I didn't know I was spoiling things," Joel drawled, at the same time giving Shelley a look of open dislike. "I'd just like to know why Shelley and her goddamn fiancé found it necessary to leave me out. Just about everyone for miles around has been invited."

"Maybe they thought they couldn't count on your good behavior, Joel," Nicole said sharply, sensing more than one passerby was looking at them.

"Why, sweetheart, of course. I didn't consider that." Joel turned his gaze on her, grinned.

Nicole spun on him. "Have you been drinking?"

Joel nodded briefly. "It's not a crime to have a beer."

"Because you know you're flying home."

"Stop fussin', Nikki. I'm fine. Say goodbye to Shelley now. She's borrowed you long enough."

Nicole felt suddenly ashamed of him, as though

what people were saying was true. Joel was unstable. "It's been lovely, Shelley. We'll be in touch."

"I'll keep a day free," Shelley promised.

"Great!"

They exchanged another brief hug, while Joel, shifting his weight from foot to foot, looked on. "See you, Joel." Shelley paused briefly to include him, despite his obvious hostility. Nicole noted the twisted smile on his face. She was glad Shelley had told her about Joel. She watched as Shelley turned and walked quickly away.

"Are you aware you upset her?" Nicole asked Joel as they walked to the corner of the main street. They needed a cab to take them to the airstrip.

"Who the hell cares!" Joel shrugged. "She and dear old Brock upset me. The big man now with all old Kingsley's authority. Who would have thought the penniless little Logan kid could land a cattle baron?"

Nicole felt her indignation rise. "Brock is very lucky to have won Shelley's hand. She's a lovely person. Clever and brave."

"Boo-hoo," Joel jeered. "She's a judgmental little bitch."

Nicole turned to him in shock. "Why ever would you say that?"

"I can see it in her eyes."

"You deliberately upset her, Joel. When you're in a mood, it affects everyone. You shouldn't drink. You're one of those people who get aggressive. You went out of your way to offend her, and there was nothing I could do to stop you."

"Look, dammit, I was angry. I could have gone to the wedding with you."

"Is that what it's all about?" Nicole said in wonderment. "You and Brock Tyson have never been friends. Why should you expect an invitation?"

"What did she tell you?" Joel's good-looking face was stony.

"About what?"

"Don't play games with me, Nikki." He took her arm in a viselike grip.

Nicole was shaken and embarrassed. People out in the street were watching them. "Stop it," she said coldly. "Let go of my arm and quit flinging yourself around."

"If anyone tried to turn you against me, I'd kill them." He released her arm but his voice remained angry.

"Don't be ridiculous," Nicole said. "You have to learn to control your temper, Joel. People perceive you as a threat. You scare them."

"You don't ever have to be scared of me." He gave her a tender look.

"I should darn well think not," she responded tartly. "I could toss you out of Eden if I chose to." Immediately as she said it she was ashamed. "I'm sorry, I didn't mean that. You have as much right to be on Eden as I have. Only, Granddad left it to me."

"Aunt Corrinne wanted me to go," he said in a voice that seemed to come from a long distance. "Did you know that?"

"Go where?"

He grimaced painfully. "Anywhere. Away from you."

On a reflex Nicole grabbed his arm. "She told you this?"

"She told Dad."

A few people were waiting at the cabstand. No cabs as yet. Nicole moved to the side of the footpath, drawing him with her. "Your father?" she said incredulously. "Why wouldn't she tell her sister? And why was she troubled?"

He touched her cheek gently. "Nikki, sometimes you are such an idiot."

She stared at him, shaking her head. "Please explain that."

His expression was drawn. "It's too hard. Far too hard. The way she carried on, Dad said anyone would have thought I was going to molest you."

"But that's horrible!" She was aghast. The anger left her.

"I thought so, too. I wouldn't hurt a hair on your head."

"I know you wouldn't, Joel." Her eyes connected with his. "What a burden for you to carry. It makes me so sad. Whatever could you have done to make my mother think like that?"

"She didn't want us to be happy." His voice was hard and emphatic.

"I refuse to believe that," Nicole said, defending her mother. "We were children together. What does Siggy say?"

"She's always refused to discuss it. She thinks my affection for you is a crashing bore."

Nicole snorted. "It practically is. Uncle Alan, what does he say?"

Joel took a deep audible breath. "He never stood a chance with Corrinne."

"What do you mean?"

"Ah, Nikki, this is too much." He looked cornered. "I know it was different for you. You were a child. I was sixteen."

"You're confusing me terribly, Joel." Nicole felt truly distressed now. She gripped Joel's arm and willed him to continue.

"Hell, it was like Corrinne was a goddess," he said at last. "Dad used to be so happy if she so much as even noticed him or spared him a word."

Her hand fell to her side. "She never would have noticed him except as Siggy's husband, her brother-in-law."

There was a faint undertone of contempt in Joel's voice. "So relationships define the feelings one is supposed to have?"

Nicole was jolted by Joel's words. "I'm saying there are taboos, surely. Societal constraints, if you like."

"Anyone can fantasize in private," Joel answered. "And falling in love is beyond our control."

Nicole had to steel herself. "Are you saying your father was in love with my mother, his sister-in-law?"

"I'm not saying that at all." Joel turned his head as though checking on the arrival of the few town cabs. "I'm saying he permitted himself to fantasize about her. Dad has an internal life none of us knows much about. I can't think he was ever in love with Mum. He married her for the money. His greatest aspiration in life had to be to marry a rich woman. He certainly didn't want to support himself. There were a lot of complicated relationships on Eden, Nikki. You were too young to see them. Corrinne was the catalyst. Certain women are like that. Beautiful, fascinating.

They make it difficult for men around them to stay out of their range. Poor old Mum! She had a rotten deal. Bloody plain with a sister that looked like a film star.''

The insult to her aunt hit Nicole hard. ''Siggy isn't plain at all. She has far more to her. When she fixes herself up, she looks quite distinguished. The thing with Siggy is she doesn't usually bother.''

''Why would you with a sister like Corrinne?'' Joel asked bitterly. ''No one would have noticed Mum if she did work her butt off to look good.''

''There is such a thing as intelligence,'' Nicole pointed out severely. ''Humor, understanding, loyalty.''

''Sure, but all in all, women are valued for their desirability. How can you doubt it? Do you think McClelland would have invited you over if you didn't fit into that category? Beautiful and fascinating. As far as I can see it's a view women hold of themselves, anyway. Once they lose their looks, they know they're out of the race.''

Nicole, the feminist, was outraged. ''Maybe they should stop being motivated by what men want.''

He laughed into her face. ''Sex is at the core of everything, Nikki. Do you think your mother's life would have ended as it did if she hadn't been such a danger to the men around her?''

''How did it end?'' Nicole asked sharply. ''That's what I want to know.''

Joel shrugged. ''One or other of them lost control. A fight resulting in an accident? Murder-suicide? Who knows? I mean, it was a long time ago.''

''I can't believe you said that. We're talking about my mother.''

Joel kept looking up the street. "She didn't like me."

To hear such a charge against her mother was devastating. "I never saw a single instance of her being unkind to you. The reverse was true."

"She turned on me." Joel's face contorted for a moment before he composed himself.

"When?"

"Don't push it, Nikki. Please," he warned. "You must be very careful what you're about. You've brooded about this for years. You always were an intense creature. No one has ever found concrete evidence of foul play. The best thing you could possibly do is forget it and get on with your life."

"And let a possible murderer go free?" She stared at Joel, shocked and appalled.

"If such a person was around, what's to stop them coming after you? I couldn't bear to think of you as a victim. Forget it, Nikki, I'm begging you."

She simply had to ask him, "Did you ever speak to Dr. Rosendahl about the burdens that were put on you?"

His eyes flashed as if someone had turned on a light. "Why mention him? Hell, I have nothing but contempt for him and all he represents. Headshrinkers. Charlatans. They can't help themselves, let alone anyone else."

Urgent questions rose to her throat, but she was uncertain how to handle Joel when he was feeling this way. "He helped me greatly," she said. "Why not you?"

Given an opening, again no response. "Why didn't

anyone advise me of his death?'' she asked next. ''Didn't anyone think I'd be interested?''

''Don't look at me,'' he said moodily, staring at some point over her head. ''I never spent any time thinking about him. I never liked the man. Always stroking his beard. I never liked those eyes of his, either. Black as night. They seemed to push you to the limit, probing into your soul. I didn't trust him.''

She gave him a look of mixed anxiety and inquiry. ''What did you have to hide? Tell me. It was nothing, isn't that true?''

''Of course it's true.'' His hand came out, closed around hers. ''All I want is for you to be happy, Nikki.''

For the life of her Nicole couldn't draw her hand away, nor could she trust herself to question him further. Joel had deliberately lied to her, but he looked so loving it deeply distressed her. Cabs started arriving.

''Let's go,'' he said, animated now as if a threat had been averted. ''I can't wait to get home.''

CHAPTER TWELVE

NICOLE SAT in the tiny parlor of her old nanny's rented cottage, dabbing at her damp eyes and looking around her. Snapshots galore! Everywhere she looked there were photographs of herself, lined up along the mantel, on top of a glass-fronted cabinet, on the coffee table in front of her, on open display on the shelves of a plain pine bookcase, which held quite a collection of romance paperbacks. Dot had always been addicted to romance novels, treating them as proof life had happy endings.

So...herself at all stages and all taken outdoors—sitting on ponies, on fences, in trees, on swings, holding a kitten up to her face, smiling widely in the magnificent pool her grandfather had built in the garden after she told him that she and Joel wanted one. All those curls! She was a pretty child. Strangely, not one snap included Joel, which she thought very odd. They were always together like brother and sister. Dot had been nanny to both of them. Clearly she had been the favorite. Poor Joel! He hadn't exactly had the best of times, which must have reinforced his idea of being different.

One small, surprisingly upbeat painting, hers—she had given it to Dot as a keepsake—highlighted the room's general bleakness, if anything could be said to be bleak in Queensland's perpetual golden sunshine and brilliant blue skies. But the room spoke of a lack of money and a general hopelessness, as though brightening things up wasn't just financially impossible but simply not worth the effort.

Dot had greeted her with tears of joy streaming down her face. Nicole found herself doing the same, crying her head off. Now Dot had hurried off to her little kitchen to make tea.

Nicole had flown in that morning with Drake, who had a cattlemen's meeting in the state capital. The premier and the minister for Primary Industries would be in attendance. Politics for Drake. For her the cover story of buying an appropriate outfit for Shelley and Brock's wedding. She had told no one, not even Drake, she had come with the express purpose of looking up Dot. She wanted to find out exactly why Dot had left Eden. Had she truly gone of her own accord, or had she been pushed? And if so, why? Siggy was gruff, but not unfeeling. Her grandmother Louise was the kindest of women. She wanted a reason from Dot she could accept.

While she waited, Nicole sat on the edge of a worn armchair, lost in the past. The collection of old photographs had stirred up so many memories. She could see herself as a little girl being very naughty and high-handed, giving Dot a difficult time; Dot not knowing where she was or what mischief she was getting up to, other times sweet and loving, her arms flung around Dot's neck. She realized now she must have been very spoiled. Her grandfather's little princess, indulged in every way. In stark contrast, much of Dot's life had been unutterably sad. Dot had scars all over her body, evidence of her husband's brutality. Early on, Nicole had felt it absolutely imperative the family look after Dot. Not only to repay the debts of her childhood, but because she, herself, had in many ways lived a life of material privilege. She knew Dot would literally have given her life for her. It almost happened once at a station waterhole when Dot, fearing her young charge was in difficulties—she was only fooling around, for she could swim like a fish—waded in after her, moving farther and farther out into deep water, arm outstretched with the hope of pulling her in. Dot, unbelievably, given she was Outback born and bred, had never learned to swim.

"Here we are now!" Audibly puffing, either from excitement or physical exertion, Dot came back into the room bearing a tray set with a white paper doily and tea things.

"I'll take that, Dot." Nicole stood up immediately. Before Dot could protest, she took the tray from her and put it down on the coffee table in front of the single sofa, upholstered in a dismal brown velvet. "Scones, how lovely!" She looked up to smile.

"I made them specially for you." Dot's thin cheeks pinked. Nicole had rung from the airport to ask if it would be okay if she paid a visit.

"I was just looking at all the old photographs, Dot. They bring back so many memories."

"All I had of you," Dot said poignantly. She lowered herself stiffly onto the sofa, which gave alarmingly. She was wearing a lot of lavender scent that wafted with her movements. Nicole was reminded how in the old days Dot had always packed her dresser drawers with sachets of their beautiful boronia. "Old bones," Dot said in wry explanation of the creaks.

"You've had your hair cut?" As long as Nicole could remember, Dot had always worn her hair in a rather straggly bun. Now it was short and mostly gray. It looked as though it hadn't had a good conditioning in some time. Nicole made a mental note to do something about that. She was dismayed by how much older Dot looked, though she said nothing. She wouldn't have offended Dot for the world. A little bent, probably from osteoporosis, Dot was all sharp jutting angles, though her short wiry frame had never carried much weight.

"A month or two ago," Dot said in response to Nicole's question, touching a hand to her head. "I don't like it, but I couldn't stand long hair in the humid heat. Brisbane is so humid, very tropical. It's dry back home." Nostalgia was easy to detect in her tone. That gave Nicole encouragement.

"Why did you leave, Dot?" she asked. "I was shocked when Siggy told me you'd gone. I thought you never wanted to leave Eden."

"Still take milk in your tea, love?" Dot asked, apparently not eager to answer questions.

"Milk, no sugar," Nicole told her absently, wanting to get back to the purpose of her visit.

Dot busied herself pouring. The scones looked light and fluffy—Nicole wasn't surprised—topped with strawberry jam.

"Had to rush out and get that," Dot said, smiling. For all her gauntness, her expression was the same as ever—sweet, patient, gentle. She indicated the jam.

"I'm so thrilled you're here, Nicole. It's like a dream."

"I always wrote to you, Dot. Kept up the phone calls," Nicole reminded her, hating to think of Dot miserable.

"I know, love. I've got all your letters. I've read and reread them so much they're falling to bits. You're so beautiful. So much like your mother but not like her, if you know what I mean. I keep your mother's portrait on my bedside table. Lovely, lovely lady. Such a tragedy you were denied her. I mustn't cry. Mustn't cry," she chided herself. A tear splashed.

"Don't upset yourself, Dot. Please don't." Nicole moved to the dreadful lumpy couch and hugged Dot's bony shoulders. "I'm so happy to see you."

"Not near as happy as me, love," Dot said promptly. "This can be a lonely life."

"Exactly!" Nicole gazed, puzzled, into her old nanny's face. "What I don't understand is why it has to be."

Again as if stalling, Dorothy passed the tea. Nicole stared at the cups and saucers, the milk jug and the sugar bowl thoughtfully. Aynsley. Rather beautiful. White with a gold and ultramarine border. She knew it.

"Your grandmother wanted me to have this," Dot said proudly. "Do you remember the piece?"

"I think I do."

"This is the first time I've ever used this china," Dot admitted. "It's too good."

Nicole leaned closer, accepting her tea. "It's meant to be used, Dot. You really must. Why do you think Gran gave it to you."

"What if I broke a piece?" Dot asked dramatically.

"I have complete confidence you won't. Anyway, it's yours."

"I know." Dot smiled with pleasure. "She gave me other things, too. Lovely linen and towels and things."

"I hope you're using them."

Dot blushed. "I think I enjoy looking at them more than using them. I'd never get the sheets and pillowcases to look like that again. So white and smooth."

"Trust me, Dot. They'll come up beautifully. Quality always does." Nicole took a sip of her tea. She wasn't much of a tea drinker—found the taste vaguely medicinal. She set the cup down into the saucer.

"Is there some mystery about why you left Eden, Dot? Something you can't answer?"

Dot bent her head, looking as if she was fighting off tears. "The truth is, love, I lost my role long ago. I was no use to anybody. I had to go."

"Never in this world!" Nicole protested strongly. "Had to, Dot? That's not right at all. Siggy said you wanted to go. Gran was under the impression you did. From what I can see, you're thoroughly miserable here on your own."

"It's okay," Dot said, grasping Nicole's hand with one sudden distraught movement. "Really it is, love. Your aunt took care of me. I can't work anymore."

"Why would you need to work?" Nicole asked gently. "You spent years and years looking after Joel and me. You can't move out just like that. In fact, I implore you to come back."

Dot looked away, red-cheeked, glittery-eyed. "I can't, love. Mr. Holt would drive me out of the house again."

Nicole was so shocked she laughed. "What does Mr. Holt have to do with anything? He holds no responsible position at Eden. He's my aunt's husband. He's tolerated. You know that. You lived with us. You saw everything."

Dot's "yes" was almost inaudible.

"Are you telling me Mr. Holt, not Siggy, wanted you sacked? I refuse to believe it."

Dot began to fidget with a fold of her skirt. "I decided it was best to go. I told Miss Sigrid I wanted to go. She questioned me just like you. She was very surprised, a bit insulted, but I knew for some time I had to go."

Nicole looked at her in bewilderment. "There's a story here, Dot," she prompted. "Please tell me. What did Joel say, for instance? You were just as good to him as you were to me. Surely he had something to say about your going."

Dot snorted her contempt for that. "Joel didn't care anything for me, or anyone else as far as I could see. His heart belongs to you. He kept out of it, but I'd say he sided with his father, not that they talk much."

"So you felt Mr. Holt wanted you gone, but he never actually said anything to you?"

Dot cocked her gray head. "That man, lovey, is a trained actor. He's anything he wants to be. If you want to know, I'm frightened of him. That's really the case."

"Good God!" Nicole's gaze turned inward. She was seeing Alan's smooth impassive face, the gentlemanly facade. "Who could be frightened of Alan?" Her voice rose in amazement. "He's never shown himself to be anything other than harmless."

"Do you really know him, love?" Dot clutched Nicole's shoulder. "I thought I knew my husband before I married him. I thought he was a good man, going to look after me. I married a monster."

Nicole gave Dot a look full of outrage for the things that had been done to Dot during her violent marriage. "He'll pay for his crimes, Dot, if he hasn't paid already. Leave him to the hereafter. But what makes you couple your husband with Mr. Holt? On the face of it, it's a mind-boggling accusation." She threw up her hands. "Alan's not physically violent. He wouldn't dream of laying a rough hand on a woman."

Dot looked painfully unconvinced. "I don't want to sully his name. All I'm saying is I have this fear of him. Deep down here." She pressed a hand to her chest.

"But there's got to be a reason," Nicole persisted, coming to the sad conclusion Dot was more than a little paranoid. Not that anyone could possibly blame her. "Has he ever done anything to make you wonder he might have some serious problems? Has he been unkind to you? Has he shouted at you? Given you dirty looks? Complained about you to Aunt Siggy?"

Dot spread her hands, the knuckles swollen and knotted. "I just sensed it, love."

That wasn't entirely sane, was it? Nicole made her voice soothing. "Could it be you had such a frightful time with your husband that some aspect of Mr. Holt's looks or behavior triggers those old feelings? You were terribly abused, Dot." Physically, mentally, sexually. Deeply traumatized. Nicole knew as well as anyone how that created lifelong problems.

"That man's got secrets," Dot said with considerable doggedness. "Like my man. They look okay. They can even act okay, but they're twisted. There's something dark inside them. If you ask me, it's the devil."

"I've never seen it, Dot." Nicole spoke the simple truth.

"Because everyone loves you. They were there to protect you. Rich powerful people. I had nothing like that. You never wanted for courage or confidence. You couldn't care less when your dad shouted at you. I had neither. Archie cleared me out of that. I lost the ability to have children. He did that to me."

Nicole rubbed Dot's arm up and down in an effort to console her. "Dot, dear, this seems to be all tied up with your husband. So many terrible things happened to you that you're still fearful. You're attaching far too much importance to Alan Holt's behavior. I'd say he's been eccentric all his life."

Dot suddenly recalled a detail of great moment. "Do you know that man was crazily in love with your mother?" she asked, her smile grim. "I'm sure of it."

Nicole braced herself for more disclosures. "Did you see something to support that?"

Put on the spot, Dot shook her head. "Nothing I could report to anyone. It was all up here." She tapped her furrowed forehead. "I know he used to claim he was somewhere when he was someplace else. I do know that for a fact, but it wouldn't have paid me to tell anyone. Not your Granddad. He despised the man. Only put up with him because of your aunt."

Nicole tensed, sitting upright on the dreadful sofa. "Where was he at the time my mother and David McClelland were killed?"

Dot met her eyes. "He claimed he was at Koomera Crossing picking up supplies."

"Are you saying he lied? People saw him, Dot. They saw him in town. They saw him sleeping in his vehicle. That was pretty much checked out. Alan was never a suspect. He had no reason…"

Dot's voice fell to a whisper. "He never came home that night."

"Much too far to drive, Dot. That's easily explained. My mother would never have been afraid of Alan."

"She was like you, love. Afraid of nothing. But it pays to watch the people around you. I always do. You never know who might be mad. He's an odd, odd man. He never helped his boy. He never took any interest in him, even though Joel has something of his father in him. More's the pity!"

Nicole was quiet for a moment, thinking. "Why don't you have any snapshots of Joel? They're all of me."

"Because you were a precious child!" Dot smiled. "I loved you. You were such a bright little girl, full of life. No malice. No spite."

"I should hope not, Dot. That sounds terrible. But I was naughty. I do remember that."

"What's naughty? Nothing!" Dot scoffed. "You were sunny and loving. 'Course, your granddad spoiled you something rotten, but it never changed your nature. You treated me right. You were affectionate, always showing your emotions. Never hid them away like your cousin."

"But you can't interpret a natural reserve as malice

and spite, can you, Dot?'' Nicole went to Joel's defense. "Joel just didn't have my temperament.''

"You always did stick up for him," Dot said. "I used to worry about it, all your taking the blame.''

"It was a two-way thing. Joel's my cousin. I love him.''

"Not as powerfully as he loves you," Dot said, groaning. "A different way. He's a bit nutty, like his father.''

Nicole heaved a deep sigh. "Dot, I want you to know there's no one on Eden to hurt you. In any case, I'm home now. How could you be frightened with me around? I want you back.''

"No, love.'' There was a tremor in Dot's voice. "I don't know what that man's going to do next.''

Nicole stared sightlessly at the bookcase, thinking that Dot might need care. "I've come especially to take you home. I want you home.''

"No, love," Dot said again, and shook her head several times, the picture of misery. "The fact is, I'm frightened to come. And I believe you should go away. Back to America. Sell Eden. Go away.''

"I can't do that, Dot. Eden is my home. I love it. It's part of me. I cannot, will not, part with it.''

Dot drew a shaky hand across her mouth as if to zip it. "I understand, love. How is Joel?''

"He's all right, though perhaps he's not the best person in the world to run Eden since Granddad died.''

"Who could match your granddad?'' Dot said simply. "How is Joel with you now you're home?''

"Fine, I guess. I'm starting to recognize he's a bit too attached to me.''

Dot listened with averted gaze. "Send him away,''

she advised in a trembling voice. "Him and his dad. Your mother wanted to."

Nicole stared at her. "You're sure of that?"

"Yes, love." Dot nodded her head emphatically.

"What about Aunt Siggy?"

"That's up to you. Miss Sigrid's a good person. Unhappy underneath. Marrying the wrong man didn't help much. Neither did seeing him fall in love with her sister. Not that Miss Corrinne ever looked his way."

Nicole flinched, running a dismayed hand through her hair. "God, Dot, I was always watching," she protested. "I never saw anything. I was just a kid, but I was never stupid. In fact, I was positively nosey."

For the first time Dot laughed. Very gently she took Nicole's face and kissed it. "Didn't I used to tell you you were too smart? Same as your mama. But you just missed that one thing, though."

By now Nicole felt unspeakably sad and confused. "I'm going to ask you a very important question, Dot. If you love me, I beg you to answer it truthfully."

Dot's face paled as if she was about to be asked more than she could answer. "What is it, child?"

"Is Heath Cavanagh my father, or did my mother deceive him?" Nicole burst out.

Dot's expression was genuinely shocked. "Why, how wrong you are to question that, Nicole!" she chided. "We're talking about your mother here. Miss Corrinne. Of course Heath Cavanagh is your father. Never doubt it. Lord, girl, you really can't see that your mother would never have married him if she'd been carrying David McClelland's child? Shame on you, Nicole. Shame."

Nicole lowered her head, feeling chastened. "I'm sorry. I couldn't stop myself asking. Heath's back on Eden. He's come home to die. He's very ill."

"And you've taken him in, believing he mightn't be your father?" Dot asked.

"Pity overcame everything else."

"Because you've got a good heart. That's one of your outstanding qualities. But sometimes you do tend to be pigheaded."

"I know. Thank you, Dot." Nicole smiled. "Isn't there something I could say to change your mind? I can't leave you here." She looked around. "You really won't come?"

"No, love." Dot sounded very sure.

Nicole patted her hand. "Then would you allow me to find you a nice little villa in a good retirement village? The best Brisbane has to offer, or the Gold Coast with its lovely beaches. You need company, friends. Quality facilities. Meals and cleaning taken care of. Attractive grounds to roam in. Would you like that?"

Dot's eyes brightened, then gradually faded. "I've got to watch the pennies, love. Miss Sigrid gave me a lot of money, but sometimes dying isn't easy. I could last for years and years. My mum died in her nineties."

"I swear you will, too. You're family," Nicole said, taking Dot's hand. "From now on, you're going to let me look after you properly, because that's what I want."

Dot reached out and squeezed Nicole's hand. Her tears of joy were the only response Nicole needed.

THE PHONE RANG in her hotel suite. Nicole, quickly unlocking the door, ran to it. It was Drake.

"How's your day been?"

"Great. How was yours?" Just the sound of his voice had her blood bubbling. When happiness comes, you can't ignore it even though it could lead to greater unhappiness, she thought, grabbing it before it was gone.

"Just a moment," he said, obviously turning away to speak to someone in the background.

A murmur of voices, then he was back on the line. "Sorry about that. The meeting went a lot better than expected. And a lot longer. The premier is a good bloke. He listens. Did you find your dress?"

"I did." Nicole had gone shopping for most of the afternoon.

"You can tell me about it over dinner. I'll pick you up around seven-thirty if that's okay? I thought we could walk from the hotel to the restaurant. Five minutes or so. It's good and it's on the river."

"I'm looking forward to it."

"So am I." Even as he was hanging up, she could hear voices in the background trying to get his attention. Probably reporters.

She'd bought more than the outfit for Shelley and Brock's wedding. She'd indulged herself further by buying a dress for tonight. A soft sexy number she found so irresistible she'd never even asked the price. It was a satin wrap dress in a beautiful shade of mulberry.

She was ready before time, incredibly because she wasn't vain taking many a long look at herself, turning this way and that. Checking. Double-checking. She knew she dressed well. She had good taste—fortunately she could afford to have—but she had never gone all out for allure. This dress was deliciously alluring and fit beautifully.

Stop looking at yourself, Nicole, she admonished, turning away determinedly from her reflection. Drake was the cause of this. He was on her mind all the time. She planned to tell him about her visit to Dot over dinner, the disturbing things Dot had said. Not familiar with retirement villages and how they were run, she had rung the family solicitors asking if one of the secretaries could check out the situation for her and get back. She wanted to see Dot settled in a more cheerful environment. She wanted to help her choose the furniture. Pick out a decent sofa, for a start. The cottage had been rented furnished, and Dot had avoided making a few purchases of her own, convinced she would outlast her mother.

THE RESTAURANT had sweeping views of the river and the city's nighttime glitter through its floor-to-ceiling windows. The decor was very classy, discreetly opulent with gilt-framed mirrors reflecting the exquisite arrangements of flowers—lots of tropical orchids—the elegant furnishings and the well-dressed guests. Probably all of them regulars who knew a gastronomic experience when they had one. The chef, they learned from the back of the beautifully presented menu, was a young Franco-Japanese who had recently won a prestigious award from a field of the country's most highly skilled and exciting chefs. The judge had been very enthusiastic in his praise for what was happening on the Australian scene and the important part the cuisine of Southeast Asia had played in it.

"Hungry?" Drake asked, letting his eyes roam over her. She looked so stunning this evening he thought he would carry the memory forever. The color of her dress, so unusual, highlighted the ruby flash of her hair and emphasized the perfection of her skin. Quite extraordinarily it also turned her eyes an iridescent blue.

"Starving!" Her smiling eyes locked with his. "I had a cup of tea and a scone with my old nanny many long hours ago. You remember Dot?"

"Of course I do. Siggy sacked her."

"No, she didn't. I'll tell you what happened if you're interested."

"I'm more interested in you." He reached out and gently touched her hand. "You look exquisite. I'm utterly bewitched."

"You've told me that before, but you can tell me again."

"I promise I'll tell you a hundred times over before the night's out. I love the dress. Never take it off unless I'm there to help you."

"You plan to?" The expression in his eyes made her toes curl.

"Are you surprised?"

"No," Nicole said softly.

THEY STUDIED THEIR MENUS, little shafts of electricity charging the air between them.

Nicole stuck to beautiful Moreton Bay's legendary seafood. Drake was torn between the carpaccio of coral-reef trout with herbs and the Red Emperor with papaya chili and coconut salsa.

"We can choose dessert later." He smiled at her.

"*You* can choose dessert later. I have to watch my figure."

"I'll watch it for you." He leaned closer. "You have the most beautiful breasts."

She put a forefinger to her mouth, exquisitely conscious of her plunging neckline. "Hush, I can't take it."

He smiled. "Don't worry. I've seen you more naked than that." He sat back, holding his fragile wineglass by the stem, the beads of champagne reflecting a golden-green.

He looked effortlessly right, Nicole thought. The breadth of his shoulders set off the fine tailoring of his charcoal jacket. His ice-white shirt worn with a stylish striped silk tie in gray, gold and black, accentuated his deep tan, the thick raven hair and his extraordinary eyes. She had a sudden mental image of them both in bed, knowing when the moment came she would welcome him.

"So tell me about Dot," he said after the waiter had taken their order and moved away from their secluded window table. "I suppose you've already set about improving her life."

"She doesn't want to come back to Eden."

"Now that surprises me. I thought she was a fixture."

Her eyes were troubled. "It might come down to Dot's mental health."

"Really?" Drake raised an eyebrow. "I would have thought Dot had her head screwed on right. So what are we talking about—early stages of dementia? That's not fair. That demon Dot married gave her hell. God knows how many times she was hospitalized during their marriage, but she kept going back to him. Inexplicable to me.''

''It happens,'' Nicole sighed. ''Perhaps the abuse turned her mind. She confessed she left Eden because she was afraid of Alan.''

''Alan?'' Drake's reaction was the same as hers. Naked disbelief. ''So she's lost it?''

''I've had to consider that, but in every other respect she's perfectly normal, the same as ever. Dot was always quiet, but she was a pretty shrewd observer. She said he's a born actor, which he is. She said he was 'crazily'—her word—in love with my mother.''

Drake shrugged. ''Okay, I can accept that. Lots of men fall for fascinating women. But it would have been a look-not-touch situation.''

''I'm certain my mother hardly noticed him.''

His look was somber. ''Given that all the action was elsewhere.''

''What tangled lives we've led,'' Nicole observed.

''It had a lot to do with sex-charged people being under the same roof. Virtually living in isolation for most of the time,'' Drake said. ''That sort of intimacy can be suffocating. So we have a hotbed of intrigue. Alan was never in love with his wife. I think we all know why he married her. Siggy was left feeling unloved and unfulfilled. Corrinne had two men madly in love with her—''

''Three, if Dot is correct.''

He grimaced slightly. ''Okay, three. Siggy is attracted to the hugely virile Heath. You've got a lot of confusion and despair there. Small wonder Joel has problems. Devalued by his grandfather, largely ignored by his father, pressured by his mother... That only left you and Louise, who spoiled the both of you. As for you and Joel—"

"Do you think we should talk about Joel if we want to enjoy ourselves? I told you our relationship is fine."

"Okay." He apparently had the sense not to push it.

In the end, after two delicious courses, Nicole couldn't resist dessert.

"Chocolate, the ultimate aphrodisiac," Drake joked, then joined Nicole in a slice of a luscious dark-chocolate truffle tart on the sweets trolley.

They lingered over coffee, both conscious of the building sexual tension. "What now?" she asked, aware her voice wasn't quite steady.

"To your suite, I hope." He was staring at her intently, his eyes drinking in her face. "I want to feel your body against mine. I want you in bed with me. Anything strange about that?"

Her skin sizzled, yet she shivered. "Sex, excitement, the two of us dressed up for dinner. What's the real agenda, I wonder?"

"You think I'm after more than your body?" He frowned.

"I know you are. They tell me you're becoming famous as a strategist."

"Tell me, what's my strategy with you? I know you have a vivid imagination."

She lifted her chin. "So I'll let it have its head. You could want to take me further into the regions of suffering. You could want revenge for your family—Callista would back you in that. You lock me into a deep relationship, an engagement, then break things off the minute you get Eden. Just like that. Over. It's been done before.''

His handsome mouth turned down at the corners. ''That's monstrous and cruel. I'd need to hate you to do that.''

''But you don't love me.'' She looked at him levelly.

''Are either of us able to move on to love, Nicole?'' he asked quietly.

''Oh, I hope so!'' Her tone was intense. ''But love might have seized up. In my experience loving is loss. I've learned to protect myself for emotional survival.''

''But the desire is there.'' He leaned forward and held her wrist. ''Neither of us can deny it. I always thought you were brave, Nicole, not scared.''

She looked down at his strong tanned hand on her narrow wrist. Against his skin, hers was the color of milk. ''Desire that flares brilliantly has the potential to destroy. We both know that.''

''Maybe we should go together for counseling,'' he suggested wryly, releasing her and leaning back.

She had to smile. ''I don't know that I'd argue with that. Another thing I wanted to mention and get your view on. Shelley Logan told me she learned from Brock that Joel had been seeing Dr. Rosendahl.''

Drake's black eyebrows drew together. ''As in doctor, patient?''

''Yes.''

''Why would Joel tell Brock that? They're not at all friendly. Never have been.''

''Their paths must have crossed. Apparently Joel didn't mean to divulge the information. It slipped out in the course of what I imagine was a heated conversation.''

"Is there any other kind with Joel?" Drake asked. "Why would he want to see Rosendahl? I thought the man rather frightened him."

"What did Joel have to be frightened about?" The notion made her feel anxious.

"Nic, darling, why don't you ask him?" he challenged.

"Maybe I will," she retorted.

"If it's true, Joel had to get to Sydney, as Rosendahl practiced there. He must have been feeling especially bad. Despite all his talk about shrinks, he must have thought the good doctor could help him as he helped you. Rosendahl knew the whole story. It's much like going to a doctor who knows your case history. It makes things easier. Joel could have been living for years with some information he wanted to get off his chest."

"Like what? Aren't you forgetting the whole family was grilled for hours by the police?"

"Joel never took the witness stand."

"He knew nothing," she protested. "He was only sixteen at the time."

"He could have lied about someone, something. He could have shoved it all to the back of his mind and thrown away the key. Forgetfulness is just another form of lying."

"Except he wouldn't have protected my—"

"Go on, say it."

She was startled, a little daunted by the darkening look on his face. "I was going to say it, Drake, if you'd given me the chance. My father, Heath."

"Finally!" He threw up a hand. "Dot's opinion—knowing you, you would have asked her—must have carried some weight."

She gazed out the window to the floodlit promenade. Couples were strolling arm in arm, enjoying the view of the city skyline and the balmy breeze off the river. A City Cat had docked a short distance off, and passengers, mostly young people, disembarked, laughing, chattering, set for a night on the town.

"It doesn't take much to scratch the surface of our renewed friendship, does it?"

He shrugged. "Keeping to safe subjects is a high-wire act. Both of us fall off. You're right in a way. Coming together sexually, marvelous as it was, has only complicated things. Our emotions are heightened. I'm not planning on making you unhappy, Nic. Believe me. I care about you. I always have."

"I wish I believed that." She smiled a little, but her face was serious.

He reached for her hand again, lean fingers causing her flesh to tingle. "I'm no psychiatrist, but you're still pretty much mixed up."

"And you want to rescue me?"

"Maybe I'm the only one who can," he said.

CHAPTER THIRTEEN

HE TOOK HER HAND as they walked back to the hotel. The breeze off the river was like black silk. The gardens that lined both sides of the promenade were filled with lush tropical plants, the gorgeous blossoms of the tuberose, the white ginger and gardenia scenting the air so heavily it was almost dripping perfume. Standing tall above the garden beds, the palms whispered sensuously as the wind stroked their long curving fronds.

Headlights beamed at them as they waited to cross the road. His hand shifted to the sensitive flesh of her upper arm, rested near her breast. She felt intoxicated, out of balance, pierced through with sexual urgency.

By the time they reached the hotel—was it minutes or hours? time had dissolved—she felt almost too shaky to walk. For someone who had lived on the outskirts of passion, her lust for him seemed shocking. They didn't speak at all in the elevator, heads near turned in opposite directions as though they were indifferent to each other. Strangers.

"Have you your entry card?" he asked outside the door of her suite. Who needed a suite? She'd only booked it because of him. Because of the inevitable. Extra privacy. Sleeping together. With the enemy?

It was a miracle they'd got this far. Once inside the

door she fell back against it as if she'd walked miles, his strong arms reaching for her, holding her up. He began to kiss her deeply, madly, without pause; all over her face, her mouth, her ears, her neck, hungry nuzzling kisses that had long moaning breaths sighing out of her. He must have worked out in advance the best way to get her out of her dress, not letting it slide to the floor, but moving her with him, so he could drop it gently over a chair.

They hadn't paused to turn on the lights. The room's illumination came from the glitter of the city's towers. Urgency mounting, he lifted her, carrying her from the sitting room to the bedroom, where he let her fall onto the bedcovers already turned back by a maid.

"The more I have, the more I want." He leaned above her in the semidarkness, his voice harsh with desire.

"You're good at everything, aren't you?" she whispered back. "Consummate lover. My knight in shining armor." The words held the merest flicker of a taunt. Such extremes of feeling were in her: love she felt she needed to cover up, at the same time an underlying resistance; yet she was yearning for him, her blood turned to mercury, allowing him to undress her so slowly, so voluptuously that in the end she was almost thrashing.

He left her naked, defenseless. Sex, even great sex, couldn't be labeled love.

"My funny Nicole!" He bent to kiss her, tempering the turbulence of his desire with a mocking lightness. "You're compelled to fight me."

Light fell on her upturned face. "I might be like

my mother. I might bring punishment down on our heads.''

He shuddered involuntarily, also carrying his share of devastating memories. ''Nic, for God's sake, stop!'' He stood away from her, deftly stripping off his clothes, totally unselfconscious in his nakedness, his erection rearing.

He was so beautiful to see. So beautiful to touch. Such a man. Nicole let her body take over.

Ungently he rolled her across the bed, stripping off the heavy quilted bedspread and heaving it on thc floor.

''Come here to me.'' He lay down, pulling her backward into his arms, allowing his rock-hard penis to slip between her legs when he wanted to sink it deep within her.

Not yet, though his veins seemed to be exploding with sparks.

She bent like a willow to him, fitting her supple back and neat buttocks to his torso. With his fingers he began applying increasing amounts of friction to the swollen nipples of her breasts, dark as mulberries against the luminosity of her skin. Excitement spurted, unbearable, panting, excruciatingly exquisite. Her body began to buck, her pelvis lifting upward and outward, following its own will.

A hundred more excitements were to follow. He flipped her this way and that, a master, fully in control of her, his eyes glowing even in the low light.

Her fluttery moans became so agitated they sounded heartbroken to his ears. Wrenched from some secret place deep within her. Somewhere she didn't want him to see, but prised out of her by passion. He eased back slightly; the need to have her so intense he felt near-insane with frustration.

"You want me? Tell me."

Her throat was so crowded with cries Nicole was soundless when she wanted to shout yes! He had her legs spread, tonguing her, every curve, every crease, every crevice, savoring texture and taste, until she thought she couldn't bear more excitement and not expire.

Now she acted on her own. She climbed over his long splendid body, her thighs shutting tight, riding him like a favorite stallion, swaying, flying, letting her tapering fingers with their long polished nails, curl around him, guiding him into the entrance to her womb, glorying in his deep plunge.

He filled her.

This was where she wanted him to be.

Tonight. Tomorrow. Forever.

DRAKE HAD TO RETURN to Kooltar, but Nicole spent several more days in Brisbane attending to unfinished business. Her solicitor's office was prompt coming up with a number of options for Dot's retirement home. In the end she and Dot chose a villa with immediate occupancy in Brisbane's beautiful bayside area. Dot was ecstatic about it, which pleased Nicole. She left her solicitors to complete the sale. They would pick up a generous fee for their time and attention. It was a simple matter to pick out suitable furniture—completed in an afternoon—delivery date to be set by Dot. At least in that direction things were moving.

"You're an angel," Dot told her, overcome by her good fortune and Nicole's generosity.

"I'm not that good. You like it? You really like it?"

"It's marvelous," Dot said, far happier than she'd been only days ago.

"I want to make you as comfortable as I can."

"You've done that, love." They were having coffee at the retirement village's attractive lakeside restaurant, Dot gazing about with interest. Most of the tables were full of pleasant-looking retirees, with others, couples and singles, wandering the shady paths down by the lake. The whole atmosphere was easy and relaxed. Nicole was sure it wouldn't take Dot long to make friends.

The business of tracking down Jacob Rosendahl's widow proved a lot harder. Nicole had met Sonya, a psychiatrist like her late husband, on many occasions. She was a woman of calm inner strength. Sonya would have been devastated by her husband's senseless death. It took a number of calls—nobody seemed to want to give out information, probably being protective—to finally get the phone number of Sonya Rosendahl's sister, Mrs. Irene Stellmach. Listening to the area code, Nicole realized Mrs. Stellmach lived in Brisbane. A great piece of luck!

She consulted the phone book. Four Stellmachs. None with the initial I. She settled herself on the side of the bed and began pushing buttons. It took three calls to finally get Irene, who sounded extremely wary until it sank in that Nicole was an ex-patient of Dr. Rosendahl's. Mrs. Rosendahl would know her, Nicole said; she'd been living in the United States and had only recently heard the sad news. She fully expected

Irene to say she would pass on the message; instead, she brought her sister to the phone.

"Why don't you come visit me," Sonya invited. "We can talk."

IT WAS SUCH a beautiful day they sat on the stone terrace at the rear of the house with steps leading down to manicured lawns and beautiful tropical gardens. The Stellmachs—he was an eminent surgeon—lived on acreage in the affluent western suburbs. The residence was large, light-filled and beautifully decorated. Clearly, the Stellmachs didn't want for money, something that was supported by Irene Stellmach's immaculate appearance. The resemblance between the sisters was marked, though Irene dressed in the height of fashion and Sonya was far less conventional. Arty, people would have called her, with her long skirts and peasant blouses, rather like a costume, long dangly earrings, her naturally blond hair a fuzzy mop, unlike her sister's classic pageboy. Both sisters had voices like cellos. Both still retained slight Hungarian accents, though they had been in the country forty years.

"There's something you want to know, Nicole, I can tell." They had been speaking for well over a half hour, Nicole finding out almost immediately the police had never tracked down the hit-and-run driver. It had been raining. Dusk had been closing in.

"It was Jacob's time," Sonya said philosophically. "We can't evade the call when it comes."

"Such a tragic waste!" Nicole sighed deeply. "It was Dr. Rosendahl who helped me get on with my life. He was the one who really started me on my painting."

"And you are already becoming famous." Sonya smiled.

"Not exactly, but my showings gave me a lot of encouragement." Nicole paused a moment before she found the courage to ask, "You never ever thought the hit-and-run may not have been an accident?"

Sonya's smile faded like a dark cloud sailing over the sun. She looked suddenly old and shaken. "My dear, why would you say that?"

"I'm so very sorry if I've upset you," Nicole apologized.

"You wouldn't do it without good reason," Sonya stated. "You're a young woman of sensitivity. Who would want to hurt my Jacob?"

"He treated a lot of disturbed people, Sonya. He treated me."

"You were always going to be cured." Sonya's mellow voice was soothing, safe.

"I still have ongoing problems, Sonya."

"Don't we all." Sonya shrugged. "It was good your cousin, Joel, found the courage to come to Jacob for help."

Nicole sat back in her chair. "So he did come?"

"But of course. That young man was churning with troubles. Didn't you know?"

"It's as I've told you, Sonya. I've only just returned. Joel has never mentioned it. Could you tell me when and for how long he saw Dr. Rosendahl?"

Sonya hesitated, looking concerned. "I suppose that would be all right. I think the final visit was shortly before Jacob's fatal accident. Let me think for a moment... I suppose he came on and off, when he could, for nearly a year."

Nicole was shocked. "That long? I can't believe it." Why had Joel never told her?

"Why, my dear? Your cousin suffered, too. Not to the extent you did. It was your beloved mother, after all, but Joel was so young. He had to live with the tragedy."

"Of course he did. I'm just amazed he never told me about it, that's all. Neither did my aunt. She realized Joel was seeing Dr. Rosendahl?"

"That, my dear, I wouldn't know. I think I can safely say your cousin, Joel, is a very secretive young man."

"Whatever happened to Dr. Rosendahl's files?"

Sonya's expression changed. "Nicole, I could never allow you to look at your cousin's file. That's confidential. My own life cracked wide open after Jacob was killed. I've had to come to Irene to find some comfort. Her husband, Carl, is a wonderful man. So understanding. When I can, I'll have Jacob's files destroyed. For now they're in a safe place. Why would you want to see your cousin's file?" Sonya stared deeply into Nicole's eyes. "You do want to see it?"

Nicole flushed. "I realize I have no right. All I'm saying is I would give a lot to know what Joel's problems are."

"Why don't you ask him?" Sonya suggested briskly. "It took me about one minute seeing you two together—that's many years ago—to realize your cousin adores you."

Nicole looked at her in dismay. "I don't want him to adore me, Sonya. Adoration isn't normal."

"Between cousins, perhaps not. The file is protected, my dear. Can you tell me anything about your ongoing problems? You know, I practiced along with Jacob for many years.''

''Yes, of course. I'm terrified, Sonya, that my mother's death wasn't an accident. My intuition about it over the years has only grown stronger. Lately it's as if my mother is urging me to discover what really happened.''

''Wouldn't that put you in danger?'' Sonya's voice was concerned.

''I don't care. My desire to find out who did it and have them punished outweighs my concerns for my own safety.''

''That can't be wise, Nicole. Surely you should approach the police, shouldn't you, my dear? If you've uncovered new evidence, even a shred?''

Nicole shook her head. ''All I'm going on is gut feelings.''

''They won't work no matter how strong they've become. The law deals with facts, not feelings. Is there someone you suspect? It's no secret you were estranged from your father. Most people knew that.''

''He's on Eden now. That's why I returned. He's come home to die.''

''Poor man!'' Sonya's finely cut features were somber. ''Of what?''

''Cirrhosis of the liver.''

''That's bad.''

Nicole nodded. ''It seems more like suicide to me. He always was a heavy drinker. I imagine his drinking got a lot worse after my mother died…the way she died. It was ghastly! The pain, the scandal, the ugliness.''

"And you want to reopen the whole terrible episode?"

"Wouldn't you, Sonya, if you thought the husband you so loved and respected was cut down in cold blood?"

Sonya's gray eyes blazed silver. "You think there's some connection between Jacob's death and your family tragedy?"

"I don't know, Sonya. Forgive me please for even mentioning it. But I'm eaten up with all sorts of bizarre theories. What's not bizarre is my conviction it was no accident. My mother loved me. She would never have left me. Not for anyone. She would never have put David McClelland's life in danger. It was suggested she might have caused him to lose control of the vehicle."

Sonya nodded. "I remember the whole business vividly. Even as a child you made a great impression on Jacob and me. Both of us would have done anything to help you."

"You did!" Nicole assured her. "It would help me enormously to know why Joel sought out Dr. Rosendahl. I know this won't concern you—so many people who don't know what they're talking about ridicule 'shrinks,' which is what Joel called them. He was like that. So it must have been something compelling to get him into therapy."

Sonya considered deeply. "Even if I knew, my dear, I couldn't tell you."

"You might if you realized not telling me could put me or some member of my family in serious danger. You may not believe this, either, but I've given my heart to Drake McClelland. If you remember, Drake is David McClelland's nephew.''

''You're in love with him?'' Sonya brightened.

''I'm madly in love with him, but I don't trust him, or me.''

Sonya's eyes widened and she gave a little gasp. ''Why not?''

''I've lost the knack of trusting, Sonya.''

''You were separated so violently and so suddenly from your mother. You don't trust life.''

''It's a little more complex than that. Drake has inherited Kooltar from his father. Kooltar is our neighbor. Drake has his maiden aunt still living with him. She hates me as much as she hated my mother.''

''I remember the story, Nicole,'' Sonya said quietly. ''You think McClelland revenge is somehow mixed up with the relationship? He and his aunt have a plan?''

Nicole gave a deep anguished sigh. ''It's such an extreme view, melodramatic, but the fact is, Drake wants Eden. He makes no bones about it, although he says he's prepared to wait until such time as it ever comes on the market.''

''You've considered selling?'' Sonya raised her eyebrows in surprise.

''No. Drake won't get it. Unless…he marries me.''

''I see.'' Sonya glanced away over the garden. ''He's been very successful so far. You said you're madly in love with him.''

''Which doesn't mean it will lead to marriage. Marriage is a very serious step.''

''You feel you would be selling yourself *and* Eden? You can't conceive he may love you for yourself alone? You're a beautiful, intelligent woman. You would never lack suitors.''

Nicole kept her eyes on the garden, its latticed walls covered in white iceberg roses. ''I know he wants me. But I torment myself with the idea I might only be part of the picture. Drake is very ambitious. He has big plans.''

''Surely you're not the only girl in the world for such a man?'' Sonya asked dryly.

''I'm the only one who owns Eden,'' Nicole said wryly. ''Eden boasts a fine stream, the Minareechi, that cuts a swathe through the station. Permanent deep water, priceless in drought.''

Sonya frowned, staring at her hands. ''Is it possible someone could be poisoning your mind? Your cousin, Joel, hasn't he been managing the station in your absence?''

''Yes, but not all that well, Sonya. No one can match my grandfather.''

''He's a hero in your mind?''

''Of course,'' Nicole answered without hesitation, though she had heard the surprise and doubt in Sonya's tone. Obviously not everyone saw her grandfather the way she did, a man who'd shown her unconditional love. ''Joel dislikes Drake. He's been jealous of him since we were children together. Drake is everything Joel is not.''

''That would motivate Joel to put Drake down at every opportunity.''

''I suppose. I rely too much on my instincts.''

''Which, my dear, can be amplified and distorted by emotions—anxiety, fear, anger, falling in love. Your Drake sounds like a dominant person. Perhaps you fear being controlled? Perhaps you fear love itself? In your mind you may not clearly be distinguishing between love and loss.''

"It's a great pity you've retired, Sonya," Nicole said with a sigh. "I'd have to come to you for further counseling."

"I can recommend an excellent colleague should you really feel the need," Sonya answered very seriously. "Staying sane is a battle when so many things work against us. Modern life, old traumas. Are you going to allow this love affair with Drake McClelland to continue?''

Nicole felt the betraying blush move over her skin. "Caution is thrown to the winds when I'm in his arms. Being in love is so...disruptive."

"It's also the most wonderful feeling in the world." Sonya smiled warmly. "Love is the great healer. It's our best chance at the future. The right man, Nicole, will be the embodiment of your dreams, as Jacob was mine. I'll think carefully on all you've told me. Would you like a stroll around the gardens? Irene and Carl have five or so acres, three of them devoted to gardens—the rest is bushland. Gardens are marvelous when one is under stress."

CHAPTER FOURTEEN

JOEL REACTED violently when Nicole found the courage to ask him about his visits to Jacob Rosendahl. She could keep quiet no longer. Joel had no right to keep that sort of information to himself.

"Who the hell told you?" Her question had robbed him of all attention. The Toyota hit a succession of deep, bone-jarring corrugations.

"Watch the road, would you?" she exclaimed in alarm. "I'm asking a simple question, Joel, so what's the problem answering? I understand perfectly you felt the need to speak to a professional. Dr. Rosendahl knew our story."

"Who told you?" Joel repeated, teeth gritted, his gray, green-flecked eyes narrowed in anger. "Was it McClelland? I've got the feeling something is going on between you two."

"Would it be any of your business if something were?" she snapped, tired of his jealousy of Drake.

"How can you say that?" He shot her a look full of reproach. "Since childhood we've told each other everything."

"So why, then, didn't you tell me you'd been seeing Dr. Rosendahl, instead of keeping it to yourself all this time? Why didn't you confide in me when I told you he'd been killed? For that matter, why didn't you tell me what was troubling you? Maybe I could have helped.''

"You're the last one who can help," he said bitterly. "Anyway you aren't here most of the time, remember? You make your escape to New York."

"I'm here now. Can't you confide in me?"

He swung the four-wheel drive off the rough track and into the shade of a stand of bauhinias decked out in bridal white.

"Answer me, Nikki. Was it McClelland?" He turned off the engine. The hot silence was complete.

"Is that an order? I don't take orders from you, Joel." Her temper was rising. "Drake knows nothing about it."

"Make sure you keep it that way," he warned, two vertical lines between his eyebrows. "So who was it? That sanctimonious little bitch, Shelley Logan? Brock must have told her. Couldn't keep his mouth shut."

"Why couldn't *you?*" she challenged. "Brock Tyson didn't need to know your private affairs."

"I didn't *tell* him." The knuckles of the hand resting on the wheel were white. "I'd had too much to drink and it just slipped out. He was bloody quick, because I know I shut up like a clam. Why are you starting this, Nikki? I've got one hell of a headache."

"I'm sorry, but you're the one getting upset. Is the problem so private you can't tell me?"

"Ah, it was nothing," he said dismissively. "I was having a few nightmares."

"About what?"

Joel swept off his akubra and ran a wretched hand through his sun-streaked hair. "You're not blaming me for going to him, are you?"

All of a sudden she was full of pity. "Joel, dear, of course not." She squeezed his arm, thinking he looked thin and hollow-eyed. "I'm your friend always. We're cousins. We share a strong bond."

"I love you, Nikki," he said with fervor, totally without embarrassment.

Nicole was suddenly very conscious that their faces were only inches away. "Of course you do. And I love you."

"Don't ever leave me."

That hit a raw nerve. "Stop it, Joel. We're in each other's lives."

"For always. That's our destiny. I'll never let you marry McClelland."

"What a break for him!" she said, hoping to make Joel veer off in another direction. "What makes you think Drake would want to marry neurotic old me?"

"He'd be a bloody fool if he didn't, and he's no fool. It's only a matter of time, Nikki, before he sets the scene for the big proposal."

"What makes you think I'd say yes?" she snapped, her nerves fraying.

"You wouldn't let him take advantage of you, I know. You're too smart. But you're going to need every ounce of your resolve. He's after you because he's after Eden."

"Whatever!" She made her voice falsely bright and uncaring. "He'll never get it."

"That's my girl." He lifted the hand nearest him and kissed it tenderly.

"Quit that," she said sharply, snatching her hand away. "Joel, I want to get someone in to help you.

Look at you! You're working yourself ragged. I don't like to see that.''

"What are we talking about here?'' He looked at her suspiciously. "Not someone over me?''

"No way!'' She shook her head. "I said someone experienced and capable to help you. You manage the station. He'll be your offsider, your overseer.''

He gripped her hand again. "Why are you saying this, Nikki? Aren't you happy with the way I'm running things?''

This time she had to wrench her hand out of his grasp. "I think we can do better, Joel. The operation is too big for just you. Siggy isn't getting any younger. Your father never does anything but take it easy. Surely you can see it's for the best.''

Joel gave her one long look. "As long as he's not over me.''

"You have my word. You're family.''

"You're a businesswoman, aren't you?'' He smiled.

"Granddad showed me the ropes.''

"The old bastard never showed me.''

"That's not true, Joel. Please don't call our grandfather a bastard. I don't like it.''

"He'd have moved heaven and earth for you, Nikki. Never me.'' Joel's voice was flat, cold.

"I have sympathy for you, Joel, but Granddad was never unkind. I never heard him raise his voice to you.''

"He didn't have to, to get things across. Good old Sir Giles, God bless him! He sure gave Dad a rough time.''

"Dear God!'' Nicole groaned, staring with exasperation out the window. "Your father has never had to lift a finger. I wouldn't call that a rough time."

"I mean, Grandfather despised him. You could see it in his eyes, the smooth way he had of talking to Dad."

"Granddad didn't despise him enough to send him on his way," Nicole answered fierily. "Neither did your father drum up the pride to go."

Joel shook his head slowly. "We aren't your kind of people, are we, Dad and me?"

"I don't know what you're talking about, Joel. You're fine. I get on well enough with your father. He doesn't really bother anyone."

"It's guys like McClelland you admire." Joel's voice was as much desperate now as angry. "McClelland, Outback Baron. Hell, he was made for the part."

"Why are you so jealous of Drake?" she asked quietly.

"Good God, don't you know?" He stared straight ahead through the windshield, not meeting her eyes.

"You feel dreadful I inherited Eden, is that it? Drake inherited Kooltar from his father. Granddad left Eden to me. It isn't fair, is it," she said sadly.

Joel plunged back into anger. "I don't give a damn about Eden. I wish to hell I'd got out of here years ago. After your mother...I should have gone then."

She shook her head as if to clear it, for a moment unable to speak. "Is this what you wanted to talk to Dr. Rosendahl about, Joel? You're tortured by your feelings? You're at war with your environment? You don't want to be a cattleman? Who cares! I guess Granddad knew you didn't really want it—but he left you rich. You're not stuck here without money dependent on me or anyone. You can do what you like. Go anywhere.''

"Away from you? You still don't get it? I would *die* away from you.''

Her voice held all her deep dismay. "Joel, please don't say that and in that way. It's so extravagant. It smacks of obsession. We're not joined at the hip like Siamese twins. You'll get married, raise a family. Hopefully when I get myself together, so will I. Why didn't I realize you were so full of resentments? They're so destructive. It's a wonder you don't hate me. You don't hate me, do you?'' she asked softly, trying to draw him out of his intensely emotional mood.

"Sometimes. Just a little.'' He gave her his attractive lopsided smile.

"What can I do to make it up to you?''

"Let me go.''

She stared back at him, breathless with shock. "Joel, I'm not forcing you to stay here on Eden. I want what you want. You're free to leave tomorrow if that's how you feel.''

His voice turned harsh. "God, you never get it! Why is that? Are you blind?''

Nicole's stomach started to churn. She had to make a move to cut Joel's dependence on her. But how? "I think I'm going to be sick.'' She opened the passenger door, lurched out onto the fiery sand covered with tufts of burnt Mitchell grass.

Within seconds Joel came around the hood to join her. He put an arm around her, his eyes holding a depth of concern that was almost fierce. "It's the heat," he said, staring at her pale face. "Why were we talking in the car? It's too bloody hot. Sit down for a moment, Nikki. I don't know what I was thinking, upsetting you so. I'll get a drink of water from the canteen."

"Thanks." Nicole lowered herself dizzily to the ground. Spent bauhinia blossoms rained on her head, on her shoulders, fell to the scorched earth. She was reluctant to face it, but Joel's attachment to her was starting to become more than a burden. It was becoming a threat.

Joel was back within seconds. "Drink up," he said, his voice still filled with anxiety. "As soon as you feel better, I'll take you home."

"Good idea." She stared past him at the crystal mirage. The mirage was a phenomenon of the desert, creating beautiful and terrible illusions. She had lived with it her whole life just as she had lived with her cousin, Joel. They were siblings—that was how she saw them. Now she had to face the hard fact that Joel had far more than brotherly feelings for her. Had she ever really known him, or had it all been illusion? Whatever the answer, she appeared to be central to Joel's life.

Didn't that put him in direct conflict with Drake?

NICOLE FOUND HERSELF driven to question Siggy privately, try to determine if Siggy had known about Joel's visits to Dr. Rosendahl, with both deciding to keep it from her.

Siggy's reaction was amazement, then outrage, as though the questions constituted extreme harassment.

Her third reaction was betrayal. "How dare he?"

"Calm down, Siggy. What do you mean, how dare he? Joel doesn't need you to grant permission."

"I'll be damned!" Siggy struck the kitchen table where she'd been writing up menus for the dour Mrs. Barrett, who just happened to save her job by being a great cook. "Aren't your kids supposed to tell you things? All right, he's no kid, but surely to God he can come to me with his problems. I'm his mother, after all!"

"You can't tell him I told you, Siggy."

"The son of a bitch!" Siggy swore from habit, her tone flinty.

"That's great, seeing as you're his mother." Nicole gave her a wry look.

"You've upset me, Nikki." Siggy dropped her head into her hands.

"I'm sorry. I don't mean to upset you, but Joel upset me."

Siggy glanced up, eyes firing. "Now, *that* I find very distressing. It has to be for the first time. I mean, he has you way up there on a pedestal."

"Where I absolutely don't want to be," Nicole said in extreme exasperation. "I hope you're not blaming me for it. The big trouble is, Joel's had no one else to put there."

"You really don't think so?" Siggy drew herself up, looking affronted.

"Lord, Siggy, I remember a time when you called him dopey on a regular basis."

"It was nothing personal." Siggy had the grace to color. "He was always forgetting things."

"I never heard you call your husband dopey. The occasional 'darling.' I used to wonder about that."

"Leave Alan out of this," Siggy warned.

"I wasn't under the impression he was ever in it. I'm worried about Joel. And that's the truth."

"Sure," Siggy agreed miserably, "I've been worrying about Joel for most of his life. If I didn't know better, I'd say I never bore him. Don't think it's easy being married to Alan, either. I swear he's never loved me."

"Shoot him," Nicole suggested lightly.

"It's tempting."

"Better yet, divorce him."

Siggy shrugged. "Might as well. I've got nothing better to do. He fell in love with Corrinne the instant he laid eyes on her. It wasn't a case of Corrinne stealing him away. Corrinne had men falling in love with her for most of her short life. She never even saw them. No one was important to her but David. She was David McClelland's girl."

"It's just that she ran off with Heath." Nicole gave her aunt a bewildered glance. "That's one hell of a bad joke, Siggy. How is Heath? He told me he was okay."

"He'll go when he gets the call," Siggy said with quiet fatalism. "He seems to be at peace. He's very grateful to you for letting him stay here."

"How would I clear it with my conscience if I didn't?" Nicole said. "To get back to Joel. Have you any idea at all why he'd go to Dr. Rosendahl? He only told me he was having nightmares."

"Nightmares," Siggy said, "have been happening to me for most of my married life." She started to laugh, then abruptly stopped. "Joel's bedroom is too far away for me to hear him if he yelled. Actually, I find myself disputing that. Joel's like his father. He sleeps like a log. He slept through all the furor that dreadful morning your mother didn't come home. My understanding is Joel didn't rate psychological testing very highly. Or the persons who conducted them. That included Rosendahl.''

Nicole rose to the doctor's defense. ''Jacob Rosendahl was a man of immense presence. Much wisdom and understanding. He was a complete person.''

''Listen, that's okay. I agree with you, but Joel was absolutely livid whenever he was obliged to talk to him back then. Maybe I'll confront Joel. I want to get this straight. See what we're dealing with.''

Nicole shook her head vigorously. ''Don't do that, Siggy. You'll be exposing me. In any case, Joel doesn't have to explain himself. If you went to him, it would get his back up.''

Siggy gave a bark of a laugh. ''Joel has a very nasty habit of always getting his back up. He has a chip on his shoulder as big as Ayer's Rock. What's your problem, anyway? You always were a little snoop.''

''Make that *sleuth* if you don't mind. All the secrets in the family made my life hard. What I want to know is, what does it all mean?''

''Why ask me?'' Siggy said forlornly. ''The older I get the less I know. At a guess I'd say nothing.''

''You're not so dumb, Siggy.'' Nicole studied her aunt with affection.

''Thank you.'' Siggy gave her a ghost of a smile. ''Tell me again when these visits took place.''

Nicole leaned closer. ''The last not long before Dr. Rosendahl was killed. The first possibly a year before that.''

"And we never knew?" Siggy looked deeply troubled.

"What did you think he was doing when he took himself off to Sydney or wherever he said he went?"

"Drawing on my knowledge of the world and my limited knowledge of men, I had the feeling it had to be sex. Women. Parties, dates, whatever. Think about it. It's pretty tame out here. There are plenty of pretty girls in Sydney. He's single, he's good-looking, he's got money. I figured he was having himself a good time."

"It's possible he was." Nicole nodded. "But there must have been something very pressing on his mind to seek out Dr. Rosendahl."

"Well, he did something right." Siggy's tone was laconic.

"So why deny it?"

"*I* would." Siggy drained her coffee and grimaced, although it had been particularly good. "If I chose to see a shrink, I'd keep my big fat mouth shut. Just like if I chose to hire a private detective."

"And have you?" Nicole asked, thinking this wasn't just Siggy being Siggy but somehow connected.

Siggy laughed harshly. "That, my dear, is a long dirty story."

"If you were checking up on your dear husband when he's away on his jaunts, I could understand it."

"I told you—my lips are sealed. You can't possibly think Joel might have had something to do with Rosendahl's death, do you?"

Nicole stared at her. "Now, *there's* a bizarre idea! Are you saying he was in Sydney at that time?"

"I only said it because he has an alibi." Siggy slapped at a lone fly that had had the temerity to breach the gauzed door. "And it would save you time."

"Has he really got an alibi?" Nicole looked at her aunt hard.

"Can you hear the two of us?" Siggy said evasively. "Can you hear what we're saying? What's happened to you, Nikki?"

"I haven't lost my mind, if that's what you think."

"Well, that's a lucky break." Siggy touched two fingers to her aching eyes.

"Something very bad happened here on Eden all those years ago, Siggy. Two people died. My mother—your sister—and David McClelland. I don't think they drove off the escarpment into Shadow Valley. I think they were forced off."

"No." Siggy made a low despairing sound.

"Yes, Siggy. The worst part of it is, it was someone we know."

"Then it was Heath." Siggy raised her head. "Who else? He was a violent man. Corrinne was unfaithful, making a fool of him. Heath is the only one who makes sense."

"I wouldn't say that. Wasn't my mother planning on sending Joel away?"

Siggy leaped to her feet. "Be careful, girl," she warned, head shaking slightly as in the early stages of Parkinson's. "Joel and I may not be great pals, but he is my son. My son. Do you understand what that means? Of course you don't!"

"Siggy, calm down. I'm sorry if I shocked you.

Let's leave Joel out of this. What about Alan? You said yourself he was in love with my mother.''

Siggy snorted. No angry display of emotion for her husband. ''Alan can't do anything more strenuous than crack his knuckles. Forget Alan. What about that kook, Callista? I'd jump out of my skin if she clamped her tiny hand on my shoulder. Or some other nutcase in the area? Someone who spent the last ten years in jail and felt like pushing the Land Cruiser off the cliff for spoiling his view. Nothing's too dreadful for a psychopath. No, Nikki, we'll never make sense of it. It was either a tragic accident or they decided to end their lives together. This family is cursed.''

''I don't accept that.''

''I do,'' Siggy muttered, looking utterly convinced.

''Then we better start fighting our way out of it. Justice has to be done.''

Siggy leaned her hands on the table. ''Even in the event you find some member of your family is a murderer? Come off it, girl!''

''Are you saying you'd let them go free?''

Siggy stiffened. ''My overriding concern is for family. You're opening up not a whole can of worms, but venomous snakes. It's safer to put it all behind us.''

Nicole, too, rose to her feet. ''I don't like your moral reasoning, Siggy. Murder is murder. You might be able to allow a murderer to go free, but I can't. It's a little problem I have.''

''Sorry, you're stuck with it,'' Siggy said brutally. ''I can promise you your grandfather left no stone unturned. He had people all over checking.''

''Maybe they were looking in the wrong place.''

Nicole gazed hard at her aunt. "You sound frightened, Siggy."

"Does that surprise you?" Siggy's tone was as sharp as a whiplash.

It didn't faze Nicole. "Someone murdered my mother and David McClelland," she responded in a low grave voice. "You've got to help me find out who."

Siggy reached out to touch her niece's shoulder. "As long as you don't intend to start on me," she said with black humor. "The authorities are the right people to catch criminals, Nikki."

"I know." Nicole nodded. "The only trouble is, the authorities believe the case is closed."

"And it will stay closed until you have something new to offer. Which you don't." Her movements oddly stiff, Siggy walked to the door, bringing the conversation to a halt.

LATER IN THE DAY Nicole received a call from Shelley Logan telling her the maid of honor she had chosen for her wedding, Jody Mitchell—Nicole knew her slightly—had had a bad fall in a three-day cross-country event, breaking her leg and collarbone. Would Nicole, Shelley wondered, consider taking over the role?

Nicole, although sorry for Jody's bad luck, was delighted to accept—but expressed concern about the bridesmaid's dress. As far as she could recall, Jody was rather short, with an entirely different sort of figure from her own.

"The color will suit you beautifully," Shelley said. "Lilac satin, but we'll have to start from scratch with

your gown. You're taller and a lot more willowy than
Jody who's sturdily built. If you'll e-mail me your
precise measurements, I'll give them to my dressmaker. The gown is strapless, the bodice tapering to a
deep V. It has a fitted waist and long billowing skirt.''

''But your dressmaker won't have much time.'' It
was less than a month to the wedding to be held on
Mulgaree.

Shelley's laugh was relieved. ''Don't worry, I've
already checked with her. She said she could do it.
She's brilliant!''

They spent a few more minutes chatting, Nicole
pausing on her way out of the homestead to tell Siggy
and her grandmother the news.

''How lovely, darling!'' Louise smiled at her.
''You'll look so beautiful!''

''Just remember not to look more beautiful than the
bride,'' Siggy warned in her customary wry tone.

NICOLE FOUND HEATH dozing in a comfortable chair
in the garden overlooking the sequined stretch of the
Minareechi and the focal point of the homestead's gardens, the waterfall. Her grandfather's design, it had
been constructed at the narrow end of the stream using
the most striking boulders he could find on station
land. Most she knew had come from Shadow Valley.
It had been a huge job, requiring an irrigation system,
but the result was their own private oasis, one of calm,
peace and tranquillity. Easy to see why this was one
of Heath's favorite spots. Balm for his tormented
spirit.

Grasses and rushes, masses and masses of Japanese
water iris and arum lilies grew on the verge and into

the water itself. To soften the boulders, a mini-forest had been created, using plants that would survive the dry heat; the trees that made up the canopy shaded the whole. Black swans with their scarlet bills banded in white sailed in state across the water's glassy dark green surface. They were joined by cobs and pens, a few of the pens with their white cygnets.

Siggy was right. As she approached soundlessly over the thick cushioning grass, she could see on Heath Cavanagh's face a rare look of peace. Of final acceptance. If he had a terrible stain on his soul and was getting ready to face his maker, could he really look like that?

His eyes flew open as she hovered over him. "Reen!" he cried out, not in agitation, but with so much joy it suggested only passionate gratitude she had come.

Nicole felt tears well up in her eyes. Oh, yes, he had loved her mother.

"It's me, Nicole," she said gently, taking the garden chair beside him. "I hope I'm not disturbing you."

"Never!" he maintained, visibly summoning up alertness and carefully sitting upright. "For a moment, with the sun behind you shining on your hair, I thought you were your mother. I thought she'd come for me. She was and remains my heart's yearning."

"I know." Nicole struggled to keep the emotion out of her voice. "You must have loved her very much."

"Loved her. Hated her. In life and in death. But I never destroyed her. That would have been the most terrible desecration. Her enemy is still out there. She used to call me a brutal man. She struggled to escape me.''

''She must have loved you once,'' Nicole, torn by pity, reminded him.

''No, child. I mesmerized her. Her feelings for David McClelland became too much for her. He was her knight in shining armor. Never me. My life has been empty with her gone. I haven't cared if I lived or died. Even when I raved against her, I still loved her. But she betrayed me. I was her husband, the father of her child.''

''Would you very kindly consider this? Sleep on it if you wish.'' She spoke gently, so very gently. ''Would you help me by volunteering a DNA sample? Just a hair of your head.''

He laughed in genuine amusement, a rich deep sound that surprised her. ''You could have pulled one just then, when I was sleeping. Or got one from my hairbrush. Lots of things you could have done.''

''I wouldn't do anything like that without your permission.'' She shook her head. ''I've come too late to the realization you're my father, but there's a complication. I've fallen in love with Drake McClelland.''

''Of course you have!'' Abruptly he lifted a fist to the sky. ''That's what this is all about. A McClelland getting square. Just as Corrinne belonged to David, you're to belong to his nephew.''

''You don't think he could love me?'' she asked simply, confronted by the fact she was an heiress.

''Who wouldn't love you?'' he said. ''Even when you were the naughtiest little girl in the world, you used to tug at my heartstrings. Maybe there's a demon in him, child. Demons live in men.'' He gave a gust of terrible laughter.

''What do you mean?''

''You're too smart not to know, Nicole. McClelland gets you, he gets Eden.''

''That would happen whoever I marry. At least up to a point. What would you like to see happen?'' She kept her eyes on him.

He rubbed at the faint stubble along his jawline. ''I don't want to see anyone harm my girl in any way,'' he said tautly. ''And yes, you can have your DNA sample. Clear up this point once and for all. No way are you McClelland's child. No way are you Drake's cousin. You should have accepted that right away.''

''Well, I have. This is for the record.'' Nicole stood up, resting her hand on his shoulder. ''Is there anything I can get you? Something to eat or drink? This is a beautiful spot. Mrs. Barrett can bring the food down here. I have to meet up with the vet. He's flying in, in about ten minutes.''

Heath lifted his head, black eyes suddenly keen. ''How's Joel taking the fact you're in love with Drake McClelland?''

She dropped her eyes. ''I haven't told him, but I wanted you to know. You're my father.''

He smiled sadly. ''Only from a short time back.''

''I'm sorry.'' She knew her voice sounded highly emotional. She bent and kissed his stubbled cheek, felt the rasp. ''I was in such a mess.''

''Don't think I don't blame myself for that!'' He caught her hand and held it. ''Between the two of us, your mother and me, we made a mess of being parents. One thing I'd like you to do for me...''

"Anything." Nicole was acutely aware just how much they'd all missed.

"Bring McClelland to see me. He's not taking you anywhere until the two of us have a long talk."

Nicole smiled through her tears, her heart twisting with pity for this strange flawed man. "I think that could be arranged."

"Good," he said firmly, nodding his head. "Make it soon. I mightn't have lived much of a life, but I know a man of substance when I see one."

CHAPTER FIFTEEN

"WHAT'S HE COMING here for?" Joel's angry voice rang out. They were at dinner in the informal dining room off the kitchen the family used when not entertaining. Heath, for the first time in days, had made the effort to come to the table, although he ate very sparingly and allowed himself just one small glass of red wine.

"I've invited him, Joel," Nicole said, thoroughly exasperated. "My father wants to meet him. He hasn't seen Drake in years."

Joel shook his blond head, not being in the least subtle with his objections. "What possible interest could he be to you, Heath?" He transferred his attention across the table. "He's a bloody McClelland. His uncle was the bastard who stole your wife."

Nicole saw her grandmother wince, Siggy's mouth tighten. Alan continued to eat slowly, apparently savoring every morsel of his beef Wellington. "Mind your language, would you?" she protested, not bothering to suppress her annoyance. Joel was becoming outrageous, or she was just starting to notice. "This is the dinner table, not the stockyards."

"I'm so sorry, Princess!" Joel jeered, tension in the taut muscles of his lean face. "Is there something going on here I don't know about?"

"What if I said yes? What would you do?" She tossed off the challenge, much as she'd defied him as a child.

For a moment Joel looked as wild as a hawk. He might well have been about to answer, "Kill myself!" Instead, he made a visible effort to pull himself together. "I hope nothing would be happening you couldn't tell me, Nikki."

Nicole responded by making her own tone quieter. "Joel, I've already told you our bitter feud with the McClellands is over. My father has made no objection, have you, Dad?"

Such open acknowledgment after the long years of estrangement returned Heath Cavanagh his dignity. "None whatever," he said, smiling back at her. "I'm interested in meeting the adult Drake. I understand he's become quite an impressive character. I'd like to see that for myself."

"Won't that upset you, Heath?" Siggy asked, looking genuinely concerned for him. There were such deep purple shadows beneath his eyes, hollows in his cheeks. He had lost so much weight.

"It might," Heath conceded. "I won't find out until I actually lay eyes on him. Does he still have the look of David?"

"We haven't seen much of him, either, Heath." Louise, seated at the head of the table, spoke in her gentle voice. "David was a handsome man."

"Yes, he looks like his bloody uncle," Joel burst out, discharging a dark kind of energy. "Only, the uncle was a wax dummy to this guy. I remember that David was a bit too much on the soft side. The gentleman, the patrician. Drake's as tough as nails. He plays the patrician when it suits him. Just like Grand-dad, arrogant bastard.''

"Please do stop swearing, dear," his grandmother pleaded, holding a hand to her temple. "You may have forgotten, but your grandfather never swore. He didn't have to play at being anything, either. He was real."

"Clearly I don't take after him," Joel said, flushing. "It's hard not to swear with what I've had to endure."

"Endure?" Siggy sat bolt upright. "How you exaggerate, Joel! What in the name of heaven have you actually suffered? Sometimes you sound damn neurotic. If you put your mind to it, you could have a really good life."

"What—like Dad?" Joel sneered, exposing his complete lack of respect for his father.

His father, however, regarded him impassively across the immaculately set table with its lace-trimmed place mats. Siggy answered for him. "Kindly leave your father out of it. He's never laid a finger on you, more's the pity."

Joel laughed. "I'm sorry to tell you, Mum, but Dad is so thick-skinned you couldn't wound him if you tried. There are givers and takers. He's a born taker."

"Thank you, my boy," Alan murmured suavely, picking up his wineglass, sniffing the fine bouquet.

"Don't mention it." Joel's face twisted with contempt.

"Look on the positive side, Joel," Siggy said, trying to appease her difficult son. "You can play an active role in life. Find your niche."

"Niche?" Joel cried as though someone had plunged a dinner fork into his arm. "Is this a setup?"

he demanded, looking from one to the other. "First Nikki talks about getting in an overseer. Now you start talking about me finding my niche. Are you about to kick me out?"

Alan stirred himself to give a piece of fatherly advice. "Do calm down, Joel, there's a good fellow."

"What, if anything, would you know about good fellows?" Joel retorted. "Everything you bloody say is like an actor playing a part. It's not you at all. You won't let you out. No one tells you anything, either. You're just a piece of furniture."

"Oh well," Alan drawled, inclining his well-shaped fair head. "At least I don't go around upsetting people and swearing at the dinner table, whereas you occasionally act quite insane."

"Insane, am I?" Joel shot to his feet, scraping back his chair. "I had to go into therapy because of having a father like you, a mother like her." He paused to point at Siggy.

"Go on," his father invited calmly, assuming the patrician look he had long since perfected from watching the late Sir Giles. "Your grandmother has always been an angel. That just leaves Nicole. We can't ignore Nicole. She figures very largely in your life. The question is, does that count as an upset."

Joel focused wild eyes on his cousin. "She gives my life meaning."

"Oh, for God's sake, Joel, sit down." Siggy's strong resonant voice pinged off the walls. "You're making an utter fool of yourself. You've hardly touched your meal."

Extraordinarily, given his abandon, Joel obeyed. "I'm very concerned about what's happening here," he said, breathing hard. "If McClelland ever crosses the line with Nicole, I'll kill him."

A disbelieving laugh rose from his father's throat, but Siggy spoke grimly. "Look, I'm sick of all this melodrama. It's hell just having to listen to it."

"Besides, Drake McClelland would be far too difficult to kill." Alan used a calm, cool analytical voice, one of his extensive range.

Siggy, clearly not expecting him to say that, looked thoroughly disconcerted. "What the devil are you talking about, Alan? I don't know what's got into you all."

"Just having a little joke, my dear, to distract you. I'm as appalled by what Joel has been saying as you."

"Good God, you're a worse dad than I am, Alan," Heath rasped, then took a sip of wine. "What motivates you? I wonder. I never did find out."

"It wasn't drink and gambling, dear boy." Alan's smile was cynical, touched with contempt. "You're dying, but you brought it all on yourself."

Heath shook his head, as untroubled as ever by Alan's opinion. "No, someone else did that. The person who killed my wife. Did you kill her, Alan?" he asked.

"Lord God, Heath, what are you rabbiting on about now?" Siggy groaned, abandoning her own meal.

"I'm much too gentle, too God-fearing, to kill, Heath," Alan answered equably. "I always thought you did it."

"The hell you did!" Heath responded promptly, his black eyes burning. "You're not an easy character to get to know—always slip sliding around, they seek him here, they seek him there—but I think I've finally got your measure.''

Louise, at the head of the table, held up a trembling hand, her magnificent jeweled rings that never came off flashing brilliantly. "Must we have these dreadful discussions at the table? It's a good thing Giles is dead. You're all making me feel ill.''

"Would you like to go to your room, Gran?'' Nicole rose immediately to her feet, thinking this discussion, disturbing as it was, might have led to some answers.

"I think that would be for the best, darling.''

Joel, suddenly remembering himself, pulled his grandmother's chair back, allowing her to stand. "I don't believe my daughter was killed by anyone,'' Louise announced, hovering between despair and continuing to hide her head in the sand. "It was an accident.''

"No, it wasn't!'' Joel said unexpectedly, pulling them all up short.

"You know something, Joel?'' Alan was very still now, the sneer wiped clear of his mouth.

"No more than the rest of you!'' Now Joel's voice sounded powerless, almost a whine. "All we can do is wait.''

"Wait?'' Nicole could keep silent no longer. "Wait for what?''

"I'll take you to your room, Mother.'' Frowning ferociously, Siggy moved to her aging mother, throwing an arm protectively around her. "The truth is, this family is mad.''

"Right on, Mum. I hope you're including yourself,'' Joel called after her.

"You're no comfort at all to your mother," Alan chided.

"Do shut up, Dad," Joel said in disgust. "What sort of man are you? Your life is just one long pretense."

"My whole life actually," his father answered mildly.

"What are we waiting for, Joel?" Nicole asked in a surprisingly steely tone.

"Surely you haven't forgotten?" He stared back at her like a combatant. "There's a killer out there."

"Or in here." Heath brought the whole thing into the open. "Something in the back of my brain keeps telling me neither of you has told the truth," he addressed father and son. "I was wrongly accused."

"That's what they all say, old boy," Alan drawled. "You had someone to place you elsewhere, didn't you? That let you off the hook." Alan spoke smoothly, but Nicole could see a vein beating away in his temple.

"Exactly! But as it turned out, so did you. And Joel." Heath's black eyes glinted.

Nicole drew in her breath sharply. "Dad, all we're doing is taking stabs in the dark. Pointing at this one and that. No actual proof of anything. Joel was out driving. He was waiting to get his license, remember. He was sixteen years old."

Heath didn't answer for a moment. "Every Outback kid can drive as soon as they can see over the wheel," he said presently. "Joel regularly took one or other of the station vehicles out. No one knew where he went. Or where anyone went, for that matter. An Outback station offers unlimited freedom of movement. In all my years here no one ever checked on anyone."

Nicole's thoughts were a chaotic mix. "Surely at least for that particular time everyone's movements *were* checked?" Being a child at the time, she'd been terribly handicapped.

"Pretty much like a city person saying I was at home all night, alone," Heath offered wryly.

"But Granddad would have investigated."

Heath considered awhile. "All these years later things seem clearer, especially when one is dying."

"Oh, great!" Joel gripped the sides of his chair. "Now we're all suspects."

"Well, it wasn't me," Heath said in a very quiet voice. "It certainly wasn't Nicole. It wasn't the illustrious Giles. Nor saintly Louise."

"You haven't commented on Mum yet," Joel crowed sarcastically.

"I've concluded Siggy had nothing to do with it, either, though I've speculated on that, as well. Siggy loved her sister, though she was horrendously jealous of her."

"There's at least one thing you should tell us," Alan said. "Didn't you and she share a brief sexual encounter? Corrinne betrayed you, you betrayed her?"

"Sure I did. Later." Heath didn't rise to Alan's taunt. In fact, he looked quite unconcerned. "But never with poor old Siggy. Apart from the fact I didn't want to add to her troubles, she never had the slightest appeal for me."

A thin foxy smile crossed Alan's face. "Well, you conveyed that often enough. Constantly humiliating her."

"Maybe I was trying to put her off," Heath suggested, which in fact might have been true, Nicole thought.

"Oh, don't let's talk about Siggy like this," she pleaded. "She's always tried to do her best in a dreadfully complicated household."

"True!" Alan declared. "Don't you think it's high time we started on the McClellands? Exotic little Callista is a near basket case. Did she ever resolve her obsessive passion for her brother? The thing is, none of us knows what really happened."

"I won't stop until I'm certain," Nicole promised, the grimness of her expression offset by her beauty.

"Well, then, you'd best mind your back," Alan murmured.

"The person who tries to harm Nicole will finish in hell," Heath stated with astonishing vigor. "I'll personally see to it if I have to. I'm not all used up yet."

FROM THE ANCIENT flat-topped mesa they had a grandstand view of Shadow Valley. It had been very difficult for Nicole to consent to coming here, but she knew the only person she could approach the valley with was Drake. Even then it was with a sense of great apprehension.

Shadow Valley was a magnificent canvas even under drought. Eminently paintable. Color-saturated. A land beyond dimensions peopled on that scorching afternoon by thousands of little leaping stick figures the mirage threw up on the burning air. The great blood-red plain sprawled away in all directions; the far horizon, aglitter with the spectacular, jeweled gibber that littered certain parts of the desert.

The eternal golden spinifex made a patchwork carpet, crisscrossed by innumerable interwoven water channels that gave the vast area its name. After heavy rains, when floodwaters broke the banks, the entire area was inundated. Billabongs ran fifty miles wide. The great plain turned into the inland sea of prehistory. It was one of the great sights of the Channel Country but no greater than when the floodwaters receded and wildflowers turned the arid Wild Heart impossibly glorious.

Beautiful, blazing, blinding, mile after mile after mile of desert flora; the white and gold paper daisies, the blue lupin and dancing Sue, the pink parakeelya, the purple moola-moola, the Morgan flower and the parrot pea, spider lilies and tomato bush, the scarlet desert peas, the pink boronia and its cousin, the divinely scented brown and yellow. Another sight that station people lived for and stored in the memory for when times were hard.

Drake drew the Land Cruiser to a halt. "Let's get out," Nicole said quickly in a voice that revealed her tension.

"Are you okay?" He rested an arm on the wheel, looking intently at her pale profile. He knew she was upset. She couldn't fail to be. He recognized the same upset in himself, but he felt comforted by the fact she had consented to come with him. That meant a lot.

She nodded, shoving on her cream akubra and adjusting it low over her eyes. "I'll know soon enough."

"Just remember, we're trying to understand how the accident happened."

Out of the vehicle, Drake came around the hood with its strong bull bar to join her. He looked up at the opal-blue sky. Clouds were gathering on the horizon. It was very hot and still, and their voices were clear and loud in the isolation. "The first of the storm is coming up," he commented. "I hope to God it amounts to something. The rest of the state has been blessed with good rains. It's got to be our turn."

"I pray every night."

"As do we all."

She glanced at him. His face with its aquiline nose was shadowed by the wide brim of his akubra. His eyes glittered, like jewels in a mask. He looked strong, balanced, whereas she felt an emotional mess.

"Do you suppose this was the spot they stopped? Or farther over?" She stared around the escarpment. Thick green swathes of bush arched away to both sides, but the broad ledge was almost free of any kind of vegetation, worn smooth by vehicles and horses.

"If we go a little nearer the edge, you might be able to pick out some landmarks." He was observing her closely. He knew she was almost messianic in her desire to find out what had really happened. "The base is littered with huge boulders."

"Don't I know it!" She shuddered. Her mother's battered body had been resting on one, face upturned, eyes open. How she wished she could lose that horrible vision, but it was almost as if she were there on that tragic day watching her mother's body be flung clear of the vehicle, bouncing from one rocky ledge to the other, until it finally reached its resting place.

"We don't have to if you don't want to," he said gently.

"I'm all right. Just hold my hand."

"I was going to, anyway." He laced her fingers through his.

"All right, let's do it." She felt pressure akin to dread build in her chest.

"You don't suffer from vertigo, do you? You never used to."

Nicole gave a short laugh. "Lots of things I didn't suffer from."

They approached the edge of the rugged escarpment, the hard-packed fiery earth bound by tussocks of grasses bleached silver. In Shadow Valley beneath them, the desert floor was littered with boulders of all shapes and sizes. Huge and small, their sides worn smooth as marbles by the abrasive action of the sand and wind. In common with all desert rocks, they changed color according to the time of day and the weather conditions. At midafternoon in the quivering golden heat, they blended with the ochre-stained earth, a rich orange-red.

"There." She pointed, grief locked away inside for now.

"You're sure?" His expression was grim. The memory of his uncle David had assumed almost mystical proportions for him. David had been such a peaceful person, with great charm of manner. He had died far too young.

As had Corrinne, the love of his life who had nonetheless betrayed him.

The huge boulder they were staring at was perfectly round, a giant's marble standing about six feet high, dwarfing the other rocks and decaying pinnacles that surrounded it. Above them soared a wedge-tailed eagle, leisurely riding the wind. No sign of the falcons, the fastest birds of prey on earth.

Nicole and Drake contemplated the desert floor for

quite a while in silence, Drake with his arms locked securely around her, holding her back against him. "What brought them here, do you suppose? The view, or was one or the other issuing an ultimatum about ending the affair? Your mother was married. She had you."

"She would never have lost custody of me," Nicole said passionately. "Granddad would have seen to it. Anyway, my father wouldn't have wanted custody."

"Why not?" Drake countered. "You don't really know that with certainty, Nic. In many ways your father was put in an impossible situation."

"Did he tell you that when you talked?" She twisted her head back to look at him. Drake had been on Eden since ten that morning.

"Not in so many words, but we covered a lot of ground."

"I told him I was in love with you," she admitted.

"Pity you haven't told me. Did you also tell him you don't trust yourself with me?"

She shook her head, her long hair arranged in a heavy braid. "You made a great impression."

"I wasn't trying to make an impression, Nicole," he said dryly.

"Maybe that's why you did. You don't give a damn what anyone thinks."

"Not true. I value the opinion of my friends and the many people I admire."

"You can't admire me. I'm a mess."

His hands came up under her breasts, encircling her rib cage. "On the contrary, I think you're very brave. I admire that."

She leaned back against him, reveling in his strength. "I'm glad you're here."

"That gives me comfort."

"My mother's last words keep coming back to me. 'We need to choose new clothes for you, darling. You're growing out of everything!' She had that lovely little smile on her face, so loving. 'I think that calls for a trip into Sydney.' Then she laughed and mussed my hair. How could she say such a thing if she was contemplating ending her life? She would never have left me. I've never for a minute believed otherwise."

He turned her about. "Why have you never said this before? Your mother's last words to you, I mean?"

She knew he was waiting for a response she couldn't give. "Because they were really private. Something between my mother and me. Just the two of us, mother and daughter."

He gave her a deep searching look. "It was all so very hard for you, Nic. You were just a child."

"I dream of her, too," she confessed. "She's always trying to tell me something, but just as she's about to, I wake up. Do you think we'll ever know? I confronted Joel about seeing Dr. Rosendahl."

"And?" he prompted.

"At first he was livid, then he settled down. Sometimes I wonder if I know Joel at all. I certainly don't know Alan. He's endlessly playacting. It's just so slick. You'll see at dinner. Family discussions have been extremely intense of late. I know I'm stirring things up, but I can't seem to stop. I thought Heath would find it draining, but he seems to have gone into some kind of remission.''

"That can happen, Nic, before the end,'' Drake said quietly.

"I know. He volunteered a DNA sample.''

"He told me.'' He guided her gently toward the car, intent on finding a way down into the valley. "Getting you to believe the truth has been one long battle.''

"I accept it now.'' She drew a deep breath. "But I want it made official.''

"You're going to tack the results on a bulletin board or run it in the local rag?''

"You know what I mean.''

"Sometimes I do. Other times you speak in tongues.'' His dark-tanned skin glittered with a light sweat. She found it incredibly erotic, imagining her tongue licking it off. She was madly, incurably in love with him, no matter where it took her.

When they reached the Land Cruiser, he took her into his arms and looked down at her intensely. "Could you love me, Nic?''

"If our lovemaking means anything, the answer must be yes.'' It wasn't commitment, but it wasn't denial.

"Would you want to marry me?''

"The impossible dream.'' There was a fluttering just above her heart. "My greatest love, my greatest fear.''

"You have to break out of your prison, Nic. Others find ways to live their dream.''

"I'm trying to,'' she said. "Desperately.''

"And I'm committed to helping you.'' He continued to stare down at her, thinking the world was vast,

but if he searched through every corner of it, he
wouldn't find a woman he wanted more than Nicole
Cavanagh, daughter of the woman his uncle had lost
his heart and his life to. "You have a siren's eyes, do
you know that?" he asked with a twisted smile.

"Sirens aren't human. I am. Only too human."

The lids of her eyes closed as his hungry mouth
came down over hers.

Gold dust fell from the sky. It spilled down over
them like a silky inescapable web.

Drake pulled his mouth away. "Isn't there someplace we can go?" he asked huskily, the urgency in
his voice sending thrill after thrill through her. "I want
you so badly I'm going to go up in smoke."

"I'm the same." Impossible to deny it.

"Tell me where." He was already starting to move.

"I'll tell you when we're driving." She ran on
ahead, her eyes suddenly teasing, taunting, free of all
melancholy.

Making love to her was the nearest he had come to
paradise, Drake thought.

STRANGE HOW HISTORY repeats itself, the figure buried
deep in the cover of the bushes agonized. His rage
was so acute it felt as if a horse had fallen on him,
crushing his chest.

The faithless Corrinne, the temptress who wanted
every man she saw, and McClelland. He hadn't seen
either of them in the longest time. Fourteen years, to
be exact. Laughable, really, how people had never suspected him! He was family, after all. Only much later
had Rosendahl started to piece things together. Rosendahl, with the most benign of expressions and yet

piercing eyes that could beam down to a man's soul. That couldn't have been allowed to happen; Rosendahl had to be removed. Just like Corrinne, who'd been planning on sending them away from Eden.

Heartless bitch!

Bright noon. It was suffocatingly hot in his place of concealment. He was sweating heavily in the dense shelter, down on his haunches. He shifted his grip on a sapling and a branch whipped back fiercely, stinging his face. He wiped off a smear of blood.

Damn! he snarled to himself. That hurt. Not a breath of breeze reached him. But as he watched, a snake came close. So close he instinctively shrank back, holding his breath in sudden panic. The thing slithered away as it sensed the unwelcome presence of a human, disappearing into the thick screen of grasses. Bloody snakes and lizards! He never felt secure with them about. Goannas could grow to a massive six feet long and were known to attack.

He hadn't sighted a living soul on his way here. Only the cattle, and they weren't about to tell. Just like the lovers of old, they were parked only a few feet from the cliff face. Almost the same spot. Uncanny! He fancied he could still see his footprints on the baked red earth, except he'd taken good care to get rid of them using the leafy head of a broken branch as a broom. He wasn't such a fool he didn't know Judah, the tracker, would cotton on to them at once.

He'd gone to David McClelland's side of the Land Cruiser first. Though startled, neither of them had suspected a thing, nor did they show the slightest shame at being discovered together. He was scarcely a risk to them, after all. He was nothing.

How many times had he relived every minute of that short encounter? He'd waved, as good as a sympathetic squeeze of the shoulder, saying he was going on his way. McClelland, always the gentleman, had actually waved back.

Nudge nudge, wink wink. The poor fool!

All it took was for him to get back into the four-wheel drive, reverse, then roar dead ahead, the massive bull bar on his vehicle slamming into the rear of the Land Cruiser, pushing it inexorably over the stony crest, just like that. Too easy! The realization of what was happening to them came too late, but he fancied he'd heard her sobbing. She continued to sob in his nightmares. It was getting so bad he had daytime echoes in his head.

Momentous events could be over in seconds. He'd yanked open his door, sneezing violently at the cloud of red dust, walked to the very edge of the escarpment and peered down. In the brilliant light, he saw her splayed across a boulder, just like a sacrifice, clearly dead. He didn't have to check on McClelland. The windshield had caved in on his head. No one could have survived that crash. He had expected and hoped the Land Cruiser would catch fire, but somehow it didn't. They'd really deserved to be immolated together. Still, he felt his cup of bitterness that had for so long overflowed, miraculously emptied....

Now Nicole. The most beautiful of women, with far more spirit than her mother. More aggression. Time for her to get what she deserved. She, too, was playing the part of whore, responding passionately to McClelland's kisses, her beautiful body delivered up to him, to his mouth and his hands. It was sickening, the two of them locked in each other's arms. She was as faithless as her mother. He was overcome by a feeling as powerful as grief, only lethal. But for the fact he didn't want to get caught, he felt like shooting them now. Or McClelland, at least. He had other plans for Nicole, the mirror image of her mother, though she was as good as dead. The heiress to a ruthless dysfunctional family hiding behind their name and privileged background, the veneer of polished gentility.

He could never try the same game with McClelland. Drake McClelland, unlike his wimp of an uncle, would be on to him at once. Even his hatred was mixed up with respect. He had to think of something else. After all, he specialized in ideas.

THEY DROVE THROUGH Shadow Valley, avoiding the area littered with boulders, traveling along the cliff face with its numerous wind-carved caves, until Nicole pointed to one of the largest. The hollowed-out entrance was almost entirely decorated with the feathery green plumes Outback people called pussytails. The plants were whipped about in the driving wind that had suddenly sprung up, companion to the rapidly advancing storm.

The sky was spectacular, shafts of brilliant sunlight like spotlights piercing the towering giants' castles of livid charcoal, purple and metallic green with slashes of silver. Rather like the palette she used in her own canvases, Nicole thought, finding great excitement in a scene that mirrored her tempestuous feelings. Anywhere else but the desert one would have battened down against an onslaught in the face of that savage sky, but both of them had witnessed countless desert spectacles in the past that had never yielded a drop of precious rain.

They parked beneath a broad overhang in the cliff face, reaching the entrance to the cave just as the sky released the first heavy drops.

For long moments neither of them took shelter, Nicole holding up her face in ecstasy at the long-awaited shower burst.

"Rain!" she cried. "It's actually rain. Isn't it wonderful!"

"And it's coming down harder!" He laughed heartily, a man of the land sharing her joy and relief, then drew her back into his arms. Neither cared they were getting wet. It was only when the sky was ripped asunder by a dangerous fork of lightning so lurid and intense it burned itself on the retina, followed by a barbaric clap of thunder, that he hauled her into the cave, shouting to her above the wind to mind her head.

Even then the storm and the rain lured them to the entrance to rejoice in the spectacle. They knelt in the soft sand, staring out at the valley lit up intermittently by extraordinary incandescence. Lightning seethed and spat, the smell of the rain intoxicating to both of them.

He turned his head to soak her in like the rain. She was so achingly beautiful, so begging to be touched. "Take off your clothes," he said, face taut, reaching out to help her with her shirt. "I want to make love to you. I don't want it to ever end."

Within moments, the storm raging outside the cave, she was naked. As she lay back on the powdery dry sand, he began to stroke her body—her shoulders, her arms, her throat, the rounds of her breasts, the slight curve of her stomach, her delicate hips—marveling at the color and texture of her skin.

"God, I'm a caveman compared to you," he murmured wryly, conscious of the dark mat of hair that covered his chest and ran in a thin deep V into his groin and down his long legs.

"I should be terrified of you, in that case." She smiled back at him, astonished by her abandon.

"I thought you were."

"Not at times like these."

He smiled and reached back for his hat; crystal-clear rainwater was still trapped in the wide brim. "Where would you like this?"

Before she could answer, languidly, erotically, he began to pour little streams of rainwater across her breasts and stomach, watching it run like a silken banner.

Her mouth pursed in a delighted gasp. The sensation was irresistibly delicious. He leaned into her, kissing her deeply. Scores of kisses. Soft. Tender. Fierce. Slowly he lowered himself over her, all male splendor and dark energy, his sex heavy at his groin. He bent his head so he could lick her rain-slicked skin with his tongue.

Her answer was a slow groan. Radiance spread through her. She could feel herself starting to enter another dimension. Her every nerve jumped as her muscles contracted. Sparks exploded behind her tightly shut lids.

Tiny rivulets of rainwater ran down over her thighs and into her cleft, soaking the light whorl of rose-tinted hair.

His eyes followed the water's progress, burning a

sizzling trail. He gripped her slender hips, hands electric, then lowered his head, his tongue slipping deeper into her with every sharp catch of her breath.

"Drake!" Her back arched up from the sand as she called her lover's name. She was trying ineffectually to hold his head from her, startled beyond belief by the degree of sexual pleasure. The excitement was too primitive, too deliriously high. She felt she was losing her grip on reality. She was lost, craving all the things he was doing to her. He had shattered her illusions that she was a low-key, cool person with a take-it-or-leave-it attitude toward sex.

Drake acting quite naturally had raised lovemaking to an art form, and such was the force of her passion she couldn't argue with it. It devoured her, changing her inner landscape forever.

Little pulses flicked here and there all over her body. He felt the shock of her beauty, her nakedness, take his breath away. Her luminescent skin gleamed in the dimness of the cave, and her masses of auburn hair formed a halo around her face. This was the woman straight out of his dreams. Miraculously, mysteriously Nicole. Both of them had traveled a long way.

The muscles in his forearms rippled as he lifted her supple legs to his shoulders.

All around them like incense was her fragrance, a powerful aphrodisiac. He inhaled it deeply, but desire was the sweetest scent of all. Now that he had found her, he knew he could never be denied her.

CHAPTER SIXTEEN

BY THE TIME he returned to the homestead, life seemed almost too difficult to bear. His sense of oppression—he'd developed it early in his godawful childhood—had never been stronger, the pressure on his aching temples like screws holding his brain together. The pain was unbearable. He'd had to drive with the storm raging all around him, despite the very real danger the chain lightning presented, pulling into makeshift shelters when visibility was next to nothing. It had been all he could do to control the vehicle, slipping and slewing, the wheels fighting for purchase in the mud.

He'd made it back to the homestead, pretending he'd been out near the JumpUp, miles away from the escarpment. God knows where they were. They weren't back yet, though the storm had settled to light rain and then the sun was out again in all its incredible brilliance. That was the Outback—drama, extremes, drought and floods, no in-betweens. His mouth tightened into an ugly line. They'd probably found themselves a nice little cave where they could shelter. At least that's what they'd tell the rest of them. He knew what they were about. Bloody sex. Even from a distance, kissing madly on the escarpment, they'd reeked of it. Lovers. She hadn't tried at all to stop McClelland disrupting their world. She'd offered herself up to him, as wanton as her mother.

God, how he hated her! He'd renounced every other feeling.

Fifteen minutes later he began to relax when he learned one of the stockmen had been attacked and badly gored by a feral boar. This wasn't the first time that particular animal had threatened a stockman who found himself in its territory. A shooting party was to be organized for the next day. Wild boar were vermin, and a real danger.

The shooting party also offered an opportunity for some unfortunate young woman known for her reck-lessness to be caught in the crossfire. It was almost certain McClelland could be talked into taking part. Harder to involve Nicole, who hated killing, but the powerful desire to be with her lover might swing things in his favor. He'd have to direct his attention to getting the two of them involved. In the old days Heath, a true hunter, had relished going after feral pigs. These days Heath would find it difficult even to sit on a horse. He'd come to understand life must have been very hard for Heath, as well. The Cavanaghs knew how to treat people badly.

A HALF A DOZEN stockmen waited for them at the Five Mile.

Nicole, like the rest of them, was a good shot; her grandfather had taught her how to handle herself around firearms. The Outback wasn't the city. Danger from feral animals was a fact of life. So was the danger presented by a trespasser, a man on the run, perhaps.

Most dangerous of all were cattle "duffers"—cattle thieves—a constant threat to the industry.

"I don't know that I want you here, Nic," Drake said, eyes narrowing at her. She was busy tying a sapphire-blue bandanna around her throat, tucking it into her cotton shirt.

"Well, I'm coming. I'm experienced. Don't worry. I'll keep out of the way. You men can do the shooting. I'll stick to my camera. I'm squeamish about killing a living thing. Even a dingo or a rogue camel."

"Then keep behind the rest of the party and the line of fire. I'll be watching out for you."

"I feel safe." She meant it. With him along—

"All set?" Joel rode up to them, apparently eager to be off on the hunt. "Watch yourself, Nikki," he cautioned her, casting her an intent look she couldn't define. "It's been a long time since you've been involved in anything like this."

"I've never been involved in a boar hunt," she reminded him. "Chasing brumbies is more my style."

"A long time since you've done that, as well," Joel pointed out.

"Relax, Joel. I'll keep an eye on her," Drake promised. "I'm surprised your father decided to join us. He didn't seem at all keen last night."

"He needs the fresh air," Joel answered, looking as though he'd undergone a transformation, more focused than Nicole had seen him in days. "Dad's stuck too much behind a desk."

"You could've fooled me," she murmured sweetly.

"Well, he's a damn good shot," Joel answered with a wry smile. "He's a better shot than me."

"I didn't even know he could handle a gun," Nicole said, looking her surprise.

"You've been out of things for quite a while, Nikki. Dad's a dark horse. I said he was a good shot. I didn't say he was a sportsman. Stay well behind the guns where Drake and I can see you."

"Right, Sarge!" She gave him a mischievous salute.

Alan sat his bay gelding twenty feet away, talking to Judah, who was carrying a beautifully decorated spear, the traditional Aboriginal way of hunting wild boar. All of them were dressed in everyday bush gear, but Alan was straight out of a magazine: checked sports jacket—much, much too hot—moleskins, glossy boots, a bandanna tucked into his cream shirt. The only thing he was wearing in common with the rest was a cream akubra, but with a very fancy crocodile-skin band. Both sides were rolled up, a rakish style that offered less protection for his face and neck. Alan had retained his good English skin. Nicole thought he'd be very pink by the end of the day.

He saw Nicole looking at him and rode toward her, a smile on his unreadable face. "Take care now, young lady," he advised.

"Why, Alan, how considerate you are!"

"Always the smart answer!" He shook a playful finger at her. "Keep away from the guns. Do you have one, by the way?"

"I do." Nicole gestured to her side. "Only for my protection, but I do know how to use it. Granddad made sure of that."

"Absolutely!" Alan said in his strangely jarring plummy voice. "Sir Giles was very thorough. I'm quite looking forward to feeling the wind on my face. I was going to let this chase go by, but Joel persuaded me. Take care now, my dear. You're very precious to us." He gave her another of his enigmatic smiles, touching the sleek flank of his gelding, oddly enough called Shotgun.

They were under way!

Forty minutes later they were still in hot pursuit. The boar wasn't in his usual haunt, in the lignum swamps, but there were birds everywhere. Eden's swamps in the Wet were vast breeding grounds for nomadic waterbirds, ibis, shags, spoonbills, herons, egrets, water hens, whistling tree ducks. The torrential storm had overnight filled the creeks and swamps, and the birds, sensing it with their fantastic antennae, had arrived in big colonies.

The members of the party were fairly scattered by the time they came on at least two dozen pigs, sows, young ones, piglets, mostly black or gray-black. No sign of the big powerfully built boar. As soon as the pigs heard the riders, they bunched up and made a run for it, plunging without hesitation into the water and swimming furiously farther down the swamp. Exhaustion would soon overcome them. Their swimming was only good over short distances, but then, the hunters were really only after the boar.

When they finally sighted the animal, it was deep in the lignum thickets, wallowing in swampy mud. Nicole felt her stomach lurch. The creature looked mad. As it lumbered onto its short legs, exposing its full power, she could see how huge and ferocious it was. It had to weigh at least four hundred pounds. From its lower jaw, two powerful tusks protruded, tusks that had landed their stockman in Koomera Bush Hospital.

"Back! Get back!" Drake shouted to her, unable to disguise the flash of excitement in his face.

Men! Nicole thought. They just loved excitement and danger. She needed no second warning. Drake and the others charged ahead, the horses' hooves sending up spouts of murky water and thick splodges of mud. Suddenly the huge brute, instead of running, decided to charge. The taste of human blood must have made it frantic to have it again.

One of the party prematurely pulled the trigger and missed, or maybe the bullet ricocheted off the animal's thick mud-coated bristles, tough as armor. Birds, shrieking their outrage, burst into the sky, a teeming cloud overhead.

"Leave it. I'll take it!" Drake called, his voice loud and authoritative over the screaming birds.

Dread and excitement had sharpened all her senses. Despite the confusion and cacophony of sound, she heard with absolute clarity the metallic click of a rifle safety catch.

Behind her? To the side? Panic ripped through her like an electric shock. Every sense of self-protection screamed she was in danger. She spun her head, anticipating a shot. A shot that had only one purpose. To kill her. She had moved right into the trap.

"Drake!" She screamed his name at the top of her lungs, not knowing he had dropped the boar with one clean shot to the brain. She heaved herself desperately out of the saddle, lunging with a loud splash into the churning waters of the swamp. The shot that was intended for her sliced directly over her horse's head, causing it to bolt. Had she not flung herself well away, the mare's flying hooves undoubtedly would have killed her. She thrashed in the water, kicking herself farther into the swamp. She was covered in mud and slime, aquatic vegetation. The stench filled her nostrils.

Up ahead, the men exploded into action, two of them giving chase to the terrified mare, another, stunned by what was happening, holding a bleeding arm that had apparently been grazed by the bullet intended for her.

Oh God, oh God… She turned her head with the most profound sense of fatalism, not all that surprised to see her assassin raise his gun to his shoulder. No doubt at all of his intentions. That was death in his eyes.

It was almost time. No one could alter the course of fate. He was taking aim at her, mouth set in the most determined line. All he wanted now was to wipe her from the face of the earth. What had caused such hatred? He looked deadly. Incredibly sinister. The blond hair, the cold pale eyes. His real self revealed. No pretense. No sweet poison.

This was it. No life hereafter. No Drake, no children, no Eden. She had found herself too late. She was to die just like her mother. At the same hands. She knew that now. At this point, the moment of death, she was utterly alone. She could feel herself bleach white as if she were already dead, the blood pooling in her limbs.

She didn't flinch or look away. Maybe courage counted for something. Let him kill her in cold blood. Let him kill her with her eyes trained on him. Even now she felt a strange compassion. She wondered how Drake would take her death. How many years he would have without her. She kept the image of him firmly in her mind. Something to hang on to.

As she awaited her fate, an eternity when it was mere seconds, another shot erupted before her assassin had time to pull the trigger. She watched as he screamed in agony or frustration, pitching forward into the vine-tangled thicket, clearly snarling the single word: "Bitch!"

"Hold on, Nic. I'm coming for you."

She didn't register Drake striding through the muddied waters like a colossus berating himself aloud for not being prepared for the danger. She was disbelieving still. Part of her knew she was saved; part of her was waiting for her assassin to rise back up and finish the job. Everything seemed unearthly quiet, though in truth it was pandemonium. She remained right where she was, half-submerged in the water, going into shock.

DRAKE REACHED HER, sweeping her up into his arms. "Hold on, my love." At her extreme pallor, the dazed look in her eyes, he thought his heart would break.

He made for the bank. Once there, a rock underfoot caused him to stumble, but he righted himself almost immediately, hearing Judah shout a frenzied warning to him.

He saw the dark shape emerge from the screen of trees. The man was upright, blood gushing profusely from his gut, but still holding the rifle. The face was vicious. Merciless. Beyond reason.

Incredible! He was still alive. The devil looked after his own.

Drake did the only thing he could do, he leaped to one side, energized by fear and an impotent rage. As he went down painfully, Nicole still in his arms, he saw a tribal spear heading like a missile straight for the enemy. Unerringly it found its target, sinking into the man's neck, cutting off all possibility of future breath.

Drake didn't think he would witness anything so miraculous again.

NICOLE SAW, too, easily now, the inevitability of it all. In retrospect, her inability to see what was happening stunned her. Drake had warned her. Her father. Dot. Shelley Logan. Even Siggy had warned her in her own way. For herself, it was a case of deliberate blindness. She had to feel responsibility, even if it was against all logic.

Joel had been deeply flawed. Increasingly unable to handle anger, anxiety or conflict. He had made of her a fantasy, instead of a real woman. He had believed from childhood she was the only one to love and understand him. But she had defected. She had destroyed a relationship that had lasted all their lives. The bond Joel thought unbreakable had been severed with one stroke. She had fallen in love with Drake McClelland. From then on, Joel's conditional love had turned to manic hate. He had simply reached a point where he could no longer cope with the hatreds and jealousies that consumed him. In his own deeply troubled mind, he must have thought he had the right to kill her just as he doubtless caused her mother's and David

McClelland's fatal accident. Whether Joel would have
died from Drake's bullet, or Judah's spear had completed the execution, she had no idea. They would
know soon enough. Joel's body would be brought
home. Probably an autopsy would be performed. She
didn't know. Nor did she care. She was numb to the
bone.

THE FAMILY SAT in the living room at Eden homestead, steeling themselves for the sound of a helicopter, signaling the arrival of the police from Koomera
Crossing. All of them, with the exception of Drake
and Heath, were in a state of shock. Heath who, instead of showing even a semblance of grief, looked
revitalized, his black eyes glowing, his body held
erect. Being thought somehow guilty of his wife's
tragic death had torn him apart. It had enslaved him
to public opinion. Now he would be totally exoner-
ated. It didn't seem possible Joel had tried to kill Nicole, the cousin he adored. But God was still in his
heaven. It wouldn't be so bad to meet him now. Joel
was dead. His beautiful daughter lived, even if his wife
had not.

Siggy, who'd raced onto the veranda in the grip of
a dreadful premonition when the shooting party returned, had made only one despairing cry—a sound of
utter desolation. Now, eyes closed, she sat in her chair,
struggling to keep herself under control. She'd lived
with such terrible suspicions about her son for so long
now that his attempt to kill Nicole and his subsequent
death weren't as massively shocking as they might
have been. She knew in her heart of hearts that Joel
was capable of anything. Years ago she'd seen him

seethe with hatred for her sister, Corrinne, who wanted to send him away. It was clear to her now that he'd killed Corrinne and David McClelland, and probably that nice psychiatrist Dr. Rosendahl, who must have come to understand Joel too well and had been about to blow the whistle on him. Why hadn't she seen the extreme danger to her niece with Drake McClelland on the scene?

She glanced at her husband. Alan's chest was heaving, and tears ran unattended down his cheeks. Did he feel a tremendous loss? Joel was his son, after all. She supposed that somewhere beneath Alan's theatrical veneer was a man capable of loving his son, if not his wife.

So Callista McClelland had been right all along, she thought. A Cavanagh *had* caused the death of her beloved brother. But much of Callista's life had been wasted blaming the *wrong* Cavanagh.

CHAPTER SEVENTEEN

JOEL WAS LAID TO REST on Eden station in a small private ceremony. Afterward the Cavanaghs and the McClellands had returned to their respective homes, still trying to come to terms with the tragedy of the present and the tragedy of the past.

Nicole, as in all times of deep stress, turned to her painting. Alone, locked away at Eden in a frenzy of activity, she made inspired use of her suffering and irrational sense of guilt, covering canvas after canvas with powerful images that not only called up the truth about the past and the present, but also soon began to reveal signs of hope and signs of healing. Her most recent work, a large desert landscape, held the promise of heart-stopping beauty. She had laid down the stormy, lurid palette that had predominated so far, turning to softer yet vibrant colors, the colors of the living desert. The time was at hand when Nicole Cavanagh was ready to lay her ghosts to rest.

SIGGY AND ALAN, separate individuals and never true partners, finding themselves confronted by accumulated guilts and griefs, agreed they could no longer carry on the pretense of their marriage. Both wanted to lead different lives, although Alan being Alan was not prepared to lose the lifestyle he had become accustomed to during his marriage. He demanded a settlement. A very large settlement. In that, he'd underestimated Nicole as head of the family, and head of the family trust. When Siggy approached her with Alan's demands, Nicole called him into the study to discuss the matter.

Twenty-five minutes later Alan emerged frowning and spluttering, threatening to take the matter to court. It never happened. Whatever Nicole said to him—neither of them divulged exactly what—Alan finally accepted a sum fair enough in the circumstances but modest compared to his outrageous initial demands.

"Which just goes to show how tough my girl can be!" was Heath's dry comment.

Very strangely, considering how frighteningly ill he'd been when he arrived on Eden, Heath was responding remarkably well to the treatment regime prescribed by Dr. Sarah McQueen. Heath, who'd always had an eye for beautiful women, had taken to the doctor at his very first visit, in no time seeing beyond her obvious attractions to what a fine doctor she was. The clearing up of his wife's death seemed to have drained a lot of the toxins from his bloodstream. Physically and psychologically he was a different man.

"I don't know what I'd do without you, Heath," Siggy often told him now, at peace in his company. After Alan had left Eden with his settlement, as much a stranger as the day he set foot on the station, Louise, Siggy and Heath began to realize how easily they rubbed along.

There were no secrets now. No dreadful inner conflicts. No blotting out things that should never have been ignored. Jacob Rosendahl's widow, Sonya, had been required by the police to release Joel's file. The police examined it thoroughly. It seemed that in their sessions, seven in all, Joel had never identified himself to Rosendahl as the person who had caused Corrinne Cavanagh's vehicle to go over the escarpment. The gifted psychiatrist, however, had his methods of getting Joel to talk about the tragic event in such a way his probing would eventually have led him to the truth. But with no actual proof beyond circumstantial evidence, the police could not be sure that Joel had committed the hit-and-run. The file would have to remain open.

THE TOWN OF Koomera Crossing came to the conclusion that the death of Joel Holt had been a disaster waiting to happen. For years Joel had given the impression he was the king of the castle, a man who would always have his way. The theory was—no one knew who had started it—that Joel had succumbed to a dangerous mental illness, a mix of paranoia and rage, after his grandfather left Eden to his cousin, Nicole, and not to him. Joel had always appeared maladjusted—no one would easily forget his violent behavior at Mick Donovan's—so it was a simple matter to deduce Joel couldn't abide a woman taking precedence over him. If a few people in town had other theories, they kept them to themselves.

The Tyson-Logan wedding went ahead, if not according to plan. Because of the shocking developments on Eden station, the best man and maid of honor decided to dissociate themselves from that happy event, marred only by their absence. So ecstatic were the bridal couple, so high was the emotion, everyone managed to have a wonderful day. The unanimous decision was to leave recent events separate from the bridal festivities. Bride and groom promised at some future date they would make it up to their friends, who had stood aside rather than cast the faintest shadow on the bride and groom's perfect day.

ON KOOLTAR STATION Drake found himself profoundly lonely even as he accepted Nicole's need for this very private time to herself. No matter Joel's failings, more terrible than anyone had ever suspected, Nicole and Joel had been raised as siblings. No matter what horrible deeds Joel had done, Nicole, Drake knew, still retained a spot for him in her heart. Joel's obsession with her had led to his death. Drake had to face the fact that he'd played a major role in Joel's demise, even if it had been Judah's spear that had finished him off and even if Joel had to die to save Nicole's life. Killing a fellow human being was abhorrent under any circumstances, and Drake actually welcomed the time to come to terms with it.

Dawn to dusk he drove himself; the evenings and the long nights he craved her. Talking to her over the phone didn't suffice. She talked about her painting. She told him how much better her father was, how Alan had taken off and good riddance—her grandmother and Siggy were coping better than she'd ever have thought. Neither of them mentioned Joel. That would have shattered the odd calm.

Finally he couldn't stand it anymore. She must have read his mind, because she asked him to come for her and take her to Kooltar.

"I need to see you, Drake," she told him. "It's time

I settled my life.'' She spoke with extreme steadiness, as though she had already made up her mind. Joel's death had arisen directly from his sexual conflicts about Nicole. That knowledge and her ability to draw men to her, like her mother, might drive her into flight. Away from him. Drake couldn't discount it as a possibility. As for him, all he wanted was to make her his wife. She could do whatever she liked with Eden. Sell it to another buyer offering the right price. Engage a properly experienced, competent overseer to run it. He could help her there. She could give it away, for all he cared. All he wanted was her. And as soon as possible. He knew her work, her painting, was very important to her.

Callista was providing him with another cause for worry. Her powerful negative feelings toward the Cavanagh family hadn't diminished in the wake of Joel's death. She spoke of sins and punishments, suffocatingly moral. At one point she said Corrinne had deserved all she got. Her brother, David, would be alive today if he hadn't come under the spell of ''that woman.'' There was no way she was sorry for the family. They'd brought it down on their own heads. Drake may have saved Nicole's life, but in doing so, didn't he see that once more a McClelland could have been the victim?

The last thing Drake wanted was to cause his aunt further unhappiness, but he had permitted her to stay on Kooltar too long. Remaining there had made it easier for her to relive the old tragedies. There was a big world beyond Kooltar. Being part of it might help her regain some kind of normality.

Before he left to pick up Nicole in the helicopter, he resolved to speak to Callista. No need to go in search of her—she was in the drawing room, at the piano.

"Cally, could I have a word with you?"

She looked up smiling, resting her hands on the keys. "But of course, dear. What is it?"

He didn't beat about the bush. "I'm going over to Eden to pick up Nicole and I'm bringing her back here. She's been under enormous stress. I can't think you'd want to add to it, Cally."

At his words she looked shattered. "What stress has she suffered we haven't, Drake?" she demanded, her teeth biting into her bottom lip. "You were forced to kill a monster to save her life."

His expression darkened. "I don't need reminding. I had no other choice. I love Nicole, Cally. I'm going to do everything in my power to get her to marry me."

Callista flinched, then rose from the piano seat and stalked off several feet. "I don't believe this!" She clutched her throat, a familiar pose. "I thought as you weren't seeing her, you'd come to your senses."

He was so angry for a moment he didn't trust himself to reply. "I was giving her space, Cally," he said at last. "I considered that important. Nicole loved her cousin, even if he did try to kill her. Can you imagine what her feelings are, knowing his love turned to such hatred he turned a gun on her?"

Callista's dark eyes glittered and her whole body trembled. "Women like Nicole Cavanagh precipitate tragedy. They're dangerous women. She and her mother. You're playing with fire, Drake."

"I'll be the judge of that, Callista, not you. I've indulged you and your difficulties long enough. You play no leading role in my life as you seem to think."

Callista caught at the back of a chair like a woman about to faint. She sat down heavily. "I love you, Drake. You're all the family I have left. I've devoted myself to your well-being."

His mouth twisted in pity. "You have in your way, Cally, and I've tried to respond by offering you a home and the freedom to do whatever you like. As it's turned out, it was a big mistake. I should have been encouraging you to find yourself, instead of allowing you to get stuck in the one role of grieving sister. The way my uncle loved you wasn't in any way the same as the way you loved him, Cally. Face it. David totally lacked your obsessive streak."

Callista looked as if the sky was falling on her. "You don't know what you're talking about. David and I couldn't have been closer. We were soul mates as much as brother and sister. It was Corrinne who destroyed our very special relationship. David adored my playing. He would sit for hours."

"Okay, so he did. He was a genuine music lover and you're a gifted pianist. Did you have to fantasize he adored you? I'm sorry for you, Cally. You've wasted your life, living in the past instead of tackling the future."

She stared at him with unconcealed rage. "Why turn on me? I'm no danger to you. *She* is. You'll pay a great price for getting mixed up with her just as David did with her mother. I'm very afraid for you."

He managed to bite back a harsh answer. "You're

better and brighter than that, Cally. You're an attractive woman. A fine musician. You're financially secure. It's time for you to make a change. Get a life of your own. Sometime in the near future I intend to bring Nicole to Kooltar as my wife. I won't have anyone show feelings of anger or hostility to her. That means you, Callista."

For the first time fear and uncertainty entered her eyes. She sat utterly still. "You're being shockingly direct, Drake. Can't you see I'm broken inside? Surely I don't deserve such condemnation. Your uncle's death was witness to a dangerous woman's power. He did die, you know, at a Cavanagh's hands. Bad blood. Doesn't that frighten you?"

"Some people might think you were slightly mad, Cally," he answered quietly, though his expression was troubled. "Nicole has been the innocent victim in all this. She's suffered, but she's fought to survive. You're simply being intolerant, small-minded, valuing all the wrong things. I suppose what I'm trying to say is you've never become an adult, an independent human being."

Callista made a horrified, choking sound. "Are you trying to tell me Nicole Cavanagh is?"

"That, and she's also very brave," he replied. "It was a dreadful thing that happened to her as a child but she managed to pull herself back from the brink. You haven't and you were an adult when it happened."

"So what's the answer?" Callista stared at him.

"Simple, Cally. You have to move out. Get a life." Drake turned to move off, every inch the cattle baron.

HE FOUND HER waiting for him at Eden's airstrip. She was pale, subdued, her beautiful hair drawn back and tied with a silk scarf.

"Hi!" he said simply, bending to kiss her cheek, not her mouth. They might have been a couple on the brink of breaking up, run out of words. "Let's go."

"How are you?" She searched his eyes.

"I'm fine." The lie out came easily. "What about you?"

She shook her head a little. "Getting there. Some mornings I wake up and think the whole thing didn't happen. That it was just a dreadful nightmare."

"I know exactly how you feel." Would he ever forget that split second of horror with Joel taking aim?

They started to walk. After a moment Nicole caught hold of his arm. "Do you think we could touch down somewhere along the way? The wildflowers are out. I want to see them from the ground, as well as from the air."

"Sure." He let his eyes rest on her, resisting the powerful urge to haul her into his arms, cover her face and throat with kisses. Always slender, she looked fragile, some flicker of expression in her beautiful eyes holding him at arm's length. Was she going to tell him she intended to return to New York? He knew she still communicated with her friends, the Bradshaws, there. What would he do then? He doubted if he could take her departure without a great deal of pain.

They climbed into the cockpit of the chopper. Drake started up the engine, listening to the roar of the rotor blades whirling above them. Nicole sat quietly, not trying to speak. In moments they lifted off vertically. Nicole's eyes were on the distant ranges. Choppers could fly high and fast. They were wonderful for viewing the landscape. They had revolutionized the cattle industry. One man in a helicopter could do the work of more than a dozen stockmen. Helicopters could land almost anywhere.

Her wounded heart craved the healing sight of the desert under a mantle of wildflowers. Perhaps man hadn't lost paradise entirely, she thought, when the earth still retained glorious wild gardens.

They were airborne only minutes, when under a peacock-blue sky a vast Persian carpet opened out before their enchanted eyes. It ran on to the far horizons. This was what the Channel Country was famous for: countless legions of paper daisies, the brightest whites and yellows she'd ever seen, feathery gold and orange blossoms, the richest pinks and purples and violets, the delicacy of pale blue, lime and lilac, the blood-red desert peas; wild gardens so prolific they could only have been sown with great handfuls of seeds the Creator scattered from the sky. Soon this miracle of natural beauty would fade and die away, but the remarkable seed pods would rise eternal, bursting through the baked sun-scorched earth the very next time conditions were right.

For now what they looked down upon was the miracle of the Inland, the miracle she and Drake had been privileged to witness from childhood. The wonder never went away.

Drake set the chopper down amid the everlastings. There was scarcely a patch of fiery red soil not embroidered by flowers. This was the same ancient magic the Aborigines had been spectators to for more than forty thousand years.

When the whirling rotors stilled, they climbed out

of the chopper to have their nostrils bewitched by the strongest sweetest scents known to man. No perfume from a bottle, no matter how exquisite, could rival the scents of nature. Was it so surprising then, that standing in the midst of these fragrant masses that ran on mile after mile, Nicole felt tears well up in her eyes? The love of beauty, of natural things, was fundamental to her existence. These spectacular desert gardens were even more wonderful with Drake here to share them with her.

Drake gazed down at her face and saw the rapture there. At just the right moment he began to speak, unburdening his heart to her. Now, before it was too late, he had to tell her how much he loved her. What she meant to him. What she meant to his life. Eden simply didn't come into it. It was *she* he wanted. He couldn't get it wrong. If he broke down all barricades, maybe, just maybe, she would do the same.

As he spoke, his voice caressing her, her face began to shine and her eyes began to blaze.

It was the most moving voice she'd ever heard from him. Deep, thrilling, the sound penetrating her whole being. He spoke without fear of exposing his heart to her. Lines from the *Song of Solomon* fell, sweetly, gently from his lips:

Rise up, my love, my fair one, and come away
For lo, the winter is past, the rain is over and gone;
The flowers appear on the earth; and the time of
the singing of birds is come.

"Has it, Nicole?" He took hold of her hand, bringing it to his mouth. "Will you stay and be my beautiful wife or will you fly away? There are tears in your eyes, my love.''

She blinked them away. ''I always cry when I'm overcome with joy,'' she said. ''In this place, with you, I feel I can let any remaining sadness about Joel and everything that happened go.'' She stared into Drake's dark eyes, losing herself there. ''Was I dreaming a lovely dream, or did you just ask me to marry you?''

''I'm waiting for your answer.'' His smile looked a little strained.

''But surely you know it already.''

''I'm not that sure of myself. I have to hear it. Nicole Cavanagh, will you marry me?''

She threw back her head, lifted her arms joyously, spreading the palms upward to the sky. ''Yes, yes, yes! A thousand times yes. Today and forever. You're my favorite person in all the world. It seems like I've been waiting for you all my life.''

''In that case, hasn't enough time elapsed?'' His touch was gentle but electric. ''I'm going to make this world a safe place for you, Nic.''

''You already have,'' she responded, her tone loving and positive. ''Everything you've said to me has touched the innermost part of me. It's let in all this marvelous fresh air. You're unafraid to tell me how you feel. Now I want to tell *you*. I've wasted so much of my life unable to drive the tragedy of my mother's death from my mind. I should tell you, though I'm sure you already know, that as a McClelland I sometimes chose to strike out at you. Always that push-pull between us, all that conflict. Even so, I couldn't let the bond between us break. You've always been important to me, Drake. Dr. Rosendahl may have helped me shed a lot of the debris from my mind, but your love for me has made me whole.'' She moved into the arms he opened wide. ''I love you. You're absolutely necessary to me. I see you as my husband, the father of my children. I'm ready to take up life with you.''

''The two of us from now on.''

''Perfect. Amen.''

For brief moments they stood enfolded within each other's arms, amid the wildflowers, then he raised her head to him, staring down into her eyes. ''Here in this paradise, I've asked you to be my wife. It makes me gloriously proud and happy you've consented. I want to store up this scene in my memory, the everlastings all around us.'' He glanced around them. ''Bridal white. I want to remember your face, its exact expression, the look in your eyes. Love lifts a man to the skies. Let's fly together, my darling heart.''

She returned his kiss, soft, deep, reverent as the occasion demanded. They were blessed and they knew it.

Gradually, melting together, they slipped to the ground, their bodies crushing the thick cushion of dazzling white daisies, releasing the scent. They made love as if for the first time, the flowering earth for a bed.

A LITTLE DISTANCE OFF amid the everlastings stood the silver-gray skeleton of a mulga. What was very curious about the desert tree was that it appeared to burn with a glowing white light. Sculpted by wind and scorching sun, it had over time taken the abstract form of a graceful young woman. The breeze appeared to toss her flowing mane as it lifted one of her bough-arms, suspending it in a wave. It created the amazing impression of offering the young lovers her blessing.

A trick of the dancing light, or some kind of magic? For in the next instant the sculpture once more became a petrified desert mulga.

The power of love. The power of nature. The power of two.

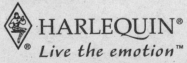

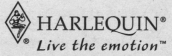

HARLEQUIN *Super* ROMANCE®

**Alouette, Michigan. Located high on the
Upper Peninsula. Home to strong men,
stalwart women and lots and lots of trees.**

NORTH COUNTRY *Stories*

Three Little Words
by Carrie Alexander
Superromance #1186

Connor Reed returns to Alouette to reconnect with his grandfather
and to escape his notorious past. He enlists the help of Tess Bucek,
the town's librarian, to help teach his grandfather to read. As
Tess and Connor start to fall in love, they learn the healing power
of words, especially three magical little ones....

Available in February 2004 wherever Harlequin books are sold.

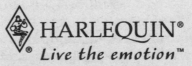

HARLEQUIN®
Live the emotion™

From the bestselling author of *Private Lives*

KAREN YOUNG

While educating teens about good choices, guidance counselor Rachel Forrest finds her own life spiraling out of control: her husband is having an affair, her aging mother collapses, and Cameron Ford is back in her life—again.

As Rachel struggles to get her life in order, her fifteen-year-old son, Nick, forges a bond with the taciturn Cameron whom he trusts with a secret that may be connected to the death of Cameron's own son, Jack, five years ago...a secret that could endanger them all.

In Confidence

"...a moving tale of second chances."
—*Romantic Times* on *Private Lives*

*Available the first week of February 2004
wherever paperbacks are sold!*